CASE WITH FOUR CLOWNS

CASE WITH 4 CLOWNS

LEO BRUCE

A Sergeant Beef Mystery

ACADEMY CHICAGO PUBLISHERS

Published in 2010 by
Academy Chicago Publishers
363 West Erie Street
Chicago, Illinois 60654

© 1939 by Leo Bruce

Printed and bound in the U.S.A.

Library of Congress Cataloging-in-Publication Data
on file with the publisher.

To
MARTIN AND IDA

CHAPTER I

WHEN my telephone bell rang that morning I had a presentiment that it was Beef. And because, as it transpired later, presentiments, not to mention predictions, became an important part of the affair in which we found ourselves involved, I remember it now. When I lifted the receiver I could hear the well-known voice making an effort to control itself, and could picture the Sergeant attempting dignity, much as he might have done in his village constable days, when the cheekiest boy in the village was explaining why there was not a lamp on his bicycle.

"I intend," he said grandly, "to investigate a new case."

This was frankly incredible. Only six months before, Beef's career, such as it had been, had obviously come to an end. The Sergeant had allowed a man to be hanged for a crime of which he was innocent, and the fact that Stewart Ferrers had committed a murder of which the Court knew nothing did not prevent Beef from being branded as a failure by the other members of his profession. In the eyes of the public Beef was a fallen star. After two startlingly successful cases he had crashed on his third, and the newspapers had not been slow to seize on his defeat. I could not believe that a client in trouble would come along and employ him as an investigator. With all the varied talents of literary detection at the disposal of anyone who needed them, not to mention Scotland Yard, it seemed scarcely likely that my blundering friend had been called in to do more than watch a suspect or examine the inside of a building.

The last time I had seen him I had tried to make him realize that, so far as he was concerned, private investigation was finished. I had not stressed the loss to me, or grumbled that my chances as a crime writer had died with his lost prestige, though I might well have done so. His wife, I knew, had been trying to persuade him to apply for a job as a cinema commissionaire, for which his appearance made him most suitable. We could both of us picture him standing with solid dignity, a firm embroidered figure, at the steps of some Renaissance or Neo-Grecian hallway. At least he would tolerate no disobedience when his orders were to "Stand in line there," and he could clear the steps of any small boys who attempted to make them a playground.

In fact, Mrs. Beef had gone so far as to unscrew the brass name-plate from his door with the explanation that the neighbors had been pulling her leg about it. But Beef had insisted that this should be stowed away carefully in the drawer of his desk.

"Never know but what I might need it," he said, and even then I thought I had detected a faint spark of hope in his voice, and had tried not to crush it too brutally.

And now, suddenly, had come his phone call. He was considering going to Yorkshire on a new case and wanted to talk it over with me. Something to do with a circus, I had gathered, but he had not been explicit. There was nothing else to do but go straight round and see him, and I got the car out with some misgivings and headed it towards the little street in the region of Baker Street which Beef had chosen as being the only possible headquarters for a private investigator.

Even in the warm spring sunshine Lilac Crescent looked no more cheerful than I had remembered it in the rain of a January afternoon. The long bare pavements were dry and dusty, the gutters littered with paper and rubbish from hawkers' carts, and the occasional smear of coal-dust around the manholes in the pavement only increased the desolation of the place. Beef's house lay on the right, in the center of a row of small unobtrusive houses which huddled together rather like a dozen monkeys sheltering from the wind on a rocky ledge. The drawn front-room blinds were shut against the brilliant stare of the sun, which was too intimate and probing for the quiet retiring life of that street.

I drew the car into the side of the road opposite Beef's front door. A hundred yards farther along stood an empty cart with a tired horse between the shafts and a man beside it in the road ringing a hand-bell. There was no sign that he had been heard, no other movement in the street.

Beef was leaning over the kitchen table on which was spread a large-scale map of Yorkshire. He stood up and held out a huge hand to me as Mrs. Beef showed me in.

"So you came," he said unnecessarily. "Well, sit down and have a cup of tea." Whereupon Mrs. Beef took the hint and bustled out of the room to leave us alone.

Beef had changed since I last saw him. Although he still seemed very pleased with himself, it struck me that perhaps he was not quite his old bumptious self. Beef had never been the man to feel ill at ease whatever happened, but now he sucked at his empty pipe, and seemed to be waiting for an opening in the matter-of-fact conversation.

"Why the map?" I asked casually, pointing to the green sheet covering the table.

Beef seemed to wave it out of existence. "Yorkshire," he said. "I was just getting my bearings. Big place, Yorkshire." He paused, looking at the map in a thoughtful way, then after a few minutes he turned and walked over to the hearth-rug, and I knew by the expression in his eyes that he was about to tell me—in his own way—the story of his new case.

"Have you ever been to one of these traveling circuses?" he said suddenly.

"Circuses?" I said, with the astonishment that was expected of me. "Why, yes, when I was a kid."

Beef looked pained. "No, I mean," he interrupted, "have

[3]

you ever thought about the way people lived in them? You know, touring around and stopping every day at a different place. Living in wagons and all that?"

"I can't say I've thought about it very much," I answered.

"No, nor don't many people. Well, my wife's nephew, he works with one. And he writes to Mrs. Beef every now and again and tells us about the sort of life he has. Exciting it must be, with animals and that and moving about seeing the country." Beef's eyes glistened for a moment, and he seemed to be thinking of the adventurous life of his fortunate nephew.

"Well?" I asked.

"Well, that's it," said Beef calmly. "This nephew has just written us a most peculiar letter. Most peculiar. I was talking to the wife about it, and she thinks I ought to follow it up, like. She says it's the chance of my career. Here, I'll show it to you." And he drew out of his pocket a piece of folded paper and handed it to me.

"Dear Uncle & Arntie [I read],

"We arrived at Scarborough this week-end and shall be moving on south next week. The season has started very well. I am very well. I hope you are the same. I must tell you Uncle about a strange thing what hapend the other day you know there is a gypsy woman with us who tells fortunes well she has just told mine. It did not cost me anything trust Albert Stiles because I fetched her water one day and and she said she wood do it for nothing. 'Misfortune will befal you,' she said. 'You will lose your job in the circus, but you will find another soon which will make you happy.' Then I asked her if they would give me the sack but she said no it wood come about difrent. She said the circus wood break up this summer because of a culammity She said there wood be a murder in the circus and that wood mean the end. I thought I wood write this to you you being interested in murders and

[4]

a detective. I think its a pity the circus will be breaking up dont you and perhaps if youve got nothing else to do just now you wood come up and stop it. I have written where we shall be every day next week so that you can find us.

> "I hope you will come,
> "Your affec. nevew,
> "Albert Stiles."

"But Beef," I said. "You're surely not going to tell me that this is your new case?"

"I don't see why not," said Beef huffily. "Albert wouldn't have written if he didn't think something was likely to happen. There's more in this than meets the eye, that's what I say. What do you think about it?"

"I think the whole thing is perfectly absurd. Some old gypsy tells your nephew's fortune. She sees he's a romantic sort, so she makes it exciting for him. Do you mean to tell me you believe in that sort of thing?"

Beef looked awkward. "Well, not exactly," he said, "but you never know. There must be something in it. Some of these gypsies know a lot more than they let on."

"So you mean to go all the way up to Yorkshire because of something a gypsy said," I snorted. "I think the whole idea is crazy."

Beef sat down slowly in his chair and his pale, watery blue eyes had a stubborn look in them.

"And," I continued, "suppose there was no murder when you got there. It wouldn't do you any good."

"Any good!" Beef burst out scornfully. "That's all you think about. The matter with you, Townsend, is that you're too careful. You like a nice ordinary murder case so's you can laugh at it for being ordinary. Everything's just a game to you, something to make a story out of. Look at my last case. You don't seem to realize that it was serious for me. The newspapers and that poking fun at me. They said I'd failed to save an innocent man and that my career was finished. What do you think that sort of thing did to me?"

"Yes, I know, Beef," I said patiently. "I know you've had a hard time over that. But how can it do you any good to go dashing off on a wild-goose chase like this?"

"How can it do me any harm?" demanded Beef truculently. "Do you know that not a soul has crossed that doorstep since my last case? I tell you I shall never get any cases coming to me now. What I've got to do is find a case for myself. And this one looks like a chance."

"But a gypsy's warning . . ." I began.

"I know it looks a bit thin," agreed Beef, "but I've got to do something. You don't know what might happen."

"And where do I come in?"

"I want you to come with me to write the case." Beef grew suddenly quite excited. "It would be something quite new," he went on. "Murder in a Circus, or something. It would probably make your name. You'd have all those other writers green with envy. There's never been a really big case in a circus, and, anyway, not this sort of case."

"This sort of case?"

"Yes. All back to front, as you might say. We go up to investigate a murder that hasn't happened yet. That's new, isn't it? I never read a book like that. Just think of it, all those people waiting for a chance to do someone in and trying to do it so that no one won't suspect them. A lot of circus folk, and no one knows who's going to murder who until the last moment. And we've got to stop them."

"And then there wouldn't be a murder at all," I protested.

"Case Without a Murder," said Beef triumphantly. "What more do you want?"

"But it wouldn't sell," I reasoned.

"You're too conservative," Beef taunted me. "Course it

would sell. You don't think people read those stories just for the murder, do you? Just being morbid? No, it's the solving they're after. Like a good puzzle to take their minds off other things, they do. But not just a professor's puzzle. Something with life in it, and excitement. That's what people like detective stories for. And something new, too. Now I'll give you an example. Look at that new bar of chocolate they brought out a while ago. 'Jupiter,' or something to do with a star. Why, it sold like anything."

"And suppose there's nothing in the whole affair?"

"We got to risk that."

Mrs. Beef came into the room bearing the promised cups of tea. "There's the insurance man at the door," she said. "Will you go and deal with him, William?"

"What do you think about this idea?" I asked Mrs. Beef as soon as the Sergeant had left the room. "Do you think we ought to go wandering in Yorkshire on such scanty evidence?"

"He would enjoy himself so," replied Mrs. Beef. "The fresh air would be good for him just now, and him so tired and miserable like he is. It'd be like a holiday for him. Do let him go, Mr. Townsend."

"But think of the waste of time," I objected, "and money."

"Oh, well. You never know," said Mrs. Beef cheerfully. "You could always write a book about the circus even if nothing else turned up, couldn't you? Lady Eleanor Smith made a good thing of it. Why shouldn't you?"

The slamming of the front door warned us that Beef's interview with the insurance man was at an end, and in a few seconds he entered the room again.

"Well?" he said.

I sighed. "Where is this circus?" I asked, with resignation.

CHAPTER II

BEEF opened one weary eye, looked out at the flat, moving country, yawned and settled his head back with a grunt. We had been driving all day along the Great North Road in order to reach the Yorkshire coast before night. The Sergeant had slept most of the way since we stopped for lunch, gurgling gently and regularly at my side, his bulky figure completely filling the seat and rolling against my arm whenever we turned a sharp corner.

The road ran almost imperceptibly into the outskirts of Doncaster, and Beef sat up and rubbed his eyes.

"Where are we?" he asked as he pulled out his watch, and then continued without waiting for my reply: "Anyway, it's time we had a little stop somewhere. You must be tired of driving all this way."

"This concern touches me," I said shortly.

Beef put his watch away. "It's ten past six," he said decisively, and began to look anxiously out of the side of the car for somewhere to park.

Not until he set his emptied glass back on the counter did he speak again.

"Same again, miss," he said, then suddenly, making violent signs to me, he pointed over the girl's head. "D'you see that there?" he asked excitedly.

I followed the direction of his wide forefinger to a bright yellow fly-bill which hung against the glass at the back of the bar. "Jacobi's Circus," read the heading, and then beneath divided off into separate squares were the lurid names of the performers, their acts and their records.

"That's the one," said Beef triumphantly. "That's the circus our Albert works for. Coming here in a week's time, it says." His voice sank to a whisper. "And for all we know it might be in this very town that a murder is committed."

"If it hasn't already *been* committed," I suggested frigidly.

I found it impossible to take this case seriously. What Beef said was no doubt true; it was this case or nothing as far as he was concerned. But, nevertheless, I could not see what we should get out of coming to Yorkshire. It boiled down to a gypsy's warning and nothing more, and to me it seemed rather fatuous that two grown men should travel over two hundred miles on such flimsy material. But Beef seemed to have made up his mind that everything would be all right, and it was not my place to attempt to discourage him. The investigator's biographer, I had learned, had no active function other than lending his car, his time, and his pen. His advice was supposed in advance to be both misleading and useless, so that when I said to Beef, "I think the whole idea is crazy," I was only doing what was expected of me, and that the case should, by all the rules, proceed to a successful conclusion in spite of me. My last remark then had been quite in keeping with my role, and I led the way out of the public-house with something of a feeling of satisfaction.

It was already growing dark by the time we reached the little seaside village of Hornsea, where the circus was playing that night, and we had very little trouble in finding the field, as every small boy we met knew, not only where it was but also how many elephants the circus had and what the clown said when one of them trod on his toe.

The evening performance had started and the sound of the band playing a brassy tango greeted us as we drove on to the field. A tall, upright young fellow in evening dress stood at the tent-flap and walked slowly over to us as we stood on the wide patch of grass before the tent looking around.

"Could you tell us where we could find Albert Stiles?" I asked.

The young man looked blank.

Beef nudged me. "Foreigner," he said. "Let me handle this." And then with wide gestures of his hands and arms he bellowed at the man: "Albert Stiles. He work for circus. See? We want see Albert Stiles. Tent hand."

The youth's face cleared. "Oah, you mean Albert," he said, with a grin. " 'E's dahn the elerphant tent." And pointing airily to the other side of the ground, he strolled back to his position by the entrance of the tent.

The elephant tent, to which he had directed us, was a large green marquee, high and square and smelling very strongly of hay and elephant manure. There was a sharp rattle of chains as we approached, and lifting the flap we saw the hind-legs of one of the animals chained to a stake at the back of the tent. The legs were crossed in an amiable, almost human way, and from the interior came the sound of heavy blowing and munching. A dim storm lantern propped up on a bale of hay was the only light, and around it sat four men playing cards. For a moment I felt that I had walked into a Goya engraving. Deep shadows were over all the tent except in the little circle of light around the card-players who cast long exaggerated images up the walls of the tent like smoky flames rising sluggishly from a cauldron. The man with his back to us was sprawled backward, using the leg of one of the elephants as a shoulder-rest, while the trunk of the animal hung over between him and the others gently tearing hay from the improvised table. When this movement threatened to upset the cards one of the men prodded fiercely at the wandering trunk.

Beef cleared his throat noisily.

"— off," said the man with his back to us.

The man facing us on the far side of the lantern scratching himself, began to re-deal the cards. There was silence for a while, broken only by the chewing of the elephants.

"Can you tell us," broke in Beef at last, "where we could find Albert Stiles?"

The card-dealer stopped short at the question and looked up at us for the first time with a card suspended in his hand. In the yellow light his face was square and ugly, the long shadows running upward from his mouth to the corners of his eyebrows with a questioning slant. He appeared to be something of a hunchback, small and round, but with long, curved arms which stretched out like a pair of jointed fire-tongs. He watched us for a moment without speaking, a dead cigarette stub hanging from the corner of his lips, and then with a slight jerk of his head he indicated the far corner of the tent.

" 'E's 'aving a kip be'ind the 'ay," he said briefly, and then returned to his dealing. The sandy-haired, broad-shouldered man on his right hand who sat cross-legged and shirtless on an upturned can picked up a piece of dirty sacking and tossed it towards the corner.

"Visitors to see you, Albert," he shouted, and the four men went back to their game.

A long bony face, topped by an untidy thatch of yellow hair with which was mixed small pieces of hay, rose over the edge of the bales and stared at us. Albert Stiles looked at us sleepily with his mouth hanging slightly open.

" 'Oo is it?" he said.

"Uncle William," said Beef, moving forward into the light. "We got your letter."

"Letter?" queried Albert drowsily.

"Yes," I interrupted. "The one where you said you thought there was going to be a mur . . ."

Albert jumped to his feet and almost threw himself across the hay to us. "Let's talk outside," he said breathlessly, and grabbing us both roughly he pushed us through the tent-flap into the open air.

"Why didn't you tell me you was coming?" he demanded

immediately. "Have you spoken to anyone else but me here?"

"Here, here," said Beef, holding up one hand, "wait a minute. Let's get this straight. Did you or did you not write a letter to us saying there was going to be a murder here?"

Albert looked round him guiltily. "Not so loud," he pleaded. "Do you want everyone to hear?"

"Look here, my lad," warned Beef in a voice which recalled his old village constable days and which might have been directed at a boy with a too accurate catapult. "I don't want any playing about from you," he continued. "Just tell us straight out what all this is about."

Albert hesitated for a moment, and then led us over to the edge of the field away from the tents. "I wish I hadn't started this now," he began.

"Come on," said Beef, settling himself down on a fallen tree-trunk, "you know what I told you."

"Well, it was like this. What I wrote in that letter was true all right, but I didn't like to tell anybody else about it."

"Why?"

"They would have laughed at me. You see, they think old Margot—that's the gypsy—is a bit cracked. They would have said she was pulling my leg, and Ginger, the man you saw in there without a shirt on, he's always got a down on me and he wouldn't have given me no peace about a thing like that. You don't know what these blokes are like when they get started on you. Regular hell it is."

"Well, that's all right," said Beef. "I can do my investigating without anybody having any suspicions. I'll just hang around and keep my eyes open."

The picture of Beef keeping his eyes open at a circus without anybody being suspicious of him struck me as particularly ludicrous, but my thoughts were interrupted by Albert.

"But if they don't know why you're 'ere," he said, " 'ow are

[12]

you going to *be* 'ere? I mean, you can't just hang around and pretend to be looking at the little birds."

"We'll have to tell the proprietor," said Beef, after a moment's thought.

"Gor, not *'im,*" said Albert. "You don't know 'im. 'E wouldn't go for nothing like that. 'E's a Tartar, 'e is. No funny business with 'im."

But Beef was already on his feet, and despite the anxious protests of his nephew, began to walk towards the tent. At last it was a resigned Albert who led us towards the large blue wagon which stood at the entrance of the field.

"This is where part of it comes true, anyway," he said. "The gypsy told me I'd lose my job."

Beef knocked briefly on the curtained door, which was opened after a slight pause by a man in evening dress.

"I want to speak to Mr. Jacobi," said Beef.

"Come in."

"Are you Mr. Jacobi?" asked Beef.

The man bowed slightly and his lean brown face creased into a faint smile. "There is no such person," he said gently. "I am the owner of Jacobi's Circus, but my name is actually Jackson. Ernest Jackson. Won't you sit down?" Then turning to Albert, who had remained at the foot of the steps, he said: "Thank you, Stiles," and began to shut the door.

"Here, wait a minute," interrupted Beef. "Let Albert in. He's got something to do with what we wanted to see you about."

Jackson seemed to hesitate for a second, and then with a short "Come in, Stiles," he held the door open while the boy sidled past him and stood awkwardly beside Beef.

"And now, Mr. Jackson," said Beef in a business-like voice, "we've come to see you about a very peculiar thing. I don't say I believe in it myself, but there won't be no harm done if it's gone into. I understand from my nephew here that you've

[13]

got an old gypsy on the ground what tells people's fortunes."

"Gypsy Margot?"

"That's her. Well, she told Albert something which I think you should know about and which I'd like to see into if you'll give me your permission." Beef turned to Stiles. "Go on, tell Mr. Jackson what she told you."

I watched Jackson's face while Albert told about the gypsy. He was a well set up man, probably about forty-five or fifty, although he carried himself like an athlete. His dark hair was almost black and plastered flat on his small, bony head. The rather wide, leathery mouth, brown skin and small ears gave him an appearance of concentrated efficiency which was emphasized by his clipped economy of speech. My first impression was one of surprise. I had expected, I suppose, an uncouth, uneducated tough; someone who dominated the circus by brute strength and muscle. This cool, precise man was a shock to me. He listened to the story with what seemed a complete absence of interest, and I could see he was unimpressed by it. His cynical eyes seemed to consider the problem as if it were an object lying on the table. He turned to Beef.

"Do you believe this story, Mr. . . . ."

"Beef," said the Sergeant, hurriedly extracting a card from his wallet and handing it to the proprietor. "Well, I won't say as I do, but then on the other hand, I can't say I don't."

"An admirably open mind on the subject," commented Jackson, with a slight smile. "And what do you wish me to do? You have told me that there is the possibility of a murder being committed in my circus. That, as you must realize, must be avoided at all costs. It would have a very bad effect on my business. But you must also realize that a circus would be the easiest place in which to commit a murder—and get away with it."

"How's that?" asked Beef.

"Every turn in the ring has a certain danger attached to it, and an unforeseen accident at almost any point might be fatal to the artist concerned. Then again there are the animals which are a constant danger to the trainers and the feeders. So that even if a murder did take place, I think you would find it very difficult, Mr. Beef, to prove that it had indeed been a murder. For myself," he continued pleasantly, with an expressive movement of his shoulders, "I do not care very much about such things so long as they do not affect the circus—and also, of course, so long as my own person is not the subject of the experiment."

It struck me as he said these words that he was being neither flippant nor cold-blooded. I suspected that in his clear, precise, business-like mind he had already rejected Beef's story as the uttermost nonsense, while at the same time looking at the question from another point of view.

"And if I stayed with the circus for a bit," Beef went on, "I could keep my eyes open and see that nothing out of the ordinary went on, couldn't I?"

Jackson smiled. "What qualifications have you for such a job?" he asked coldly.

Beef bridled. "Well, after solving three murder mysteries already what no one else could solve, and after years of experience as a sergeant in the Force, I should think I knew how to keep a lookout for a possible murderer."

"Quite honestly," said Jackson, after a pause, "it makes very little difference to me whether you gentlemen tour round with the circus or whether you don't. You would, of course, pay your own expenses . . ."

"Of course," echoed Beef.

". . . so that the question hardly affects me. To tell you the truth, the whole affair sounds to me rather fantastic, but," he waved his hand in the air, "if you wish to proceed with it . . ."

Beef was a little damped by this frankness, but he recovered himself in time to ask whether there was a tent or an empty wagon which we could use while with the circus.

"As a matter of fact," said Jackson, "there is an empty wagon which I'd been thinking of selling. I could hire that out to you for a time if you liked. Of course, there are no blankets or crockery in it now. But there's a couple of bunks, and some chairs and a table, I think. The knife-throwing act used to live in it until they split."

"I've always wanted to see a knife-throwing act," said Beef naïvely. "Why did they split up?"

Jackson smiled. "He wasn't a very good knife-thrower," he said, and left us to guess the rest.

As we left Jackson's wagon. Albert suddenly turned to Beef. "There's something I'd clean forgotten," he said suddenly. "When I asked old Margot when all this was going to happen, she said it would come off before the end of four weeks."

Beef opened his notebook and produced Albert's letter. "You wrote this," he commented, "on the fourteenth of April. How long before you wrote this did Margot tell your fortune?"

"I can't remember that far back," said Albert.

"Well, what week was it?"

"Must have been just over the week before I wrote."

"Do you remember the day?"

Albert thought for a minute, and then: "Yes, it must have been the Saturday. I remember we were one day out of Grimsby, so that makes it Saturday all right."

I referred quickly to my diary. "In that case," I said, "it must have been the fifth of April when you heard all this."

"I expect so," said Albert. "I know it was a Saturday because . . ."

"We heard that last time," said Beef abruptly, and Albert subsided meekly into silence.

CHAPTER III

I was awakened next morning before it was light by the sound of shouting and lorry engines being started. I prodded Beef sharply, but he refused to wake up, turning his face to the side of the wagon and burying his head under the blankets with a groan. One of us, I realized, had to get up before the circus moved on to the next camping-place. The trailer we were using as a living-wagon would be hitched on to one of the lorries, but my car had to be driven on separately. It was in something of a bad humor that I stepped out on to the bare, cold boards and began to dress.

The scene of last night's camp presented a complete change. The big top had been packed away on the lorries; the elephant tent had disappeared; the Wild Animal Zoo had been transformed into neat wagons and trailers waiting to start. The elephants had been sent on some time before, traveling on foot with one man to look after them—a job usually, I learned later, assigned to Tug, the hunchback. There was a strong smell of gasoline fumes in the air which bit sharply at the back of my throat.

One large lorry was being backed slowly and cautiously over the turf towards our trailer. Ginger, the top half of his body leaning out of the driving-cab, waved cheerfully at me.

"Where's Uncle?" he shouted. I did not immediately realize that he was referring to Beef. It was a nickname, I reflected, that would probably stick to Beef for good.

"Asleep inside," I replied. "Shall I wake him?"

"No, that's all right. We'll tow your trailer along just as it is. I'll try not to disturb his beauty sleep too much," he added.

In a few minutes the trailer was securely hitched up to the lorry, and I watched the sleeping Beef being drawn out of the field and join the tail of the long, colored procession of circus wagons already on the move.

It was the last one, and looking round I saw that the field was empty now except for my car and one old-fashioned caravan over by the far hedge, and between the shafts of which stood an ancient horse. Unlike the motor-driven, paint-smart, streamlined buses and trailers that the others in the circus were using, this wagon was one of the old traditional gypsy type which have always represented the Romany in book illustrations of the more romantic sort of story. It was painted a brilliant red with intricate carvings under the eaves of its railway-carriage roof. I had seen wagons like this often before; on the main roads back from Kent at the end of the hopping season; on the Downs at Epsom; in some little deserted lane off the Great North Road. In fact, I had imagined that the circus people lived in similar vehicles until I had seen the up-to-dateness of the huge converted buses and four-wheeled trailers standing around the big tent the night before. A light curl of smoke wandered slowly out of the narrow tin chimney, but otherwise there was no sign nor sound of life from it.

"Good morning," said a pleasant voice at my elbow. "Are you an artist or a writer?"

I turned sharply to find myself staring at a tall, dark girl who must have been standing close behind me for some moments. She was extremely attractive, even at that hour of the morning, with dark, emphasized features and black wavy hair. The long nose, small pointed chin and almost violet eyes gave her a Latin appearance, although she was dressed in smart, and very English, riding-breeches and white shirt.

"Must I be one or the other?" I asked, evading the question.

"They mostly are."

"Who are *they?*"

"Oh, the people who travel with us for a time. There's

always somebody following us around, either painting pictures of people in the ring, of the wagons or the horses, or writing books and stories about circus life. Boris Bleane, the novelist, was with us for a month or so last season, and he wrote in his last book that we were a people 'living precariously on the bedraggled hem of that gown which Dame Nature calls her Civilization Dress.' "

I laughed. "You're something to do with the circus then?" I asked.

The girl spread her arms above her head in a characteristic ring gesture. "I'm Gypsy Margot's daughter," she said, with mock gravity, "but I'm also one of the Concinis—my sister and I do a riding act together."

At that moment a bent figure emerged from the wagon at the far side of the field and began to beckon to the girl calling: "Anita, Anita."

"My mother," explained the girl. "You must come and see our act some time," and she turned and walked quickly across the field away from me.

There had been a peculiar tinge of condescension in her voice when she had explained that the beckoning figure was her mother. As I started up the car I wondered vaguely what it had signified. Nothing very important probably, and yet since I was here with Jacobi's Circus helping Beef to investigate a possible murder, it was only following the correct line laid down by my elders and betters in my profession to "wonder vaguely" about anything which did not present a completely innocent and normal face.

I had to pull up at the gate of the field to allow the red gypsy wagon to draw out on to the road. As I drew level the face of Anita appeared at the window and grinned cheerfully at me. Then, like a reflection in a mirror, a second face appeared beside hers, and the two girls waved to me as I drove past. I had not been warned that the Concinis were twins, and I was slightly bewildered as I drove on ahead to the next camping-place. Beef's cases had been quite complicated enough up to now without the added Shakespearian complexity of twins, and I foresaw an almost inevitably bewildered Beef, who would certainly never be able to avoid making a fool of himself in a situation like this.

The Sergeant, however, was completely unconscious of this, for when in half an hour's time I climbed into his wagon again he was just sitting up on the edge of his bunk and sleepily scratching his head.

"I thought," he said, yawning, "these people got up early. It's half-past eight already." And pushing his watch back under the pillow, he rose slowly to his feet and drew aside the curtains.

"Wouldn't hardly have thought it possible," he said ruminatively, after a prolonged stare out of the window.

"What?" I queried suspiciously.

"Nature's a marvelous thing," he said. "Now look at that bed of nettles over there. It wasn't there last night. Just simply shot up from nothing. Marvelous I call it."

It may have been the fact that I had not yet had breakfast which made me say abruptly: "We moved while you were asleep," rather than give the painstaking explanation of this phenomenon which was expected of me. In any case, I thought I detected a faint glint of mockery in Beef's eye which warned me not to take his remarks at their face value.

"And now," he said, when we had finished our meal and his pipe was drawing well, "the question is, where do we start?"

I explained to him briefly what had already occurred that morning while he had been asleep.

"Twins, eh?" he said. "Awkward sort of Do, that is. I got a cousin who married a chap called Fred Gomme. Couldn't tell him apart from his brother except when they were together.

Caused her any amount of trouble that did until Fred fell downstairs one day and broke his nose. Only thing that stopped a divorce, she used to say." And Beef gave one of his loud unexpected guffaws which he seemed to reserve for his own stories.

"Still, we can see into that later," he went on when he had recovered from his amusement. "What we ought to do first, I suppose, is to go and see that old baggage, and find out what she really knows about this murder business."

"By 'baggage,' " I said coldly, "I suppose you mean Gypsy Margot?"

"That's right," said Beef. "And then we ought to get a bit friendly with some of the people here so's to know what's going on. In which line of investigation," he continued ponderously, "you seem to have already made some progress." And still chuckling, he led the way out of the wagon.

Not many yards away Ginger was driving a long iron peg into the turf, and he paused to look up at Beef and me. As previously he wore no shirt, and his broad shoulders were an even brown from continual exposure. His oil-stained flannel trousers were tucked into a pair of rubber boots.

" 'Morning, Uncle," he shouted.

Beef looked around himself suspiciously before coming to the conclusion that the "Uncle" in question was himself, and answered the query with a rather watery smile.

" 'Ow d'you like the tober?" asked Ginger.

"Tober?" Beef looked mystified.

"Yes. This 'ere," said Ginger, hitting the peg vindictively with his hammer.

"Do you mean that peg?" asked Beef.

Ginger's face wore a pained expression. "Gor lumme," he said, leaning forward on his hammer and staring at us, "where was you brought up? Tober, I said. Tober. This 'ere," and he swept his arm round to indicate the field in which the circus was standing.

Beef's face seemed to shine suddenly with understanding. "Oh," he said, "you mean the camping-place?"

"That's right," said Ginger. "Tober." Whereupon he returned to his work with renewed vigor.

"Funny," said Beef as we walked on. "Never heard that word before."

"Perhaps," I suggested, "it's a circus word. I've heard it said that circus people have a whole vocabulary of their own."

Beef grunted. "I'd better make a note of it then," he said, and he drew from his pocket that solid official-looking note-book which had played so dependable part in his previous cases. Beef did not desert old friends, and this reminder of his constable days gave me a peculiar feeling of confidence.

The "big top" had been built up while we were eating our breakfast, and the dim interior was empty except for two men constructing the large cage for the lion act. The long boards and trestles looked bare and empty, and the central ring had not yet been prepared. Beef and I strolled towards the front entrance of the tent, on the left of which stood the proprietor's wagon commanding the whole of the field. Farther up, nearer the gate, stood a small canvas construction rather like the beach-tents used for changing. The old woman whom I remembered beckoning to her daughter early that morning was now attempting, unsuccessfully, to drive one of the small pegs into the ground.

" 'The mattock tottered in her hand,' " I said.

"That's not a mattock," said Beef, with perverted realism. "Let's go and help the old girl."

But the "old girl" did not seem to appreciate Beef's intention, for when he approached her she straightened herself up and stared uncompromisingly at him.

"What do you want?" she asked in a toneless voice. "I can

manage by myself, young man. You mind your own business."

It was difficult to judge her age since her face had the leathery preservation of a person who has spent most of his life out of doors. She might have been anywhere between fifty and a hundred and fifty. She had a long, fleshless nose over which the brown skin was stretched tight and shining and reflected the light as if it had been polished with oil. Her eyes were large and dark, so that it was impossible to tell which was pupil and which iris. She stood staring at us both for a minute or more, her long, bony hands on her hips and her head thrust suspiciously forward so that two heavy gold earrings swung out from under her hair and rested against the withered skin of her cheeks.

Then, with a quick turn which made her black skirt flare outwards, she walked into the little tent. There was a peculiar woodenness in her movements, like that of a man who has had to learn to walk a second time after an accident which has deprived him of the use of his legs for more than a year— something which is learned by reason rather than by imitation. She used long precise strides, her shoulders were level, and her arms swung with unbent elbows. In a moment she had emerged from the tent again, this time carrying a placard which she leaned against the front of it. It read:

GYPSY MARGOT

will tell, by the shadow of your future in the crystal, by the symbol of your death in the stars which were at your nativity, by your hand which is the instrument of your future; and by your eyes, which are the windows of your soul,

YOUR FORTUNE

"You know," I commented, "there's style in that. I should think that she's a very unusual woman."

Beef appeared not to be listening.

"Education," I went on. "Of a queer sort, I expect. A feeling for words. In any case, not what one usually expects from a fortune-teller on a fair-ground."

Beef still did not hear me. His lips moved silently as he finished reading the notice, and then he made a sudden dive for the opening of the tent.

"Here," I heard his voice saying, "I want to have a talk with you."

CHAPTER IV

THE old woman looked at Beef with calculating eyes. "Cross the gypsy's hand with silver," she said.

But Beef disregarded her, pulling out his notebook and sitting down at the table in the center of the tent. Margot slowly took her place in the deep arm-chair on the other side, and her eyes moved restlessly from Beef to myself and then back again to Beef.

"We don't want our fortunes told, old lady," said Beef cheerfully. "We want to find out what you know about this here murder story you've been telling my nephew."

"Murder," began Margot, "I see in the crystal the gathering shadows of angry men and women. Why are they angry? Ah, they walk back. What lies at their feet? It is the body of someone killed. They are crying, I hear the sounds of their crying like the distant cries of gulls circling the cliffs. They are lost in a forest of crying trees and no one can show them the way. They are wandering . . ."

"Here," said Beef, "I can't hardly follow all that fancy business. I want to know how you know there's going to be a murder—if there is going to be a murder—and what made you tell Albert. Couldn't you leave out the trimmings and tell us what you know?"

The old gypsy closed her eyes and rocked backwards and forwards in her seat, then suddenly folding her arms she stared straight at Beef and began to speak very quickly in a high-pitched whine. "Beware of a dark woman. She is not to be trusted. She will ask you to follow her on a journey, but you must resist the temptation. For you the future is best when you do not obey impulses. Return to the fair woman I see waiting patiently at home for you. Nevertheless, you will make a journey and return home with something of value, though it will not be gold. People will admire you for it, though they cannot see it . . ."

Beef looked up at me in despair. "What can you do with a case like this?" he asked dismally. "She don't want to speak plain. What's all this about journeys and dark women?"

"Tell her what we're doing here," I suggested.

"Look here," said Beef, turning back towards the old gypsy and speaking slowly and distinctly, as if to a child. "We came up here because of what you told Albert about there going to be a murder in the circus. We're detectives, see. We want to find out about it." He looked imploringly at the silent figure facing him, but she gave no sign that any of the words had been heard. Beef tried a new tack. "Do you know Albert?" he asked.

Margot nodded.

"Will he leave the circus?"

She nodded again.

"Why?"

"The circus," she said slowly, as if she were spitting out the words, "will break up."

"But why should it?" I asked, "it's doing pretty well."

Margot shook her head violently, so that the heavy gold rings which hung from her ears jingled as they swung from side to side. For a moment she seemed to be considering us, then she began to speak in a slow measured voice, flat, as if she did not realize what she was saying, almost automatic.

"There is much hate in the circus," she said. "I have seen it suddenly lighting an eye or directing a hand. It is like oil in the wheels; the circus is run on hate. Then suddenly a hand is raised in anger and a man is struck to the ground. When he rises there is bitterness in his heart which he tries to conceal. He will mark the slate with his anger, and the mark will only be washed away with blood. A woman drops through the air like a falling peregrine and behind her in the air is hate. Two men have watched her like animals, frightened to come out of the shadow of the undergrowth into the light where she stands. Their hands are clenched over daggers. There is death in their eyes. And the circus which is built on these foundations will crumble and fall. I smell blood in the air, and terror which feeds on the heart at night. The cold lights shine over the empty tober and a cold wind blows where once was the circus."

"Poetic, isn't she?" said Beef admiringly.

"Poetic nonsense," I said shortly; "we shan't get anything out of her."

"Who's going to get bumped off?" asked Beef, "that's what I want to know."

The gypsy looked at him blankly.

"Is it a man or a woman?"

But she had obviously said all that she would say, and simply stared at us with an expressionless face until we got up and left the tent.

"So that's your hope of regaining your reputation as a private investigator," I said bitterly. "The word of a gypsy fortune-teller?"

"I wouldn't go so far as to say she didn't know nothing," said Beef.

"Obviously," I continued, "she knew a great deal. At least, that's my guess. Personally, I think she's a very clever woman. The question is, what does this murder prediction actually mean?"

"What does it mean?" echoed Beef.

"Yes. Why did she tell Albert? There are two possibilities, I suppose. Either she thinks there is going to be an attempted murder—and we won't worry just now about how she might know that—or else she has a very special reason for trying to make people *think* there's going to be one."

[27]

"And which do you think is the correct one?" asked Beef.

"I don't know, and what's more I don't think it's very important. It's quite possible she thinks there is going to be some trouble here. But I don't see any such possibility myself. I think we're wasting our time."

"Oh, you do," said Beef stubbornly. "Well, I'm going to stay on and see into it. If you take my advice you'll stay on too. Where are you going to get the book from if you go home?" he ended triumphantly.

"My work has never been that of writing funny stories," I said tartly, "and that's about all I'm likely to get here."

Beef's mouth drooped downward in a ludicrous fashion, like a boy just beginning to cry. "All right," he said dismally, "if that's the way you feel about it. But I'm going to stay on and see this through. I think . . ."

But I never heard what it was he thought, for at that moment there was a commotion outside and looking out we saw a group of people come slowly into view. One of the elephants formed the center of the crowd, walking slowly and steadily forward, taking no apparent notice of the noise. Its trunk was held high in the air wrapped tightly round the struggling figure of Albert.

"Let me down," he was shouting desperately, but his demand was only greeted by a fresh outburst of laughter from the crowd. Albert's fists punched uselessly at the thick gray trunk which held securely to his waist and his feet kicked wildly in the air.

"Uncle," he shouted suddenly, as he caught sight of Beef and me hurrying towards him. "Uncle, tell them to make him put me down. I can't breathe. I want to get down."

"Here," said Beef commandingly, "what's all this about?" But though his voice might have made petty thieves tremble in the little town of Wraxham, where he had been a Sergeant, he had a rather different problem to deal with now. The crowd swept by us without taking any notice.

"Here," said Beef again, and then, because there was nothing else to do, we joined in the procession behind the elephant and walked slowly out of the field and into the main street of the village. The elephant appeared to know the way, for it turned confidently down towards the market-place. By this time most of the population of the village had collected and were joining in the laughter at the free show. Beef angrily elbowed his way to the front of the crowd to where Tug, the hunchback we had first met in the elephant tent, was marching, a broad grin on his face, at the head of the elephant.

"Here," said Beef once again, laying his hand on the man's shoulder, "who's supposed to be looking after this animal?"

"S'right," said Tug cheerfully, "that's me."

"Well, can't you make him put young Albert down?" asked Beef.

Tug looked at Beef as if he found something immensely funny in this last sentence. "Can't make an elephant do anything," he said. "At least, not unless he wants to. And when he wants to do something, then you can't stop him. Not unless, that is, he wants to be stopped."

This somewhat involved statement was interrupted however by the elephant itself, who had moved on ahead of the arguing couple and had reached the market-place and made its way over to a large slimy pond which occupied one corner of it. Walking in until the water was above its knees, it suddenly released the shouting Albert and began unconcernedly to squirt water over its own back. Albert struggled to the edge of the pond and climbed out on to the bank as Beef and Tug arrived on the scene.

"You did that on purpose," he shouted at the hunchback, in a voice which had become high pitched with anger.

Tug, who obviously thought himself something of a "funny

man," shrugged his shoulders innocently and looked round at his audience with an imploring gesture of his hands.

"Yes you did," persisted Albert. "That elephant wouldn't have done a thing like that on its own. You told it to."

"The elephant," said Tug, "never forgets." Which witticism raised a howl of laughter from the audience.

But Albert was apparently not in a joking mood. He pushed forward until only an inch or two separated him from the hunchback.

"I'm not a fool," he said angrily. And then, as the people seemed to be taking this as a joke too, he turned suddenly on them. "Yes, I know you think so," he went on, "you think this is a great joke. You're always doing this sort of thing to me. That's all I'm here for—to be laughed at. Well, I've just about had enough of it."

An anonymous voice from the center of the crowd called out, "Poor little Albert. He's getting all hot and bothered. Let's put him back in the nice cool water."

Beef turned to me and said quietly: "I'm going to put a stop to this."

"You'd better keep out of it," I told him, with a vision of the Sergeant himself following his nephew into the pond.

"Can't have so many of them on to one," said Beef, and stepped forward. He stood square in front of Tug, who seemed, as much as anyone, the leader of the demonstration.

"Now then," he said, "this has gone far enough."

"What the —— is it to do with you?" Tug asked.

"Never mind about that," said Beef calmly. "You leave the boy alone and get back to your jobs. The whole lot of you." And he slowly moved an authoritative hand in the direction of the circus tents.

I watched him with keen interest, and once again found myself startled by Beef's success. It really is an extraordinary thing about him that whenever I am most confident that he is going to make a fool of himself, the Sergeant comes out on top. One would have imagined that a middle-aged ex-police-man, holding up his hand as though to control traffic, would have been no obstacle to these people. And even had he been in uniform one could visualize helmets flying. But there was something about Beef, I had to admit. It may have been good humor, or it may have been some odd individual version of what is called personality. At any rate, there it was. They stopped.

"If you don't want to get back to work," said Beef, with something of a grin, "I recommend the 'Five Carpenters' over there. Nice drop of bitter, and very pleasant people . . ."

This announcement left me wondering at what point Beef had found time to "slip out" or "slip in," to use a phrase he himself adopted when speaking of public-houses.

". . . But at any rate, leave the boy alone. He's had enough for one morning."

They grinned quite easily, and started to talk among them-selves and move away. I thought that Tug Wilson had an unpleasant look, as though of some special hostility towards the Sergeant. It may have been my imagination, or he may have been genuinely angered in seeing his mob leadership destroyed by Beef's easy methods. He walked away alone.

When Beef and I were left together, I turned to him with some irritation.

"That's just about the last straw," I said.

Beef looked hurt. "Why?" he asked. "It wasn't his fault, was it?"

"That's not the point. It's the whole position I'm objecting to. First of all, we find out that the old gypsy won't give us anything reasonable to support her fantastic prediction. And now this incident, which shows that your nephew is nothing but the fool of the show. Everyone pulls his leg and bullies him. How do we know that Gypsy Margot wasn't having a little joke with him? If she was, we've been taken in nicely, that's all I can say."

"I don't say as you may not be right," said Beef, "but on the other hand . . ."

CHAPTER V

Not for the first time I found Beef's genius for non-committal pronouncements very unsatisfying. This was a time when he should have taken me into his confidence and I felt hurt that he should continue to treat me as no more than an appendage to himself and his investigations. What reason had he for thinking that something definite would emerge from this case? To me it seemed pure fantasy. How was he going to "investigate" on such a vague and undecided basis? And so at last, when we had finished our lunch, I turned to him with the intention of getting some decisive statement.

"Look here," I said, "you've got to tell me something about this case. At the moment I'm completely in the dark."

"No more than I am," said Beef, removing his tooth-pick for a moment and grinning broadly. "But something'll come of it, you see."

"Do mean to tell me," I asked incredulously, "that you have no other evidence to go on than what that crazy gypsy told you?"

"And," said Beef with dignity, "my past experience in matters of crime and murder."

"And you mean to stay on here on the chance of there being a murder?"

"I do," said Beef, "and if you've any sense, you'll stay with me."

"But Beef," I protested, "at least give me something solid to go on. At present the whole thing is fantastic. Can't you give me some good reason why I shouldn't be wasting my time if I stayed on here?"

"You take my advice," said Beef, "and you won't go far wrong."

But this was not enough for me. We might hang about with this circus for months and discover nothing unusual. "How do you intend to go about this case then?" I asked. "How are you going to look for evidence? How, as a matter of curiosity, do you know what to look *for?*"

"Well," said Beef, "I'm glad you asked me that, because I've got it all worked out nice. I thought to myself, the way to stop a murder what might happen anytime is to find out first who might want to murder who, and second, how he or she might do it. Now, it stands to reason that if this here murder was premeditated—and we can assume it will be—then the person responsible will want it to look like an accident. Especially since they'll know that I'm on the scene. All right then. This is what we do. We go to the performance this evening and keep our eyes open. We look around and make a note of all the ways someone might be killed and everybody think it was an accident. You heard what Mr. Jackson said? He said there was danger in everything that was done in the ring. So we've got to find just where the danger lies. And everything's straightforward." He looked at me in triumph.

"There was a boy at school with me," I said thoughtfully, "who had an original way of birds-nesting."

"Here," said Beef, "what's that got to do with this case?"

"You'll see," I answered. "The method this boy used was to go round all the hedges in his neighborhood and look for the places where he thought birds might possibly nest when the spring came. Then he cut away the brambles and nettles and put nails in the trees, so that when the birds did nest there he would be able to reach their eggs without any trouble."

"Well," demanded Beef, "what happened?"

"Nothing," I answered, "the birds never nested in the places he'd chosen for them. And that is where your method strikes me as being useless. The birds—if they nest at all—won't nest in your pet trees."

"So you don't think it will work?" asked Beef.

"Most decidedly not."

"Then what do you suggest?"

"Going straight home," I said shortly. "At least that's what I'm going to do, and I think you'd better come with me. Now look here, Beef, be honest with yourself. Do you really think there's going to be anything of a case in this place? Or do you just like the circus atmosphere and are using it as an excuse for a holiday away from your wife?"

"You would put it like that," snorted Beef, "and I can tell you straight that's got nothing to do with it. You go on home if you want to. I'm going to stay here and get to the bottom of it. But I'll tell you one thing. If you go home now you'll be missing what looks like the most interesting case of my career. But that's your affair." And beyond that he refused to say another word.

It was, I thought to myself, as I wandered out on to the ground, not a very easy question to decide. I quite honestly felt that our staying on now was little more than a gamble, and I hardly felt like wasting so much time and money on so small a chance. I decided in the end to put the question out of my mind until after the afternoon show. Time enough to make decisions then.

Most of the artists were in their wagons, changing, and there was peculiar quietness about the camp. A small crowd had gathered by the gate, but it was impossible to tell whether they were simply curious, or whether they intended coming to the show and did not like to be first. The band, tuning, practicing, or simply running up and down the scale on their instruments, could be heard quite clearly, and then, after a brief silence, they struck up together with a Souza march. This seemed to be the signal, for people began to enter the ground and line up in front of the empty pay-box. In ones and twos at first, and then in a steady stream, until soon the queue reached to the gate and out into the road.

For some reason that I was unable to identify I began to feel a growing excitement. Familiar sounds took on a new significance; the snarling of the lions in the lion-tunnel, where they awaited their act; a tent hand driving home a shaky peg; the groom hissing between his teeth as he put the finishing touches to the horses; the sudden sound of a primus stove as one of the wagon doors opened and then closed again; the chatter and laughter from the waiting crowd; all of it seemed to build up into a clearly-defined crescendo. Then Mrs. Jackson came down the steps of the proprietor's wagon with a jingling cash-box under her arm, and the sound was like the pause in a symphony, the faint reiteration by the leading violin of the theme, before the whole orchestra takes it up to the final climax.

The tent-flaps were thrown open and the crowd began to file into their seats. The cool tent, which had smelt only of green grass and sawdust, began to warm to the sound of quick laughter, pennies chinking, the cries of the program sellers, and the expectation on each face as it stared for a moment at the empty ring and the clean sawdust under the white lights in the tent top.

It seemed to me amazing that such a finely-graduated atmosphere of suspense could be possible. Not only in the audience, where it was more understandable, but in the circus people themselves. Even though it must be sheer routine to them, yet somehow, unconsciously, as the moment for the beginning of the show drew nearer, I felt them becoming tense, keyed up, more animated.

I took a seat near the entrance, and was joined almost immediately by the Sergeant, who grinned but said nothing, as he sat carefully beside me on the narrow planking which served for seats. The band suddenly changed to another tune, a bright rhythmical one, and the talking people became silent.

"It's the Concinis first," said Beef, who seemed already to know much more about the show than I did.

As he spoke the twins came through the artists' entrance at the back of the ring, riding two pure white horses.

"I wonder which is Anita?" I whispered to Beef.

"Well you ought to know," he chuckled in a tone of voice which instantly made me wish I had not asked the question and I turned my attention quickly back to the ring.

It was impossible to find any difference between the two girls. Both looked extremely beautiful in their bright costumes, with red leather boots and astrakhan hats in the Cossack style. As one of them passed round our side of the ring she seemed to be searching the crowd with a faint smile on her face, and then, catching my eye, she quickly raised one hand in salute. At least, then, I knew which was Anita. It was only a question of not getting mixed up. But the other twin, passing at that moment, interrupted my self-satisfied thoughts by saluting me in a similar way. I heard Beef's chuckle beside me.

"They must have arranged that between them before they started," he said. "You want to look out for yourself or you'll find yourself in no end of a mess."

"I don't know what you mean," I replied coldly.

There is nothing quite so cynical, I thought to myself, as the expression of a circus horse. It gallops steadily round the ring, while some human being performs numerous antics on its back for the amusement of more humans seated round the ring. The horse runs on, imperturbable, a little amused, almost condescendingly. I folded my arms, sat back, and watched the horses, feeling myself rather aloof.

But slowly the mood vanished. The Concinis were doing so much more than what I had smugly called "antics." There was, I discovered, a delicate artistry in the patterns they wove over and across their horses' backs, passing, changing. It was not the difficulty of the act that counted, but the confident ease with which it was performed. For me, they seemed to extract pure motion from the flesh and blood which was creating it, and like music, or the dipping swallows in the summer, they left behind them the evanescent curves of a beautiful design. A design which had disappeared as soon as it was formed, but which left its impression on the mind. I felt a little sad at the quickness of its vanishing.

Too soon the act was finished, and the stormy applause from the audience aroused me as the two white horses galloped out of the ring side by side as they had entered. I found myself applauding vigorously.

"Of course," I heard Beef's voice sarcastically beside me, "it wouldn't do to say you was biased, would it?"

Feeling misjudged, I kept silent, and watched the far side of the ring for the next turn. It was the performing seal—known as Eustace—which Corinne Jackson showed. She entered now, her arms held above her head, introducing herself in the traditional circus manner, while the seal followed her in, sprawling along in the sawdust and giving an occasional coughing sound, as if in self-encouragement.

I found the turn rather dull, although I heard Beef chuckling with the rest of the audience when, after each particular trick, Eustace lay on his side in the ring and slapped his flippers together to show his own appreciation of what he had just done. A sudden whispering at the entrance to the tent diverted my attention, and I turned to see two of the attendants talking earnestly together.

"Varda me parlari, col," one of them called quietly across the ring, and then followed a dozen or so sentences in the circus language which I did not understand, but which were answered by one of the attendants in the ring. In a few moments half a dozen men were making their way as unobtrusively as possible towards the exit, while Corinne continued her act as if nothing were happening, and the audience seemed completely unaware that anything unusual had occurred. I turned to Beef.

"Come on," he said briskly, "something's happening."

"What were they saying?" I asked.

"Well, I only caught some of it, but there's been an accident or something outside," said Beef as we made our way out into the open. For a moment I could see nothing unusual as I looked quickly round the tober, but then I noticed a small crowd of six or seven people grouped by the steps of the Concinis' wagon. Jackson hurried past us in that direction, and Beef and I followed, pushing our way quickly up the steps.

The wagon seemed crowded with the artists and hands, so that it was impossible to move, but Beef took the situation in at a glance.

"Come on," he said firmly to everybody in general, "no good hanging about like this. Let's have the wagon to ourselves for a bit, will you?"

Silently they obeyed him, leaving only five of us in the narrow wagon, and at last I saw what no doubt Beef had already noticed or guessed at; the still form of one of the twins lying on the bed. Gypsy Margot was crouched beside her on the floor, staring as one mesmerized and vainly rubbing the girl's hands.

Beef walked briskly over to the bed and bent over the figure. The girl's back was bare, as if she had been changing after her act, and she lay across the bed, sprawling, as if from a fall, with one foot just touching the floor.

"Which one is this?" asked Beef. "Anita or Helen?"

"Anita," answered Margot. "How could it have happened? I was only out of the wag . . ."

"All right," said Beef. "We can save that till afterwards. Let's have a look at her."

His thick fingers gently touched the flesh around a long bleeding wound on Anita's back.

"Water—lint—bandages," he said curtly.

When they were brought to him he proceeded to bind the wound, passing the strips of linen over and round Anita's shoulder. His usually clumsy-looking fingers seemed adroit and expert as he worked, unrolling the bandage with a neat, sure touch. Finally, when he had finished, he lifted the girl in his arms, while Margot drew back the bedcovers, and placed Anita in the bed.

"She'll be all right," he said turning to us. "Only a flesh-wound. Her shoulder-blade stopped it being anything more serious. Still, we might send for a doctor, just in case."

"Is it absolutely necessary?" asked Jackson.

"Well," answered Beef, "it's a clean wound."

"Then we won't fetch a doctor," stated Jackson. Gypsy Margot nodded her agreement with this, and Beef merely shrugged his shoulders. I realized that doctors were almost unheard of to circus people. Only extreme cases were taken to them. Used to dealing with the wounds of their animals or their. fellow artists, they regarded interference from outside with an almost superstitious eye.

"In any case," I said abruptly, "we ought to call in the police."

"Police," said Beef scornfully. "What do we want them in here for?"

Jackson and Margot were violent in their repudiation of my idea, and feeling slightly crushed, I looked at Beef in bewilderment.

"And now," said the Sergeant, "we want to get to the bottom of this. What I want to know is just what happened in here."

Nobody answered. Jackson stood sullenly leaning against the door, Mrs. Jackson was quietly clearing away the remains of the bandages, lint and water that Beef had been using, Helen was sitting on a low stool by the bed staring unblinkingly at her sister's face, and Gypsy Margot was mumbling gently to herself apparently oblivious of all that was going on.

"Now come on," said Beef impatiently. "Some of you must know what happened."

Helen suddenly moved her eyes and looked full at the Sergeant. "I did it," she said, and her voice had a vague, uncomprehending quality which changed almost to a scream as she went on, "I did it. I stabbed her. I don't know what made me . . . I saw her . . . her back . . . I . . ."

"Now don't go getting yourself all excited," said Beef calmly. And then, turning to the others, he went on: "Look, I'd just like to have a little talk with Helen alone, if you don't mind. Perhaps she'll be better if there's not so many people about."

We moved towards the door, but he gave me a slight sign that I was to stay. The other three left without a word, and I closed the door softly behind them. Beef turned to Helen.

"Now tell me just what happened," he said.

CHAPTER VI

HELEN looked at the Sergeant for a moment before she began to speak. She seemed to be weighing something in her mind, and I thought she was probably wondering how much she could tell us.

"You needn't be afraid," said Beef. "We're not trying to trap you, or anything like that. I just want to hear what happened after you left the tent. Start from there. Start where you came out of the ring."

"I don't know that I can explain it really," said Helen. "I still feel that it can't really have happened to me. I mean, the whole thing is like a dream. But I'll try. When we came out of the ring we took our horses round to the groom, and then walked to the wagon. We were laughing at a little joke we'd had with Mr. Townsend—you know, so that he wouldn't know which of us was Anita."

"Yes, I know," grinned Beef. "Took him in proper, it did, too."

"I think perhaps that's what started it," said Helen.

"What do you mean? The joke you played on Mr. Townsend? Did you have a quarrel over it then?"

"No, not that. I'll try and tell you. You see, as we were walking along Anita made some remark about how Mr. Townsend hadn't been able to tell the difference between us. I said: 'Perhaps it would be better for us if he could; if everybody could.' I don't know what made me say that. It just came out. 'Why, what do you mean?' said Anita. 'I don't know,' I said, 'It's just that I feel tired of us being so alike, I suppose.'"

"And what did she say to that?" asked Beef.

"Nothing, she just laughed. We'd got to the wagon by then,

and we started changing. She said she was going round into the tent to speak to you and Mr. Townsend, and then she suddenly had the idea that I should go instead of her. She tried to persuade me, but I wouldn't do it. It wasn't because I didn't like a joke sometimes. I felt something worse than that; something I can't describe."

"You mean," I asked, "that you thought it wasn't in very good taste. You didn't think it was a joke at all?"

"No. Nothing like that. It's a feeling I've had before sometimes. Every time we do something that proves I'm exactly like Anita I feel a little the same. It's almost as if she were stealing something of mine. As if it weren't my own life I'm leading at all, but only half of hers. I don't know if you see what I mean, it's so hard to put it into words."

"Yes," said Beef thoughtfully, "I think I do. What it comes to is this. When you look at your sister and she's doing something—we might say like tying her shoe-lace up—then it seems to you that it's like looking at yourself in the mirror. Only you know you're not doing that thing at all, so you're sort of jealous, because it looks as though she's taken something away from you. Is that what you mean?"

"In a way, I suppose it is," agreed Helen. "But I don't ever think it out clearly like that."

"All right," said Beef. "And then what happened?"

"Well, then we went on changing and talking together as we always do. But then I happened to look round and Anita was with her back to me by the bed. Her back was bare, and the skin was just like I knew mine would look if I turned round to the mirror. I thought suddenly that if a fly settled on her it would probably make me itch as well as her. And then I picked up a knife."

"Where was it?" asked Beef. "Did you take it out of a drawer?"

"No, it was on the dressing-table. One of the knives they

sometimes use in the ring. Not a proper one, but made of steel, only blunted. It was always hanging about the place."

"And then what?"

"Then I stabbed her, I suppose. I don't really remember doing it. I just felt that I had to. It didn't seem to me that Anita was a person at all—more like a cardboard figure. I wanted to cut at it with something. I didn't hate her or anything like that. I just forgot she was a person at all. And then she fell across the bed with a sort of moan and I knew what I had done. Oh, it was horrible . . ."

Helen suddenly stopped speaking and crouched down with her head in her hands crying softly to herself. "I must have been mad," she said. "Whatever could have made me want to do a thing like that?"

As she spoke we heard coming from the tent the sound of the band playing and of the clowns shouting. It seemed to seep through slowly, as if our attention had now become relaxed, and we were able to notice things outside of this wagon again. Anita too, must have been disturbed by the sound for she stirred for a moment on the bed, and then opened her eyes.

"Well," said Beef, "and how are you feeling, young lady? You gave us a bit of a fright, you did."

Anita smiled vaguely and tried to sit up. But the smile turned to a wry expression of pain as she felt the wound.

"Best thing you can do is to lie still," ordered Beef. "Do you think you could tell us what happened?"

"I think so," said Anita, "I feel all right really. My back hurts a little, that's all."

The clear voice of Eric, the proprietor's son, rang out clearly from the big top, speaking some traditional clown's patter with the Yorkshire accent he was assuming for the benefit of the crowd.

'This morn I arose
From my sweet repose.
I goes
Out among the trees that grows
To shoot the crows,
And meet one of my British foes.

Anita's story was substantially the same as her sister's. She was a little embarrassed by my eye as she told of her suggestion to prolong the joke of mixed identity with me.

"It was only a joke," she explained to Beef, although she looked at me with her eyebrows slightly raised, as if to see how I was taking it. "But Helen wouldn't do it. She seemed a little cross with the idea, so I didn't say any more."

We have some words that quickly come to blows;
He hits me on the nose,
Down I goes,
Into the gutter where all the muddy water flows.

Eric's voice seemed to be forcing its way through tears as he told of this fictitious tragedy. Then came the unvalorous sequel, the man who knows he is bested and does the common-sense thing about it.

Up I arose,
Straight home I goes,
I takes off my wet clothes—

"And then," said Anita, "just as I was taking off my things I happened to glance up into the little mirror over the bed. I saw Helen's arm, with a knife, coming down towards me. I tried to move, but it was too late. Then I suppose I must have fainted."

[45]

"That move you made," commented Beef, "just about saved your life."

Helen gave a low soft moan at these words and looked across at her sister. Anita stretched out her hand, and Helen suddenly went across to the bed, kneeling against the side of it, and buried her face in Anita's shoulder.

> —And into bed I goes.
> I turns up my toes,
> I tallows my nose,
> I has a sweet repose—
> And that's all I knows.

There was a light tapping sound on the door of the wagon and the head of Mrs. Jackson looked nervously in.

"Can I came in, Mr. Beef?" she asked. "I brought some tea. I thought the two girls could do with a cup. I always say it steadies you when anything goes wrong."

Beef motioned her in.

"There," said Mrs. Jackson, giving the two girls a cup each, "drink it up. You'll feel much better. Really," she went on half-turning to Beef and me, "I don't know what's coming over the circus these days. What with one thing and another. First we have Mr. Beef here. I don't know what Mr. Jackson is about. And then this talk of murder . . ."

"Murder?" said Helen suddenly. "Who's been talking about a murder?"

"Oh, it's nothing to do with you, dear, I'm sure. As if anyone would think about a thing like that. No, it's something that silly boy Albert Stiles has been spreading about. As if anyone couldn't see he was having his leg pulled."

Is that ALL you know? asked the level voice of Jackson from the big tent.

No, said Eric,
That's not all I know
I knows,
And you knows,
And everybody else knows,

Mrs. Jackson stopped talking abruptly when she heard her husband's voice, as if she were afraid of interrupting him. She was a small slight woman, on whom the circus life appeared to have had its effects. Nervous, so that her hands seemed to flutter continually from her lap to her hair without ever doing anything useful when they got there. She had the startled look of one of those who have grown used to bullying and sought now only to avoid it. Her white lumpy face was kind and showed concern easily.

That a nice beef steak
And a nice mutton chop
Makes a hungry man's mouth
Go flipperty-flop—
            like a lamb's tail.

"Well," said Mrs. Jackson. "I must go to put the supper on. If you've done with the cups, dears, I'll take them with me." The band in the tent had begun to play the music for the last turn, and Mrs. Jackson stood as if it had been a command and opened the door. "Well, good-by, dear," she said. "These little trials do us good sometimes, I always say." And forgetting to shut the door, she was gone, half-running, half-walking across to the proprietor's wagon.

"I often wonder," said Beef ruminatively, "how it is some of these people get into a circus. Why they join up with you. Now people like your mother, I suppose, were born in the circus. But how do those like Mrs. Jackson ever come to be here at all?"

"Your guess is quite wrong, Sergeant," said Anita. "Actually mother wasn't born in a circus at all. She used to be on the halls. That was a long time ago, of course. But she had an act with her brother."

"What did they do?" asked Beef.

"Oh, some sort of a mind-reading act. It depended a lot on hypnotism, you know."

"Hypnotism?" said Beef. "Can your mother hypnotize people then?"

"Depends on the person," answered Anita. "She can't hypnotize me, for instance. I'm the wrong sort of material. But she hypnotizes Helen sometimes."

"Has she done so lately?" I asked. "I mean within the last few weeks?"

"Why, yes," Helen said. "Actually, she hypnotized me this morning. Why do you ask?"

I looked at Beef. "Well?" I asked, "what do you think about it?"

"Townsend means," explained Beef, "that there might be some possibility of your mother putting Helen under the influence, so to speak, so that she'd try and stab you."

But both the girls disagreed completely with the possibility of this half-formed theory. They said that their mother could not control them to that extent—at least she had never done so in their experience. She was only able to put them into a sort of trance which, if anything, made one physically weaker. Beef seemed to be persuaded by them, and eventually led me out of the wagon. I was still unconvinced, but it was no use to argue with Beef. I saw that the only thing to do was to keep it in mind.

"Well," said Beef with a broad grin as we left the wagon, "do you still want to go home?"

"Most certainly not," I answered. "Things are just beginning to look exciting."

As I lay awake in bed that night I let my thoughts wander over what we had already witnessed in the circus, and its difference from the sort of life led by the rest of society. It was, I thought, exciting enough without the promise of a case. There seemed to me so much more vitality in the people. Already there had been an attempt at a murder, and I felt, as I lay there, that almost anything might happen in the future. That was the whole point about circus folk. They were not predictable, as most other people were. One felt that one had to be prepared for anything, when one was with them. It might be something quite small and ridiculous, or it might be something huge and terrifying. One could not foresee it anyway. But it was exciting. I decided that I would stay on with Beef.

Since so many little things happened each day which were not in the usual logical order of our previous "cases," I realized that it would be best to keep a continual account of them in the form of a rather full journal. Then, if anything did happen, I should have all the possible details of what led up to it already written down. It would certainly save time later. That was, of course, if a case ever came of the business. And even if it did not, I thought to myself, it would still be worth staying on.

I turned to Beef to tell him about my decision, but he was already asleep, snoring gently with his face to the wall.

CHAPTER VII

April 27th.

BEEF was already up and dressed when I awoke. He was sitting on the edge of his bunk examining a long yellow sheet which he held in his hands, and when I spoke to him he brought it over to me.

"This is one of the circus bills," he explained.

"Have you found a clue or something on it?" I asked drowsily.

"Clue?" said Beef. "No, I got an idea, that's all. You know what we ought to do today? We ought to make a thorough round of everybody in the show; go along to everybody and see what they're like, and that. Might come in handy afterwards."

"So that bill is a sort of checking list, is it?" I asked.

"That's right. Take a look at it." And Beef handed me the bill. This is what I read:

JACOBI'S CIRCUS.

Twice   Daily.
4-30   8-0

Seats at 1/-, 1/3, 2/4, and 3/6.
Children *half-price* at matinees.

THE CONCINIS.
THE GREATEST LADY TRICK RIDERS IN THE WORLD.

Incredible equestrian feats—grace and color on a galloping horse.

CORINNE JACOBI
& her
ARAB HORSES.
Equine elegance and good manners under the eye of the
graceful Corinne.

The DARIENNE BROTHERS AND SUZANNE.
GREATEST AERIAL ACT OF ALL TIME.
Thrills!   Thrills!!   THRILLS!!!

HERR KURT
AND HIS MAN-EATING LIONS.
The bravest man on earth.

PETROV DAROGA.
ECSTASY ON THE TIGHT WIRE.

EUSTACE
THE UNBELIEVABLE SEAL
Shown by our own Corinne Jacobi.

ARCHIE, SAM, and TINY
the funniest clowns in existence.
You scream, YOU ROAR, YOU YELL!!

JACOBI'S FAMOUS ELEPHANTS
SHOWN BY PETROV DAROGA
Watch Hoodlums stand on his head!

MANY OTHER LAUGHS, THRILLS, AND DISPLAYS.

"Simple, isn't it?" said Beef as soon as I had finished reading
it. "We just go round to each of those in turn, and there you
are."

"I suppose you know what you are doing," I said, "but
personally I can't see the use of it. You can't very well collect
evidence at this stage, can you?"

"Evidence? Of course not," said Beef scornfully, "that's all you seem to think about. My idea is to get to know some of the people. Make myself at home like. You never know what might come of it."

"True," I said. And in a few minutes we had started on our tour.

Beef made first for the proprietor's wagon. Jackson was alone and let us in immediately Beef knocked.

"Well," he said, "I suppose you've got your murder now, Sergeant. Although you can hardly call it a murder when the girl was little more than scratched, can you?"

"As a matter of fact," said Beef slowly, "I don't somehow think this is the murder I've been looking for. In the first place, it was too clumsy, wasn't premeditated, as they say. More what they call in France a crime of passion, if you ask me. And then, of course, as you say, it wasn't a murder at all. Now, I've spoken to both of the young ladies, and although I won't bother you by going into the full story, it seems to me that it's something to do with them being twins, if you see what I mean?"

"I'm afraid I don't," replied Jackson.

"Well, it's rather difficult to explain," said the Sergeant slowly. "Look at it like this. Here you have two girls, as like as two peas. Now, in an ordinary family living in a town say, that might cause a bit of fun sometimes, but nobody wouldn't take it serious. But here things are a bit different. Those two girls weren't leading more than one life between the two of them. Everything one could do the other might get the credit for, everybody one knew, the other knew as well. There was nothing private between them at all. Well, I think that's what was the cause of this little business. Nothing very serious, mind you, but just enough to make one of them lash out."

"I'm sure your theory is very interesting, Mr. Beef," said Jackson in a rather flat voice, "but I fail to see where it's getting you."

"That's what I was coming to," said Beef eagerly. "Now, it may not mean anything in itself, so to speak, but it gives me just the opportunity I want to go round and talk to all the people here. I don't want to question them like a policeman. Don't think that, Mr. Jackson. I just want to have a friendly little talk with them all, so's I can get to know them and get an idea of the circus as a whole. You see what I mean?"

"Quite, but why come to me about it? You're perfectly free to have these little 'chats' if you wish. It is no affair of mine, so long as you don't interfere with the working hours of the circus, that is a question which only affects the people themselves."

"Still," said Beef, uncrushed, "I just thought I'd like to get your approval. Well, that's all right then." And at that he rose, and we left the wagon.

When we were outside he drew me aside, and with an expression of childish pleasure, opened his large hand and showed me what lay in the palm of it.

"Found this on the floor in there," he said.

It was a small colored button with five or six letters printed across the center. It looked a very ordinary object to me. Perhaps a badge for some circus society, or one of those "clubs" which the makers of some proprietory articles actually persuade people to join in order to advertise their wares.

"Well, what about it?" I asked.

"I like little things like that," Beef said. "Especially coming out of Jackson's wagon. I've got my eye on him, you know."

"But what does it mean?"

"How should I know?" protested Beef. "Give us a chance. I only just picked it up. I shall make an examination of it later," he added grandly. "And now I think we'll go and see the Dariennes."

"Oh yes, I know," I said, "the greatest aerial act of all time."

"I don't know about that," admitted Beef, not recognizing my quotation from the circus bill, "but I've heard they're very good trapeze artists. French, too. I like anything French."

"They have a partner, haven't they?"

"Um," said Beef. "Suzanne. But she's not French. More like Camden Town, I should say. But she's All Right though."

When we entered the Dariennes' wagon we found that Suzanne was with them, and it was she who invited us to that universal cup of tea which will always be associated in my mind with visits to circus people. It was hot, and sticky, and sweet; a rich dark brown in color, and made with tinned milk. Since Beef seemed completely occupied with the noisy consumption of this I felt that it was incumbent on me to open the conversation, which I conscientiously did, touching on such commonplace subjects as the weather, the dullness of the Yorkshire people, and the possibilities of a good house that evening. Meanwhile, I was closely examining the Darienne brothers.

I had already heard strange rumors of these two, although I was determined to let Beef find out all that I knew for himself. Theirs was the most highly-paid act on the show, and topped the bill in the sense that they were given the largest type in all Jacobi's posters. But what had struck Ginger, my informant on the subject, was the relationship between the two brothers. The Concinis were bound by their similarity, but between the Dariennes there was a more subtle bond. "Paul, that's the oldest one," Ginger had explained, "watches his brother like a cat with a mouse." I appreciated this somewhat trite simile when I looked at Paul when he sat in the wagon. He had string-colored hair, which was cut so short that it stood straight up over his forehead in the old pre-war German fashion, and his face was large, heavy, and brooding. There was a sour and worried look on his solid features, and his big fleshy jowls were set uncompromisingly. Christophe was a very different type. He was slight, blond, and in the true sense of the word, gay. His clear-cut features were almost pretty, and his movements were swift and eager. He talked a great deal more than Paul, and had a little chiming laugh, the effect of which I found altogether charming. Both of them spoke English with a strong French accent, which gave to their conversation a special, if artificial, attraction, like the love-making speeches of Chevalier in the more obvious of his films.

Both the brothers were a queer mixture of delicacy and hardness. It was easier to understand this when they began to talk about their early life. Born in France, they had lost both father and mother before the age of ten, and had chosen then, rather than live with an elderly aunt in the south, to go on the roads and earn their own living as best they could. It had been a very hard life, and was a case of being strong and agile, or dying. Somehow they had survived, and by the time they were sixteen and thirteen respectively, they had been taken on as tent hands in a small circus. From that time their progress had been steady, and, as Paul put it, completely without exciting details. They had come to England because they heard the pay was better, and because they wanted to travel. They had been together, dependent on each other, since infancy.

Suzanne, who had been sitting silent, now spoke directly to Beef for the first time. "I mother them, Mr. Beef," she said and although the phrase was lightly spoken, it seemed to carry more significance than a joke normally does. Suzanne Beckett was still a very pretty woman. She gave one the impression of having once been a very beautiful one, and in the irregular, nervous movements of her hands, there was still something exquisite left, something extremely graceful. She might have been almost any age, but when she told Beef that she was thirty-five I could see that he believed her. And Beef generally knew when people were lying to him. A widow, past the peak of her career, she should not normally have been very interesting, and Beef would probably have taken little notice of her had it not been for one little incident which occurred just before we left.

While we had chatted, Beef had solemnly, steadily, loudly drunk the whole of his large cup of tea. It was not until he had set the cup down empty that he seemed really to turn his attention to the matter in hand.

"Now," he began heavily, "you're the top of the bill, aren't you?"

"Why, yes," said Christophe cheerfully, "of course we are." And he launched in to a long explanation of why such an important act as theirs should have deigned to travel with a tenting show at all.

At the end of it Suzanne gave him a quick smile, and turning aside to him as though she did not want us, or perhaps even Paul, to understand, she made a remark in French in a very low voice.

Beef might have missed this, but I saw Paul look up sharply and his eyes traveled from one to the other of his partners. At first it seemed that he was not going to speak, but at last he said slowly and in English: "Suzanne, I never knew you spoke French!"

The emphasis of this remark was as strange as the subject of it. How could it be, I wondered, that the girl who worked with them every day, who seemed to be looking after them now, should speak his language without him knowing it?

Even Christophe seemed flummoxed. "I've been teaching her a little," he said, and reaching over for Suzanne's spoon, he hurriedly stirred his tea.

Nothing more noteworthy took place during our interview, which ended with the cordial invitation from all three of them to come and see them again, and the hope that we would enjoy their act. Beef thanked them, and climbing down the steps of the wagon backwards, he set off in the direction of his next interview.

In any case the next wagon, which belonged to Peter Ansell, who worked as lion-feeder for Herr Kurt, the trainer, was empty, so Beef made his way over to the enclosed zoo where Ansell was most likely to be at that time of the day. The zoo, which was attached to Jacobi's circus, was actually a small enclosure of cages drawn round in a rough square and fenced round with canvas and rope to keep out prying eyes. Each of these cages was in reality the wagon or trailer in which the animals were towed from place to place on the tour, and became a cage when the front boards were taken down each day. Some of the animals behind these bars were those used in the ring, such as the lion and the seal, while the others were the more well-known "oddities" of the animal world which are always an attraction, and which were taken round as a side-show to the circus.

Beside the three lions which Kurt showed in the ring, there were three cubs, which he was still training, a fourth lion which, although full-grown, had not been trained because "he'd never had time to get down to the job," and a tiger and a jaguar, also untrained. The smaller animals, beside Eustace the seal, consisted of a hyena, a three-toed sloth, a fox, numerous monkeys, a porcupine, a kangaroo, a wolf, an owl, a vulture, and a skunk. It was, apparently, Ansell's job to look after these animals. He had to feed them, clean out the cages, act as vet and nursemaid, should the need arise, and see that nothing went wrong while they were traveling from place to place.

"Funny," commented Beef, "having a fourth lion just like the others, and never using it."

I was a little bored with the number of things the Sergeant found "funny." "I don't see why," I answered, and walked on ahead.

We learned later that, for the most part, the village people who paid their tuppences to go into the zoo after the circus show had finished, had never until then seen any of the animals shown there. It is surprising how few people who live in the country have seen a fox more than fleetingly. The circus is often their only chance of seeing other animals than the most ordinary and common ones of the countryside.

We discovered Peter Ansell digging just outside the zoo, with the slender gray kangaroo hopping slowly around him, nibbling here and there at a blade of grass. It crinkled its nostrils at Beef, but then appeared to forget him, and went on with its exploration. Ansell stood up when Beef greeted him, and sat on the edge of a wagon with his feet dangling over the side.

He must have been about thirty-five or six, with a slow cultured voice and an appearance of frankness. It did not take many questions from Beef to start him talking about himself, and the information he revealed was astonishing.

"How did I come to work in the circus?" he said, repeating Beef's question. "One drifts, I suppose. At least I've always drifted, and this simply happens to be another port. I ran away from home—or should I say school—at the age of fifteen and have only seen my parents once since then. My father was 'something in the city,' as Henry James says. Actually, he was a sugar-broker, whatever that may imply. Anyway, it was something extremely dull. I was sent to a public school and forgotten. Really, you can't imagine what a public school is like unless you've been to one, Sergeant. Take the food, for example."

"Bad, was it?" asked Beef hopefully.

"Horrible. Nearly all the boys' parents had estates, and during the Christmas term we had to eat partridges and pheasants for lunch every day. Sickening. I ran away."

"And then what did you do?" asked Beef.

"Oh, almost everything. I just wandered around most of the time. Tramp, estate agent, in prison, work-houses, farm laborer, commercial traveler, you know the sort of thing. And do you know I think the happiest years of my life have been spent in prison? Funny, isn't it? But I get this itch to move on, not the so-called 'wanderlust,' but something much more negative. You should read Ernest Hemingway, Sergeant, for a full description of what I mean. Everything goes to hell inside you, and you move away from things rather than towards. Fear of the known and monotonous, so you jump for the unknown every time. Until it turns out as bad as the other, and then you jump again. The difference is that the 'wanderlust' makes you walk forward with hope, my feeling makes me go backwards in fear. Well, that's my signature tune, Sergeant, and for the rest I'm fairly happy at the moment feeding horse-flesh to lions and cleaning cages."

"Who is it exactly employs you then?" asked Beef.

"Well, it's Kurt who pays my wages, so I suppose he's the employer. He engaged me, too. That was rather a funny affair. Perhaps you'd like to hear it." And without waiting for us to answer him, Ansell leaned easily against the side of one of the cages and began to tell us.

"A few years ago," said Ansell, "I was wandering through Westmoreland when I happened to pass through a town that had one of those small private zoos. A chap in a coffee-stall, where I stopped for a few minutes, told me that the man who usually looked after the lions at this zoo had been killed only that day. Apparently he'd been clawed to death through some sort of carelessness. Anyway, the point was, this fellow who told me the story added that he thought they'd have difficulty in getting anyone to take that job now. It gave me an idea. I'd been on the road for more than a month unable to find any work to do, and I thought this was a real gift of fortune. Of course, I went straight to the zoo and asked for the job."

"Weren't you scared?" asked Beef.

"Scared? Of course I was. But I was also hungry—and that's much more important. As it happened, I didn't get the job at all. When I rolled up to the office I found that there was a queue of about fifty or sixty chaps all waiting for the same reason. What was the good of me waiting? I knew nothing about animals, so I was bound to be turned down. I don't know what fetched all those others. I suppose it was because the other chap who had been killed had got his name in the papers over the affair (even if he wasn't alive to read them), so these blokes thought it was a romantic sort of a job, and along they came. Or perhaps they were hungry too. Anyway, I saw it was hardly worth waiting, but instead of clearing straight out I wandered round the zoo first to have a look at the animals. Might as well get a free show while I could, I thought. But when I got to the lion-house, who should come in but the owner of the zoo himself. I knew who it was because he was talking to a man he had with him about selling some lion cubs. I edged up near them and listened to what they were saying, and then when the bargain was concluded I went up to the chap who'd bought them and suggested that he might need some help in getting them away.

" 'I've got a lorry outside,' he said. But I pointed out that he couldn't manage the cubs by himself.

" 'Do you know anything about lions?' he asked. I admitted I didn't, and he seemed to think that was rather funny. Anyway, he was so tickled with the idea of my knowing nothing about them but offering to handle them for him, that he said he'd give me ten bob if I got them into the lorry.

"And I did. I haven't the slightest idea how I did it. I was scared stiff. But ten bob was a lot of money to me just then, so I grabbed them one at a time by the scuff of the neck and pitched them into the lorry. The man was amazed. He just stood there looking at me.

" 'Did you say you knew nothing about animals?' he asked me when I'd finished.

" 'Not a thing,' I said, feeling very pleased with myself now that the job was over.

" 'Then it must be instinct,' said the chap. 'I like people who have the right instinct with animals. Would you like a job with me? I'm a lion-trainer.'

"And there the job was. Of course I took it. And as you have no doubt guessed, the gentleman who gave it to me was Herr Kurt, lion-tamer to Jacobi's Circus."

As he finished his story Ansell picked up his shovel again and recommenced his work as if we did not any longer exist.

"He's a rum sort of a bird," commented Beef as we left the enclosure.

"I think he's very pleasant," I said. "I like the grateful way he told the story of his job and about Kurt. He's not the sort of man you'd expect to be grateful over anything."

"That's why he's rum," said Beef shortly.

"But surely," I protested, "the fact that he sounded grateful to Kurt should make you revise your estimate of him?"

"I know the type," said Beef confidently. "He's not really grateful to anyone, you mark my words. He's got something up his sleeve, you'll see. A man with an education like that just wasting his time pottering around in all sorts of jobs. Feeding animals. Grateful!" Beef ended scornfully. "Not him. I know the type."

CHAPTER VIII

April 27th (continued).

PETE DAROGA, the wire-walker, was seated on the steps of his neat brown wagon bending over a length of wire. He was splicing the end with a concentration which prevented him from hearing us approach, so that I had time to study the man before Beef spoke.

Although more than sixty years old, Daroga was still nearly six feet tall. He held himself upright, and had shrunk very little with age, unlike most people of his years. In his prime he must have been an unusually large man, for although now he was sinewy, his firm, wide frame seemed to have been little reduced by age, and one could see in the broad shoulders and steadily posied neck the signs of immense strength. His fingers, as they moved over the unraveled wire, were light and hooked, moving with pecking, finicky jerks as though the task were distasteful to him. He was the sort of man to whom inanimate objects offer no resistance, the small pieces of wire under his hand seeming to fall readily into place.

His face was the almost unbelievable leathery brown of a Breton peasant, twisted and ugly and far too small for his large body. The deep-cut wrinkles, sinking almost to the bone, gave his face a cushiony appearance. And on it the long ugly scar which started on his right cheek-bone and ended at his misshapen ear seemed like a hasty darn in which the wrong shade of wool had been used.

Becoming aware of Beef, Daroga looked up quickly, wrinkling his eyes as though trying to recognize the newcomer.

"I've seen you about somewhere before, haven't I?" he asked.

Beef nodded. "S'right," he said, and then almost shyly, like a small boy giving his name to the Mayor's wife: "Sergeant Beef," he volunteered.

"Oh yes, of course. You were just here in time for that little business between Helen and Anita, weren't you?" said Daroga.

Beef squatted down at the foot of the steps as if prepared for a long conversation. "Well, I don't know about that," he said. "I don't think there was anything very serious in that. Though, mind you, it's as funny a case as ever I came across. Nor I wouldn't say it was over yet."

"What makes you think that?" asked Daroga curiously.

"I couldn't exactly say," said Beef mysteriously. "Now I can understand some people; Mr. Jackson, for instance . . ."

"Can you?" said Daroga sharply.

"Can I what?"

"Understand Jackson," answered Daroga impatiently.

"Well, in a manner of speaking. I mean he's a straightforward sort of chap when you know the type." Beef suddenly seemed to realize that he was answering instead of asking questions, and quickly turned to his companion. "What do you think of him then?" he asked.

"Treats everybody like dirt under his feet," burst out the wire-walker suddenly, and then as if he had quickly controlled himself, he bent, and picking up the wire he had been splicing he shrugged his shoulders. "But he's the boss around here, anyway," he finished flatly.

"Do you like him?" asked Beef.

"We get along," said Daroga, and Beef sensed by his tone that he did not wish to pursue the subject any further.

"You know," the Sergeant went on after a pause, "I like it here. Everybody's so friendly and nice. Generally they behave a bit suspicious towards a policeman. Not that I'm in the Force any more, but you know what I mean."

If Daroga knew what he meant he did not take the trouble

to show it, but remained silent, inspecting the length of wire in his hands.

Beef tried again. "And this moving around," he said. "You see a lot of the country, and so on. Gives you experience."

Daroga did not look up, and except for a slight grunt it was impossible to tell whether he had heard Beef at all. The Sergeant stood up.

"Well," he said, "I suppose you want to get ready for the show. I don't want to get in anybody's way."

A further grunt from the wire-walker was the only farewell which he received.

"Wonder what makes him so surly?" muttered Beef, but he appeared not to expect an answer, so I followed him on.

The long converted bus which stood next to Daroga's neat wagon was known as the Clowns' Wagon. The long body, divided into three rooms, was often the meeting-place of many of the artists in the evenings after the show, but when Beef stood outside inspecting the peeling paintwork plastered with torn and faded circus bills, there were only two people inside it: Sid Bolton, known as "Tiny" in the ring, and Clem Gail, or "Archie."

Beef knocked cautiously and was greeted with a loud shout of "Come in." Clem Gail was seated in front of the mirror, dressed already in his clown's costume, and decorating his face with the traditional red and white grease-paint and sticking the fantastic pieces of hair on his chin and cheeks with spirit gum. It was difficult to recognize in this parody the handsome young man I had noticed about the grounds, and whom Albert Stiles had pointed out to me as Clem Gail. It was his voice that invited us in, and he looked up with comically squinting eyes.

"Hullo, Sergeant," he said. "Will you join us?"

Beef grinned. "Shall I be in the way here?" he asked. "I

just thought I'd like to drop in for a bit of a chat before the show started."

"Come in and sit down," said Clem Gail. "That is, if Sid isn't using all the chairs."

Sid Bolton, thus referred to, waved Beef to the only unoccupied seat, while his other hand continued to rub cold-cream into his large gleaming face. In the restricted space of the wagon his huge bulk seemed more than usually oppressive. It seemed that there was no way of escaping him, that sooner or later, wherever one moved in the wagon, one was bound to collide with him. Even Beef, who was no stripling himself, looked as though he thought it would be unwise to move from the rickety stool on which he now sat.

Yet "Tiny" Bolton was not the usual conception of "fat man." There was little flabbiness about him, and except for the roll of flesh under his ears which quivered whenever he turned his head or laughed, he was muscular and overgrown rather than paunchy or dropsical. His movements were swift and sure, and his long, rather fine hands, were ludicrous on so large a body. They reminded one of a deep-sea diver, in his solid inflated costume, and yet from which protrudes his naked unprotected hands. Nevertheless, his bulk was, at close quarters, slightly embarrassing, and Beef found it difficult to hit immediately on a topic of conversation. His eyes, roving round the wagon hopefully, were caught by the mounted mask of a large badger which hung above the door.

"That's a nice badger's head," he said. "I've got one nearly as large as that over the hat-stand in my hall. What do you carry a thing like that around for? Luck?"

Clem looked up at the mask curiously, as if seeing it for the first time. "A farmer gave us that," he said. "After he'd seen the show he said he wanted to give us a present. But he was too hard up or something, and all he could afford was the stuffed head of that badger which had been killed on his ground a few weeks before. We kept it here because of its face. It suits us, you know."

"Suits you?" queried Beef.

"Yes. You know the country name for the badger? Brock. Brock the badger. Old Clown Face. We thought it was a good mascot—so there it is."

Beef had no intention of entering into a discussion on the fauna of these isles, so he became ruminative for a while, and then at last said: "You know, I've often wondered how one starts on a job like yours. I mean, did you always want to be a clown, or did you just drift into it like any other job?"

Sid Bolton chuckled rumblingly. "In my case there wasn't anything else to do," he said.

"How was that?" asked Beef.

"I used to be shown as a fat boy on the fair-grounds," explained Sid. "But after about six years of that I stopped being what you might call a boy, and I stopped getting any fatter. So there I was in a cleft-stick. I was too old to be a fat boy, and too small to be a fat man. I tried to go on the music-halls and sing comic songs, but I didn't go down very well. The managers used to get letters saying how disgusting it was me being on the stage, and after a time they refused to engage me. I couldn't take an ordinary job—I get in my own way too much—so here I am in the circus. It makes the kids laugh, anyway."

Sid grinned cheerfully at Beef, almost as if he had been telling of the misfortunes of a stranger, and not of his own life. He seemed to find something irresistibly funny in the potted biography he had just given Beef, and turned back to the mirror with a wide grin on his face.

"Well, I don't know," said Beef. "It's a funny world. When I was a kid I used to go to circuses, and I didn't used to think the clowns were really men at all. Special sort of animal, I used to think they were. Funny and so on, but not really human."

"Most children think something like that," commented Clem.

"But the kids are the ones that enjoy clowns the most, aren't they?" asked Beef.

"Not really," said Clem. "Now you can tell that by the sort of show we put up. If you've noticed, the afternoon show isn't quite so good as the evening one. Same jokes, same turns and everything. But it hasn't got the go in it somehow. In a way, it's the audience that makes the show. Now you take the show we shall be putting on in a fortnight's time. That's the best show we shall do in the whole tour. It's a special Jubilee show on the Circus's 25th birthday. Every year on the day the Circus started we have a special performance, and it's the feeling of it being something extraordinary that makes the artists do the best they possibly can. You ought to stay and see it, then you'd know what I mean."

"What date is it?" asked Beef.

"The 3rd of May. It's a red letter day for us," said Clem, grinning.

"Red Letter Day?" queried Beef.

"Yes, that's what it is. Birthday and Christmas rolled into one. We have a good time that day."

"Wouldn't like to miss that for anything," said Beef, and with that we left the wagon.

"This is making me feel a bit dizzy," Beef told me. "I feel as if we're canvassing for an election, or something, and have to keep all bright and breezy all the time." He looked at his bill again. "Might as well go and see Corinne Jackson now," he said, and went to the proprietor's wagon.

Jackson was not in the wagon when Beef knocked, but Mrs. Jackson was there, and also Corinne and Eric Jackson, the son and daughter of the proprietor. Mrs. Jackson, who invited the

Sergeant in, quickly bustled away to make a cup of tea, this occupation seeming to be her surest standby in any and every situation, and Beef was left sitting awkwardly with Corinne and Eric. For a long time there was silence, punctuated only by Mrs. Jackson's trite opinion of the weather given every time she had cause to pass through the central room of the wagon. Eric had grunted shortly when Beef first entered and had since made no remark whatever, and Corinne seemed to be unaware of the Sergeant's presence in any way. Beef regarded her perfect profile with something of awe.

Corinne Jackson was beautiful in an altogether uncircuslike way. She had none of the rich coloring of the Latin, being so different from her father that it made one look at her mother with a new interest. Had Mrs. Jackson actually been beautiful as a young woman? Corinne would seem to argue this. Her fair, closely waved hair seemed to fit close to her head, carved and set like the head of a Greek statue. Only her nostrils, with their slight arrogant curve, betrayed a trace of selfishness. Slowly and carefully she was painting her eyelashes with mascara. Beef gazed at her, his mouth slightly open.

"Don't you find it difficult to see where you're going with that stuff on?" he blurted out at last.

Corinne stared at him coldly for a moment, and then returned to her mirror without saying anything. Eric Jackson, however, gave a quickly suppressed giggle, and Beef turned to him as a likely ally.

"Well, I mean," he said explanatorily, "it must be uncomfortable, mustn't it?"

"Corinne Jacobi," said Eric grandly. "The beautiful Corinne must not disappoint her public."

"Corinne Jacobi?" queried Beef.

"That's her ring name," explained Eric, with a smile. "Jackson wouldn't look very good on the bill."

"Oh, I see," said Beef. "Like Sid Bolton calls himself 'Tiny.' Is that what you mean?"

Once again Eric chuckled. "Well, something like that," he agreed.

"Here," said Beef suddenly, glancing at the clown's get-up which Eric wore, "you're another of these clowns, aren't you?"

This time it was Corinne who laughed. "Just another of them," she said. Beef looked at her in amazement.

"Yes, it talks," said Eric snappily. "If you press the right button, that is." And he jerked his thumb in the direction of his sister, who was furiously dabbing her face with powder.

Beef seemed bewildered by this atmosphere of animosity, and sat looking from one to the other of the two Jacksons. They appeared only to be using his presence as a means of attacking one another, and if one had believed Beef to be in reality the well-meaning simpleton that he sometimes appeared, one would have thought him uncomfortable and a little resentful about it.

"Well, I'd better go and change," said Eric after a long pause, and he walked through into the little partitioned room at the end of the wagon, leaving Beef and the coldly silent Corinne awkwardly together.

Corinne, unmoved, continued with her make-up, while Beef sought for some commonplace phrase he might use to start a conversation.

"Why don't you ask her for her autograph, Sergeant?" came Eric's voice over the partition.

Corinne appeared to be completely oblivious of all that was going on around her. When she had completed her make-up to her own satisfaction, she slipped her dressing-gown off her shoulders and commenced to powder her back. She was dressed in a scanty riding-costume, and Beef averted his eyes with haste. When, however, she began to apply the powder-puff to her long elegant legs Beef stood up awkwardly.

[69]

"I'm afraid I'm in the way," he mumbled, searching for the handle of the door and trying to look anywhere but at the girl.

Corinne looked at him with faint surprise. "Oh no," she said, "you're not in *my* way."

But Beef's hand had discovered the door-handle and he slipped quickly out of the wagon with a heavy sigh of relief.

"Don't go much on that sort of thing," he said, and it seemed to be an adequate expression of his pent-up feelings.

Herr Kurt, the lion-tamer, known to the Registrar's Office in Hoxton as George Franks, was in his wagon. At least, the light which shone through the drawn curtains would seem to argue this, although Beef's tattoo on the door brought no reply. The Sergeant waited for a few minutes, and then knocked again. This time the curtain over the glass top of the door was parted and the red, full-fed face of Kurt peered out on us. But there was no answer to the knock.

"Perhaps he didn't see us," I suggested. "Try again."

But as the Sergeant raised his hand again, the door opened suddenly and Beef almost toppled inside.

"What do you want?" demanded Kurt sharply.

"Er . . ." Beef was momentarily at a loss.

"Well, clear off and don't bother me at this time of the day," Kurt bellowed, and the door slammed within an inch of Beef's face.

Beef stared for a moment blankly at the door, and then he turned to me with a rueful grin.

"Well," he said, "there's no mistake about that being Kurt. Curt, see?" he grinned.

We turned and wandered slowly down towards the entrance to the tober. By this time crowds had already begun to form in front of the pay-box for the evening show, and for a little while we watched them in silence.

"Not much good trying to see anybody else just now," said Beef. "They'll be changing for the show. They won't want to be bothered." And he thrust his hands into his trouser pockets and concentrated his attention on the crowd.

"I say, mister," said a small but clear voice beside us. We looked down to find two very small boys clutching each other by the hands and looking up at Beef with an expression of awe. "I say, mister," one of them repeated, "Billie wants to know if you're the man who comes on with the elephants?"

A broad, flattered smile spread over Beef's face, and I could see that he considered the question to be a compliment.

"No, sonny," he said kindly. But after they had gone away he turned to me with a perturbed expression. "We do look a bit like commissionaires, don't we?" he said. "Let's stroll around a bit."

But we had not gone many yards when our attention was caught by the neat, quiet figure of a man sitting on the running-board of the lorry which supplied lighting to the tent, and we walked over to him.

"Cigarette?" offered Beef.

"Thanks, no. I don't smoke till after the show."

Beef studied the man with interest; not because he had refused a cigarette, but because that refusal seemed to point to the man being one of the artists. Yet anything less like a circus artist could scarcely be imagined. He was small and rather rotund in figure with a contented oval face rather sleepy in expression. When he replied to Beef's question he spoke very slowly, and then only after an unusually long pause in which he seemed to be repeating the other's words and testing them as a barman does a coin by throwing it into the back of the till. Another in his place would probably have said "what" and used the time taken up by a repetition of the question to think slowly of an answer. He could not have been more than thirty-five or six years old, yet his fair fluffy hair stood out around a prematurely bald spot. It looked like a halo which had been put on like a bowler-hat instead of being worn serenely untethered. His small brown eyes did not seem to take the trouble to inspect Beef, and yet one had the conviction that they had noticed all there was of importance to notice about the Sergeant.

"Are you one of the artists here, then?" asked Beef, voicing his thoughts. "I don't remember seeing you in the ring."

"Not exactly," said the man. "I'm the jack-of-all-trades. You know—odds and sods. Electrician, scene-shifter, shoe-mender; general handyman, in fact. Len Waterman, that's me. And I suppose you're Sergeant Beef?"

Beef nodded with a pleased expression.

"I've read about you," the man went on, "in those three cases of yours."

"Have you?" said Beef, almost incredulously. "And what did you think of them?"

The little man who had called himself Len Waterman seemed to be considering the question. "Well," he said slowly, "I don't want to hurt anybody's feelings about this, but since you've asked me, I'll tell you. I think you did a pretty smart piece of work in all three cases, Sergeant, but I've got one bit of criticism."

"And what's that?" asked Beef doubtfully.

"That chap Townsend," said Len Waterman. "Can't you do something about him? I mean, he puts you off, the way he mucks about with the story. He calls himself your 'old friend,' but all he does is to make fun of you all the time. Now what you ought to do is to get someone with some sense. Someone who would write your cases for you just as they really are without any of this funny business."

"It's funny you saying that," said Beef, "because this gentleman here happens to be Mr. Townsend."

The little man was only momentarily taken aback. "I'm very sorry if I've said anything I oughtn't," he apologized. But then he returned to the attack along a new line. "But you must admit, Mr. Townsend," he said to me, "that there's a lot in what I say."

"I'm afraid I don't quite see your point," I said in a chilly voice. "Perhaps if you'd be good enough to explain."

"*And* I'd be glad to," said Len Waterman. "Now look at it this way. Point one, you like to have a little laugh at the Sergeant when you get the chance, don't you? Right," he hurried on before I had time to interrupt. "But suppose he doesn't give you a chance. Then you have to make one. Right again. And what's better than publishing a book that ruins the Sergeant's career? It places you right in his hands, Sergeant," the man continued, turning to Beef. "Now what would these other detective story-writers do if their investigators couldn't solve a crime?"

"Well, what would they do?" I countered.

"They'd hush the whole matter up," said Waterman decisively. "That's what they'd do, they'd hush it up. They don't want to bring their heroes into ridicule and contempt, do they? Of course not. You can't tell me that that there Lord Simon Plimsol don't ever make a mistake. I bet he does, but we never hear of them. It wouldn't do."

"You suggest, then," I said, "that I should have been dishonest over the Sergeant's last case, and not written it?"

"That's right," said Len Waterman. "And what's more, when he gets a case again, if I was you I should do it serious. Write as if you really meant it. Stop making the Sergeant look a fool. Well, that's what I think. No offense meant, I'm sure."

Before I had time to assure him that I took his criticisms in the spirit in which they were offered, a voice from the tent could be heard sharply calling for "Len."

"That's me," he said, as he moved away. "Something gone wrong with the lights, I expect. Well, we'll have a little talk some time, shall we?" and with this he ducked under the side of the tent.

CHAPTER IX

April 27th (continued).

AFTER the evening show Beef and I watched the business of "pulling down." Every day this happens in the tenting show; every day, at the end of the performances and somewhere around ten o'clock at night, the whole of the tent has to be pulled down and packed away, the gear tidied and stacked into the lorries, the animals fed and shut up in their cages, and everything got ready for the early start next morning. Boy Scouts would no doubt have called it "striking camp," but what Beef and I watched was considerably outside the scope of the usual Scout's training.

Even before the show had completely finished the tent hands were running round loosening the guy-ropes, holding them in position until the last note of "God Save the King" had sounded. Then the walls of the tent came down with a rush, and almost before the first person was out of the tent in the open air, it was being rolled into large heavy bundles and moved away ready for the lorries. The light from the tent top flooded out over the tober and made the work easier, and a special light fixed to the head of the electricity lorry helped the work. The crowd moved out slowly. The older ones only lingered a few minutes and were soon on the road home, but the younger ones hung about in groups, some of them waiting their turn at the fortune-telling booths, some of them visiting the zoo, and others simply gathering into small knots of people and talking.

As I watched the hands and artists alike at work on the tent I realized that each person had his own particular job, and that the task of pulling down had been rationalized to its limit. There was a certain order of tasks, and people to do

[74]

them, and this was the method which got the work finished in the shortest possible time. Some of them were dismantling the seating and stacking it into one of the lorries, others were collecting the quarter-poles, others taking out the pegs and collecting them, others on the canvas itself, rolling it into separate bundles which would need three or four men to lift them.

"Standing at the corner watching other people work," sang out Ginger as he strode past us carrying three poles on his bare, gleaming shoulder.

"*And* very nice, too," answered Beef.

At last the two king poles were carried away, and the last bundle of canvas thrown into the back of the lorry. Only one or two of the smaller tasks remained to be finished and the artists had disappeared, leaving these to the tent hands.

"Let's go along to the clowns' wagon," suggested Beef, already on the move towards it. "I could do with a cup of tea and a bit of a chat."

We got both with no trouble at all. Sid Bolton, still in his make-up and clown's costume, was juggling with the tea-pot when we entered and poured us out a cup each before we had even spoken. Clem was seated in front of the mirror wiping his face, tearing away the false tufts of hair and trying to get the grease-paint off as fast as he could work. The color ran into one mixed mess all over his face as his fingers moved briskly over the skin. Then, rubbing with an old greasy rag, he sluiced his face quickly in warm water and stood before the mirror again drying himself thoughtfully with a towel. The face which emerged from under the make-up was an exceptionally good one. Clear, unwrinkled eyes, straight, firm nose, and wide humorous mouth.

"That's the trouble," he said suddenly aloud.

"What's the trouble?" asked Beef.

"This face."

"Seems all right to me," said Beef, inspecting it carefully.

"That's just what I mean. It *is* all right. And that's the trouble."

"Sorry," said Beef. "Would you mind telling us what you're talking about?"

"Well, it's like this," said Clem Gail, stripping off his clown's costume as he talked. "Now, I'm a bit ambitious. I like people to think I'm a good clown, that I do my job well and all that. But how can I when they never know it's me who does it?"

"But your name's on the bill," said Beef.

"No, it isn't. 'Archie' is. You see, I'm two different people. There's me now, with quite a good face, and there's me in the ring, with a funny face. But people never connect the two. If the others walk down the street the people nudge one another and say, 'Look, that's the trapeze artists, isn't it?' or 'Isn't that the wire-walker?' But they never say that about me because they wouldn't recognize me."

"First we get two people who are so alike people think they are one," I interrupted softly, "and now we've got one person who people think is two. Fine state of affairs. I suppose this chap will have to stab himself." But Beef nudged me heavily to shut up.

"What did you say?" asked Clem, who had not heard.

"Nothing," said Beef hurriedly. "He was just trying to be funny, that's all. Go on."

"Well, that's all, I suppose," grinned Clem. He was dressed now, and flicked the comb through his hair. "The only other grouch I've got," he went on, and I heard Sid Bolton groan behind me as if at a much-heard tale, "is that I have to change after pulling down, and by the time I get out on to the tober . . ."

"The tent hands have bagged all the best girls," finished Sid, with a chuckle.

"So that's what you're hurrying for," observed Beef. "I thought perhaps it was for our benefit."

Clem turned at the door to grin at us. "Not—likely," he said, and ran quickly down the steps.

"He's a fine one," said Sid as we got up to leave. "Always grumbling about never being able to pick up any girls. Seems to get one most nights, though."

"What's his trouble then?" I asked.

"Well, you see," explained Sid, "he was saying to me just now as we were pulling down that he'd seen a nice girl over by the Zoo and he wanted to get out before one of the hands got hold of her. They usually pick out all the best ones, you see."

As we left the wagon I noticed that Beef seemed to be exceedingly pleased with himself. He was smiling broadly and every now and again a quiet chuckle would escape from him.

"Well, what is it?" I asked. "What do you find so funny?"

"I got a job for you," he burst out. "A nice little bit of investigating that's just about up your street."

"Yes?" I said doubtfully.

"Yes. I want you to follow that young Clem Gail and see what he does."

"But suppose he picks up this girl?" I objected.

"You just go on watching what he does," said Beef. "Cor, I've had worse jobs than that in my time."

"But it's spying on his private affairs," I said. "I'm not going to do it. Where would it get us, anyway? That's got nothing to do with the case."

"How do you know?" said Beef blandly. "You just do as I say, and then come back and tell me all that happened. That's a real nice little job, and I think you ought to be pleased with it."

"Well, I'm not," I said shortly. "And what's more, if you want to know—and I can't see what use it would be to you at your age—if you want to know how a young fellow picks up a girl, then you can do your own dirty work."

"Look here," said Beef firmly. "Are you on this case with me, or aren't you? Either one way or the other. I'm not asking much."

"I'll do it," I said, "if you swear it's something to do with the case. But otherwise not."

" 'Course it's something to do with the case," said Beef. "Anything to do with the circus people is something to do with the case at this stage. How shall we know where we are unless we know something about the people mixed up in it?"

"I suppose you're right," I said reluctantly, "but . . ."

"That's right," said Beef, with a grin. "I thought you'd see it that way. Now run along or it'll be all over before you get there."

I "ran along," as Beef so tactlessly put it. I could see Clem over by the gate talking to one of the hands, and looking often at the figure of a girl who was standing by herself outside the fortune-telling tent. As I approached he left his companion and approached the girl and began speaking to her. I walked quickly round behind the wagon nearest them and listened, hoping hard that no one would come along and notice I was eavesdropping.

"Has he run away and left you?" Clem's voice asked.

"Who?" asked the girl.

"Why, the boy friend, I suppose."

"I'm waiting," said the girl, almost coldly, "for my mother."

"If she's having her fortune told, she'll be hours," said Clem. "Old Margot always takes a wet week. Come and have a look at the animals while you're waiting."

From where I stood I could see the girl's face, and knew that she would eventually say yes to this proposal. She was a tall, good-looking girl, graceful in a way I suspected she had learned from an intensive study of Ginger Rogers. The way she swung her small blue hat carelessly by the brim must have made me think of this. And possibly the way she had her hair done. Now she turned to Clem and faced him for the first time.

"Are you with the circus?" she asked at last.

"That's right," said Clem. "Now what about those animals?"

"But suppose Mother comes before I get back? She'll think I've gone home."

"You can just pop your head in the tent and tell her you're going off for a minute."

The girl paused for a moment, and then turned quickly and walked towards Margot's booth. When she emerged again she was smiling. "Mother says she'll go on home without me," she said. "Now I'm ready."

Clem seemed to think for a while. "We could go and see the elephant-tent first," he suggested. "Have you seen the elephant-tent?"

"But it's dark. There'll be nothing to see!" the girl protested.

"That's why," said Clem briskly, and grabbed her arm.

For a moment she hung back, and I thought he had misjudged his tactics. But suddenly she laughed and moved away with him. "Really, you *are* a surprise," were the last words I heard her say. "I like people to be straightforward."

Cursing myself for being so stupid as to take this job, and the couple because they couldn't stand in one place, I slipped from behind the wagon to see where they were going. Sure enough they were walking slowly across the field towards the elephant-tent, and I had to get quickly around the edge of it in order to get there before them so that they would not see me.

I paused for a moment behind one of the wagons which they would have to pass in order to hear, if possible, what they were saying. They were walking arm-in-arm and I could tell by the way their heads moved that they were speaking.

"What do you do in the circus?" I heard the girl ask.

Clem's reply was indistinct, but the girl took him up and repeated it. "On the trapeze?" she said. "That's funny, I don't recognize you."

"We look different without the make-up on," Clem mumbled.

"Yes, I suppose you do. Anyway, you were moving so fast I couldn't get a good look at your face. I think your turn is marvelous. I wish you wouldn't have all those clowns, though. Some of them are clever, I suppose, but they make me yawn."

"Oh, I don't know," said Clem defensively. "It wouldn't be much of a circus without the clowns. Why, they're the oldest part of it. Anyway, they're for the children, and I expect you laughed at them yourself, really."

"No, I didn't. They just made me tired."

There was a slight pause. Clem was obviously finding this subject a little tiresome and was searching for something less controversial. "What's your name?" he asked at last.

"Alice."

"Mine's Clem. My real name, of course. We all use other names in the ring; it sounds better."

The couple walked past me and on towards the elephant-tent, and this time I waited until they had disappeared inside before I moved. The last thing I wanted to happen was Clem or some of the other circus people to see what I was doing. Beef no doubt had a reason for this absurdly uncomfortable "job" he had given me. But, nevertheless, I found it in the worst of taste. I watched Clem hold the flap of the tent open for the girl, and then it dropped behind both of them, and I emerged from behind the wagon and walked as softly as I could across to it. I went round to the back, where I was out of the light from the tober, and here it was pitch black and impossible to see anything. So much so that I stumbled and fell over one of the tent-pegs.

"What was that noise?" Alice's voice asked urgently from inside the tent.

Clem was calm and reassuring. "One of the elephants, I expect. Nobody will come around here, you needn't worry. Why, you're trembling."

The girl gave a short, nervous laugh. "That's not because I'm frightened," she said.

"Why is it, then?"

She gave no answer, and for quite a while neither of them said anything. When they began talking again it was in so quiet a voice that I was unable to catch more than a word here and there. What, I wondered, did Beef expect me to do now? Was I supposed to worm my way into the tent itself and *see* what was happening? I could not imagine Beef being so cruel or unthinking as that. I sat, shivering slightly, in the cold grass, cursing everything and the Sergeant in particular.

"Oh, but it's warm here," said the girl's voice suddenly. "I could stay here all night."

"You'd have to sleep with the elephant-man then," said Clem.

She laughed lightly. "I shall have to go in a minute, anyway," she said. "Whatever will Mother think of me?"

"No. Not yet," said Clem, and for a little while again there was silence. "You look all misty, like a cloud," said Clem's voice after a while. "Your face is just a white patch floating about on the hay. And your hands seem to move about as if they had nothing to do with anything else."

The girl laughed softly and drowsily. "I must go now," she said reluctantly. "Really I must."

In a moment I heard the tent-flap open and the long

shadows of the pair stretched along the grass close beside me. I kept completely out of sight and hoped that Clem would not take it into his head to walk round the tent. They stood for some time in that position, and their shadows told me that they were kissing, although I didn't dare to confirm this in case I was seen.

"Come on, then," said Clem abruptly. "Would you like me to see you home?"

"No, it's only just down the road. I'll find my way. Good night, Clem."

They walked slowly together to the center of the tober, which was now clear and open, then the girl walked on by herself to the gate and Clem stood still there and watched her until she had disappeared and I could no longer hear even the hard sounds of her heels on the road. Then he turned and walked to his wagon.

"Cushti palone, col?" shouted a voice, and the head of Peter Ansell stuck out of the window of his wagon.

"What the hell's that to you?" demanded Clem snappily, and slammed the door of his wagon behind him.

Beef was sitting up in his bunk reading when I entered our trailer. "Well?" he asked cheerfully, laying the book face down on the covers.

"Is that all you've been doing all the time I've been crawling around in the wet grass spying for you?" I counter-attacked.

"Never you mind what I've been doing," said Beef severely. "What I want to know is how you got on."

"I think the whole idea of yours was thoroughly ungentle-manly, and in extremely bad taste," I protested.

"You are a one," said Beef, grinning. "I bet you enjoyed it, listening in, and that."

"I did not," I replied sharply. "I found it most degrading and uncomfortable. Suppose someone had seen me?"

"But they didn't," commented Beef. "Well, tell us what you saw."

"I'm very much afraid," I said, "that Clem Gail is something of a Don Juan." And I went on to relate all that I had heard and seen that evening.

CHAPTER X

April 28th.

It MUST have been very early when I awoke, for I lay in bed for some considerable time before I heard any noise of stirring from the tober. I stretched pleasantly. As always waking early seems to give one longer in bed, and one can take advantage of this by thinking unhurriedly over the small things one seldom has time to consider more than once in a while.

Beef had truly surprised me over this case so far. It was not only that I had discovered something new in him, but that I had begun to realize that it had always been there and I probably too blind to notice it before. It had been so easy to pick out his fooling, his ludicrous behavior under some circumstances. But in the last few days I had been forced to see an efficiency and a control over other people which had possibly put all his past behavior in a different light.

In any case, it was pleasant being here and watching him. Pleasant to see how well he got on with these circus people. He seemed to make no effort, but was just the same old friendly, boyish, natural Beef. The circus people themselves were something so unexpectedly new. Their code of morals, their behavior, their attitude, were somehow subtly different from the rest of society. It was strange country, though not strange enough to make one feel uncomfortable. In these few days' experience of them I began to look at them in a new light. What Jackson had said on that first day about the possibility of a murder in the circus, now assumed a new importance.

I felt now that almost any member of the circus we had so far met would be capable of committing a murder under certain circumstances. Perhaps that is true of everybody, but with the circus folk one felt there would be nothing particularly outrageous in that occurrence. It would be in a different category to the numerous other trials for murder reported weekly in the papers.

Normally one feels that the people one knows best are those least likely to commit a murder. It is because one knows them that one feels this. But in this case it was the reverse. Knowing the circus people a little, I felt that there was scarcely one of them who would surprise me by killing one of their fellow-artists. And Lord knows there were plenty of motives scattered through their lives. Beef and I had already come across enough motives to settle any ordinary case. They seemed to thrive on jealousy, enmities.

And it was not to condemn them that one said any one of them might commit a murder. It was rather a recognition of their peculiar vitality, their quickness, the life in which they lived continually so much closer to violence, accidental or purposeful, than the normal Englishman.

While I had been lying dreamily thinking of these things the sky outside the window had begun to grow and recede with faint streaks of light. The sun had not yet risen, but already the air was warmer and more alive. I decided to get up straight away and drive on before the circus this morning instead of arriving, as usual, after most of the work had been done and the big top pitched.

It was colder than I had expected, and it was difficult to restrain the first impulse to get back under the covers, but after a minute or so, as I moved around the wagon dressing, the blood began to circulate and I felt healthy and cheerful and had begun to whistle to myself until I realized that Beef still slept.

The dew was still on the grass outside, so that the whole tober shone grayly. Long black smears here and there, crossing and re-crossing the center, showed where the horses had wandered grazing, and around the door of many of the

[85]

wagons the trampled grass proved that I had been wrong in thinking that no one was stirring because I had heard no noise of it.

"Cup of tea, Mr. Townsend?" called a voice across the field, and I noticed the head of Sid Bolton sticking out of the window of the clowns' wagon beckoning to me. Many of the hands were crowded into the hot, stuffy interior of the wagon drinking the early morning tea, which was all the food any of them had until the tent was pitched at the next tober. They were cheery and talkative and I felt vaguely pleased that I had stolen a march on Beef by leaving him sleeping.

As the lorries were being started and run a little while in order to warm the engines, I asked Sid Bolton for details of the next tober. My idea was to run on ahead and attempt to get some idea of what the circus looked like to the people in the village where it was arriving. I wanted to see the whole thing from the beginning, as it were.

My cheerful mood persisted as I drove along the main road towards Hull. The sun was just above the horizon and threw an elongated shadow of the car along the road in front of me. There was still a faint ground mist, which, I had been told, meant that the day "would be a real stinker," filling some of the small hollows so that only the tops of the trees showed above it. It might have been ladled out in great spoonfuls here and there in an attempt to level the country as a road-worker levels a road with tarred stones in the summer. It was scarcely half an hour's journey to the next village where we were to pitch for the day, but then my car was not loaded and made far better speed than the huge circus lorries. I passed the elephants, which must have started more than two hours before the dawn, within three miles of the village, and the man who rode beside them on horseback gave a careless wave when he saw who I was. It was Tug Wilson, and his face, in the short glimpse I caught of it, looked sour and disgruntled.

I gathered that getting up early for the elephants was not calculated to improve the temper—unless, of course, in a process of wearing it down.

I found the village, when I reached it, to be small and almost indistinguishable from the other villages we had been stopping at for the last few days. It was built around a crossing of two narrow roads, none of which went to anywhere particularly important, but led eventually to other villages such as this one. As the street entered between the houses it grew far narrower than it had been in the open country, but there was no traffic other than my car, so I had no chance of observing the constriction which would be inevitable when the main body of the circus reached it later in the morning. Every other shop window, and every pub, displayed the bright yellow bill of Jacobi's Circus, but they were of little help to me in discovering the tober. I asked the only occupant of the street; an elderly, vague man, who was staring at me as if I had been a procession of Red Indians in full war-paint.

"Circus?" he repeated.

"Yes," I said. "Can you tell me where the circus usually pitches when it comes to this village?"

"Is a circus coming here?" he asked.

"Yes," I said. "Can you tell me," and so on.

"Is it the same one was here a month ago?" he asked. "Called itself Boggles or Woggles or something?"

"No," I said patiently, and repeated my original question.

This time it drew response, and the man directed me to a field on the edge of the village. "That's where they usually go," he said. And I took his word for it and drove the car down to the gate. I did not enter the field, but parked the car just outside on the road, and sat there waiting for the circus to arrive. I had not long to wait, for in something under an hour the first lorry drove up, closely followed by the rest of the caravan. Daroga waved and drove the first lorry in.

Pete Daroga's was always the first wagon to enter the new tober. He drove it over to the far end, leaped out and was inspecting the ground by the time the next wagon had drawn in. Selecting the flattest portion of the field as the place on which to pitch the tent, he proceeded to supervise the raising of the king-poles into position. Within half an hour the iron pegs had been driven home and the swaying canvas was being hauled slowly up into the air. Most of the other wagons had arrived and had arranged themselves in a rough circle round the field, each in its special position facing the big top. Jackson's wagon was the last to arrive, and as the large blue trailer was pulled into position the proprietor himself opened the door and stood grimly on the grass watching the operations. For a while he did not speak, but watched the men moving backward and forward. His mouth was set in a hard thin line, and his eyes were concentrated on the figure of Pete Daroga as he moved among the men giving them instructions. Not until he had moved over to the front of the field did he speak.

"I suppose you know, Daroga, that you are building up on the wrong tober?" he said, and his voice was cold and biting as he spoke.

Pete turned quickly at his voice. "This is the tober you told me," he said abruptly.

"We all know," said Jackson suavely, "that you are infallible, Daroga. But in the present instance—although I am *sure* it is not your fault—what you have done will have to be undone. Unless, of course, you would like to pay the rent of this field out of your own earnings."

Pete flushed at the cold insult in these words and walked slowly across the field towards the proprietor. "Are you trying to tell me that we've got to take the blasted tent down and move it into another field?" he asked.

Jackson shrugged as if he were not interested in the question, and would have turned to walk into his wagon if Pete had not grabbed him roughly by the sleeve. Jackson shook off the hand impatiently, but nevertheless waited for the man to speak.

"This was the field we built up in ten years ago, isn't it?" asked Pete.

Jackson shrugged again. "Ten years ago—certainly. But it so happens that the arrangement has been changed since then and the landlord prefers that we use the smaller field across the road."

"Then you'd better go and persuade him otherwise," said Pete bluntly. "Don't go trying to put the results of your own dam' carelessness on to me. The tent's nearly up now, and it won't be shifted for you nor all the landlords in the village. Carry on, men," he shouted at the hands, who had been standing about watching the quarrel. "Get those quarter-poles in."

The two men stood facing each other with less than a yard separating them. Neither of them moved, but stared straight into each other's faces. Pete was tall and almost loose-jointed, his hands on his hips and his feet slightly apart pushing his battered, ugly face forward from between his shoulders as if inviting anyone to hit him. Jackson, small, slick, with glossy hair and a faint sardonic grin, watched him as if in contempt.

"You know who's boss here, Daroga?" he asked quietly.

Pete spat on the grass to one side. "I know one or two things more than that," he said. "And that makes us even."

Jackson's eyes flickered for a moment, and he turned them away and looked over towards the tent where the men had begun work again. "I'll see what I can do," he said at last.

Pete said nothing, but turned his back abruptly on the little man and did not even trouble to watch him climb into his car and drive off down the road to the village. The work continued in silence now, for the men had seen the battle and looked respectfully at the old man who had apparently won it. They were not very concerned as to how Pete had achieved it, they merely admired him for being able to get the better of a boss they all hated—and thoroughly feared.

Within ten minutes Jackson was back, and as he climbed up the steps of the wagon he waved Pete over to him. Pete took his time, sauntering slowly across the grass issuing instructions as he went.

"The tent can stay where it is," said Jackson. "I arranged it with the landlord."

Pete's mouth curved in a pitying grin, and then he turned to the men and shouted: "Mr. Jackson says the tent can stay where it is. You don't need to take it down after all."

Jackson's face went white, and he took a step forward as if to speak. But suddenly changing his mind he retreated to his wagon and slammed the door ferociously.

After that the morning's work went on fairly peacefully. The tent was finished and most of the seating unloaded. Although it was a weekday and well past school-time, the field seemed full of small groups of children who wandered around getting in the men's way and listening curiously to the sounds which came from the animal wagons which had not yet been opened.

"Can't you put them chavvies to work, Pete?" Ginger shouted, indicating the children. But he was too late, for at that moment the elephants arrived and the whole mob went tearing off across the field to watch them come in through the gate.

The elephants ignored them, and without any direction from Albert they made straight for the elephant-tent. The children ran around them shouting, scattering if a trunk seemed to sway out a little too much, rushing in to touch the thick, rough hide when the attention of one of the animals was elsewhere.

One of the elephant-men, a negro, stood holding the canvas

flap up for them and shouting at the kids to "Git away," but they took no notice of him unless he made a threatening movement of his arms or legs, and even then they were back as soon as his back was turned, peering under the tent to see the shackling chains fixed to the elephants' hind legs.

Pete strolled over with a grin on his battered face. "Here, you," he shouted, "give us a hand with the lion-cage."

The children immediately surged round him pelting him with questions, leaving only two rather cynical little souls, determined that it was a ruse to get them from the elephant-tent, and so stolidly refusing to help with the lion-cage.

With twenty or thirty children breathlessly leaning on the ropes, the animal cages were slowly drawn round to form three sides of a square. Brightly painted wings were swung out from two of the wagons and bolted together to discover that "Jacobi's Wild Animal Zoo" had been created.

By the middle of the morning the camp had begun to take on a look of permanence. The white canvas was steady in the sun, and the wagons had begun to collect oddments around them, pails, boxes, chairs, which gave the impression that the inhabitants were settling in. A long clothes-line tethered the proprietor's wagon to the nearest tree, and Corinne stood lazily under it, her mouth filled with clothes-pegs, hanging out a long series of clean tights and circus costumes in the sun. The ancient gypsy wagon was similarly decorated, and by the front door, seated in a rickety arm-chair, Anita lay half asleep, letting the warmth soak through her.

Most of the children had disappeared home to their lunch, although here and there a short-cropped head would push its way under a canvas sheet and glance distrustfully around before emerging fully into the zoo, the elephant-tent, or the big top. All the work of building up was finished. Most of the men had gone down the street to the pub, one or two others lounged around the ground talking or simply lying silent in the sun and smoking.

When a neat young man walked on to the field only two people saw him. Corinne quickly emptied her mouth of pegs and watched him out of the corner of her eye, and Herr Kurt, the lion-trainer, stopped hammering at the lion-tunnel for a moment. He forgot to bring the hammer down, and just sat cross-legged on the top of the box with his hand in the air and his brows knit almost into a straight line.

Yet there was nothing particular about the stranger to make people look more than once at him. He was dressed in a light fawn suit and walked with a buoyant step. His eyes looked quickly over the tents and wagons with a sort of amusement. He was probably a young commercial traveler or a car salesman; fairly well off for a bachelor, cynical, not over-burdened with work, rather complacent, but with a curiosity sometimes at odds with that complacency. He noticed Anita sitting in the sunshine and Corinne pegging out clothes.

Herr Kurt, whose real name incidentally, and that by which he was generally known among the circus people, was George Franks, did not attempt to hide his hostility as he watched the young man. When he laid the hammer down on the board beside him and folded his arms he looked more than ever like a figure of judgment. Actually his feelings were those of bitter resignation. From experience he knew that sooner or later the young man would approach Corinne and begin a conversation.

"You know," he said to me, "this is always happening. Not that it worries me, you understand. But every village we go to she seems to pick up one of these young whipper-snappers, and gets him to follow the show around for a couple of days. I don't know what they expect to get for it. They sit in the most expensive seats, and she gives them each a special smile from the ring. Perhaps they have a little talk after the show's over. And then, of course, they fade away directly we get too far along the road for them to be able to come to the show in the evening."

I could tell from Kurt's voice that he did not take this so philosophically as he pretended to. For some reason he sounded hurt over it. But I asked no questions, and when he picked up his hammer and began to bang nails home with the maximum possible noise, I left him and went along to rouse Beef. He had already slept well on to the middle of the morning, and I wondered if perhaps he was feeling ill. Such behavior was not usual with him.

CHAPTER XI

> "Piebald horses
> And ribald music
> Circle around
> A spangled lady."

BEEF was just on the point of getting out of bed when I entered the wagon. He smiled sleepily at me, and rubbing his eyes with the backs of his clenched hands, asked: "Well, what's the news?"

"Nothing more important than that it's nearly eleven o'clock," I said.

"Good," commented Beef, beginning to search around for his clothes, "they're open, then."

Experience had told me what "they" were, so I waited silently for the Sergeant to complete his dressing, and then accompanied him in the direction of the village. Most of the circus folks had mentioned "The Jolly Shepherds," and this turned out to be the first pub on the route.

"Very sensible, too," said Beef, and I followed him into the public bar.

The atmosphere here was thick with smoke and hostility. Five of the villagers sat in a line along one of the wooden benches and drank in silence. Now and again one of them would make a short remark to his neighbor about a purely local problem. On the other hand, the visitors from the circus ignored the other occupants of the bar and continued their conversation as if they had been alone. It struck me that they were probably used to this sort of hostile greeting, and were using their most effective defense against it; circus language and "toughness."

I observed to Beef that these people, in the presence of strangers, tended to make their talk more and more unintelligible and filled with a mixture of Romany, Italian, German, Spanish, Russian, and even Hindustani, words and phrases. This language—the circus language—born out of the isolation of the early circus people, served now to increase that separation from ordinary society. From being a defensive weapon it had now, under modern conditions, become a method of attack. Beef, however, seemed unimpressed by my theorizing, and with a brief, "I shouldn't be surprised if you wasn't right," he went over to join the group at the dart-board.

There were perhaps a dozen of us crowded into that small bar, all talking, drinking, laughing among ourselves and taking no notice of the five villagers on the bench. Clem was playing darts with Sid Bolton, and Peter Ansell was scoring for them. Peter Ansell, the ex-public school boy, a man who had seen the inside of a prison, a wanderer who seemed for the present to have found his home among professional wanderers. His pale, rather thin hair was brushed back closely, his face long and sensitive, with a faint yellowish tinge in the skin, which gave him a semi-mournful, semi-humorous expression.

In a corner, and a little apart from the others, sat the two trapeze artists, Paul and Christophe Darienne, speaking quietly together in French. From what Ginger had told me, and after watching them during the last few days, this apparent isolation of the two brothers had assumed a clearer importance than I had first guessed. It seemed to me now that in their reserve, in their frequent silences, in their use of French as a secret yet common language, was the clue to the relationship between them. It could hardly be called "love." That abused and almost meaningless term was something far less than the bond which seemed to unite the two Darienne brothers. As individuals they were different in almost every way, and yet together one felt that they were complementary rather than "different." I had little doubt in my own mind that such experiences as telepathy were common, if unconscious, between them. I had noticed, for instance, that if one brother saw something, he did not need to say to the other, "Look," because the act of his seeing seemed to carry itself to his brother without the word or gesture that other people need to convey experience.

But there was more to it than that. It was not simply that they were attuned to each other, as the expression is. It was rather that existence to either of them actually included the other in the definition. The ordinary individual sees himself as separable from all his surroundings. Honesty compels him to admit that if he were transferred to the other side of the world, where every person and every item of the surroundings was utterly foreign and unknown to him, yet he would still live as that same individual. Changed perhaps or rapidly changing, but nevertheless most people can envisage such an occurrence, and farther, can see themselves continuing in those new surroundings. But in the case of the Dariennes I felt that this was not true. For Paul, existence has no meaning when it is separated from Christophe's existence, and for Christophe, though I suspected in a somewhat lesser measure, the same held true.

As I watched them now I realized that there was nothing unfriendly in their concentration in each other. When remarks were thrown at them they always answered. They were not outside the circus "atmosphere," but seemed to have seized a small corner of it for themselves.

And in this atmosphere I suddenly realized that Beef was completely at home. He walked over to the dart players, who had just finished their game. "Hullo," he said, "what's all this? A family party?"

"Hullo, Uncle," said Ginger, "what about a game of darts?"

"And now," said Beef with a grin, "you *are* asking for it."

"You're going to have your work cut out," said Ansell quietly, as he ruled a new page for the scoring, "Ginger's our champion dart player. Hasn't been beaten this season."

"Have to see if we can't do something about that," said Beef, and he arranged his large feet carefully behind the throwing line.

I noticed that the whole group of the circus folk in the pub were taking much more than a casual interest in this game between Beef and Ginger, and it took me some minutes to discover why. Then it struck me that when Ginger had called Beef Uncle there had been something more than leg-pulling in it. The fact was that Beef had got himself accepted here as I should never be able to. With his humorous, natural behavior he had conquered a vast difference of outlook and character. He had made himself liked and popular with people to whom I should always remain a friendly stranger. And he had done it quite simply, because he was that sort of a person. And that, I suppose, is one of the biggest compliments one can pay anybody.

The game progressed amid growing excitement. Beef won the first leg, and Ginger the second. It was going to be a close finish. I moved over towards the board in order to watch it. They were both throwing for their final double, and it was Beef's turn. He seemed to be unperturbed as he stood stolidly, hefting his dart for a moment before he threw it, and then—"Office," shouted the whole group together.

"Good old Uncle," said another of the hands, and I realized again that this nickname was not the sort that people use when they wish to show a faint contempt for a person. It was more as if Beef had earned the right to be known by a familiar diminutive. I sipped my beer and watched his success, feeling a slight tinge of jealousy as I did so.

The first to leave the bar were the Darienne brothers. There was nothing secretive in their behavior as they rose from their seat and slipped out of the door, but they gave the impression of a self-sufficiency. I could see them through the crooked glass of the bar window as they walked down the empty main street, walking slowly, moving their heads and shoulders as they talked, and their hands occasionally illustrating or emphasizing a point.

Since the others looked like staying on for some time yet (Ginger was talking darkly about a return match), I decided to catch up with the Dariennes. They interested me intensely, and I felt I should be doing more to help the "case" by talking to them than Beef was doing by playing darts. I felt that this was probably only another facet of my jealousy of his success, but, nevertheless, I hurried after the two brothers.

I caught them up at the gate and noticed at the same time that Anita Concini was seated outside her wagon. She waved to us and we walked over to her, passing as we did so Corinne, deep in conversation with the young man of the day before.

"Who is that?" Paul asked Anita as soon as we had reached her.

Anita laughed. "A man," she said.

"The complete answer," grinned Christophe. "At least the most important fact as far as Corinne is concerned, eh?"

"Watch George on top of the lion-tunnel," said Anita, indicating Kurt, "and see if you can guess what he's thinking. He ought to be used to that sort of thing by now. Yet he's been squatting there for the last twenty minutes wishing he had a machine-gun, by the look on his face. I don't know what he'd do if he had one—probably shoot them both."

"That's absurd," protested Paul. "One must have the right before it is possible to feel jealous; or at least before one should show one's jealousy. George has none. We all know that he's in love with Corinne—it's something he couldn't hide anyway if he wanted to—but that doesn't give him the right to be possessive, does it?"

Anita seemed to be on the point of speaking, and then she shook her head and laughed quietly. "You know, Paul," she said, "either you two are very honest and innocent, or else you're very good actors."

"Innocent?" said Paul. "What do you mean by that? The English language is very difficult sometimes."

But Anita refused to explain any further, and after a while the two boys walked off, shaking their heads in a puzzled fashion.

"Why does Corinne behave like that?" I asked Anita as soon as we were alone.

"Corinne has one main idea," explained Anita, "and in a way everything she does has something to do with it."

"And that is?" I probed.

"It's quite simple. She wants to leave the circus."

"So she hopes one of these young men will fall in love with her and take her 'away from it'?" I asked. "A very romantic idea, but scarcely likely, is it?"

"Oh, no. It's not that at all," replied Anita. "I don't think this is meant for anything really. But I suppose these young fellows who follow her around represent the outside world to her. She doesn't expect anything from them, or they from her, I don't suppose. But they fascinate her. I'm surprised she hasn't had a try at yourself or the Sergeant."

"Miaow," I said.

"Yes, I know. But you did ask me, didn't you?"

When I looked back towards the pair by Jackson's wagon again, I discovered that the young man was on his way out of the gate, and that Corinne was walking slowly towards Kurt, who was banging fiercely, as if he had not seen her coming.

"Watch this, Sherlock," said Anita. "I don't know what she's going to say to him, but in about two minutes from now she'll have George as sweet as pie, and eating out of her hand."

And Anita was quite right. I watched Kurt's face, and from the dour expression which he wore when he greeted Corinne, I watched a gradual change, until in a few minutes he had climbed down off the top of the lion-tunnel and was grinning like a beauty-struck yokel.

CHAPTER XII

BACK in the wagon, and alone, I felt that it was a good opportunity to take stock of the situation. There were so many people involved that I thought I was bound to get muddled unless I put the whole thing straight in my mind as far as it had gone. It had not, it is true, gone very far. There was nothing one could call clues or evidence in the usual way, but nevertheless we had discovered something about the characters of the various people among whom we were living. I took a sheet of paper and began to run through them.

In the first place, because he was fresh in my memory, was the young clown, Clem Gail. There was the strange contradiction which ruled his life; that he should be unrecognizable in the ring and comparatively unhonored for his skill. This was, at any rate, something new in the private life of a clown. The normal story seems to be that the clown laughs, and hides a breaking heart; that most clowns suffer from chronic dyspepsia, or keep aged mothers. Clem was certainly a departure from the accepted normal. And, moreover, he seemed to see himself as something of a Don Juan, a fact which was again in contradiction to his anonymous self in the ring. But there was little else about him that we had so far discovered. Nothing which seemed to involve him directly in this strange, hypothetical case.

Next there was Corinne Jackson. She quite obviously wanted to get away from the circus life. In the ring she was almost condescending. And this linked her with the numerous attachments she made with young men outside the show. Yet she was not what one might call the scheming type. The young men who seemed to gather round her at every new village made little impression on her. It appeared to me that she hardly looked on them as means of escaping from the circus life, but rather as expressions of her dislike for all that the circus stood for. Her relationship with her brother seemed to be that of friendly bickering, which characterizes so many brother and sister relations. With her father she was cold and distant, and with her mother offhand and casual. Where did Kurt come in?

Herr Kurt, or George Franks, to give him his correct name, was quite clearly in love with Corinne. He was jealous of every new friendship she struck up, but since this did not in any way deter her from making them, I assumed that she was not in love with him. And yet we had had an example of Corinne taking pains to dispel that jealousy. It might have been through some special vanity which made her want to be on good terms with all the men in the show, or it might have been that she really did like the lion-trainer and his jealousy flattered her. This was obviously a problem which we should have to solve later.

There was something, too, in the attitude of Daroga, the wire-walker, to Jackson, which defied definition at this stage. The little incident when we had set up on the wrong tober was illuminating. Jackson was not the sort of boss who is generally laughed at by his staff, and yet Daroga had won in that little tussle. Daroga himself seemed to treat Jackson in a very casual way, which was not completely in keeping with the proprietor's reputation as an autocrat. What was there between those two? It was something which had not come out into the open so far.

And then the Dariennes. The younger brother had been teaching Suzanne French, and Paul had been both hurt and surprised at the discovery. The closeness of the two lads, their immense friendship for each other, seemed to argue that this was something out of the ordinary. Where did Suzanne come in in that peculiar relationship? There seemed to be no room for her. And yet there was little doubt that some link did exist between them. Again, only the future could reveal it.

And why had old Gypsy Margot predicted a murder in the circus? Surely, there was nothing in this fortune-telling business. And yet, unless she thought such a murder would actually take place, she would hardly have told Albert so. Generally, fortune-tellers take good care not to say anything which can easily be proved wrong. Had she some special reason for thinking a murder would occur? The charge of madness seemed hardly correct. She did not act like a mad woman, and from our experience of her I thought she was most probably very astute under her seer's guise. Was it important that she was a hypnotist? And the attempted stabbing of Anita by Helen; had that any connection with the murder idea? The original prediction, so Albert had since told us, had been fairly specific. It would take place, the old woman had said, within a month. And that had been quite early in April. It was now the twenty-eighth.

In relation to all these doubtful points the Concinis seemed fairly simple. There seemed no doubt that Helen had stabbed her sister in a fit of unreasonable self-pity. In actual fact, she loved her sister, but the similarity between the two had produced a sort of jealousy. But an explanation of it did not mean that the whole affair might not happen again in some new form. And the next time the knife might not strike a shoulder-blade. The next time it might possibly be murder. Was that the case we were here to investigate? It was difficult to discover exactly what Beef thought about this. He gave one very little help.

And as if in answer to my doubts the Sergeant at that moment came into the wagon.

"So you came back?" I said.

"Looks like it, doesn't it?" grinned Beef.

"Where are all the others?"

"Oh, most of them are still down the bevvy, but I . . ."

"Bevvy?" I asked. "What's a bevvy?"

"Boozer," said Beef shortly. "You know, pub. It's a circus word."

"The good detective," I said acidly, "always tries to merge with his background. Is that what you're doing?"

"There's no call for you to be sarcastic," said Beef. "I just picked up a few words here and there. Must be sociable."

"And the result of a morning's work," I persisted, "is that we now know that 'bevvy' is the circus word for pub. Very useful I'm sure."

"Don't you run away with the idea that that's all I've been doing," protested Beef. "I've been watching Kurt with some lion cubs in the ring. That's why I came across here. I thought you might be interested."

"Interested," I said, "but not very useful."

"Oh, I don't know," said Beef. "You never know. Anyway, I like watching them. Come on."

The huge white tent spread comfortably over the whole field, its canvas top rippling gently in the slight wind. Sun, warm and still, gave the impression of complete inactivity in the circus. At any rate, it was one of the few hours the circus people had free during the day and they generally spent them either in rehearsals, in sleep, in the pub or in each other's wagons. The field was empty now, except for half a dozen or so school-children, who peered curiously into each tent and wagon, and were never discouraged by the shouts or abuse of the circus folk. It seemed to me that the circus was the peculiar prerogative of children; the one place where their curiosity was a right instead of a nuisance.

I followed Beef into the big empty tent, where it was cool out of the sun. The strong smell of trodden grass, mixed with that of fresh sawdust, filled the air. The seating stood around in a large circle, empty and bare, and looked much too uneasy and rough to bear the weight of the crowd I knew would fill it at the evening performance. At the moment, however, Beef and I were the only audience, and he directed my attention to the lion cage, where Kurt was trying to persuade the two lion cubs to perform some simple trick.

Beef seemed to know quite a lot about the business of lion-trainer, and I soon realized that he had certainly not been wasting his time in the few days he had had at the circus.

"You see how he does it?" he said. "These cubs are only six or seven months old and rather young for training, and he has to be very patient with them. All he's done so far is to teach them to sit still on their stools, and they won't always do that. Now watch."

The two half-grown cubs were now sitting with a rather bored expression on their faces on the two stools at one side of the cage, while Kurt stood in front of them, talking gently in a soft monotonous voice, repeating the same words over and over again.

"Goooood *boy*," he said. "Goooood *boy*."

The lions appeared to take no notice whatever of this flattery. Then Kurt took a small piece of meat from his pocket, and sticking it on the top of a short pole, he waved it in front of one of the cubs. The cub pawed at it playfully, trying to grab it, but failed. Then Kurt drew the pole just out of the lion's reach.

"Down," he said, "down."

The cub seemed to reflect a moment, and then came slowly off his stool and approached the meat which Kurt brought nearer and nearer to himself and at last dropped on the ground quite close to his feet. The cub approached suspiciously and slowly, and then finally sank flat on the ground and took the meat. Kurt cracked his whip suddenly and the cub ran back to its stool in the corner and sat down.

"Why," I said, "they look as tame as tabby cats. I thought this was supposed to be a dangerous game."

"I wouldn't like to go in there anyway," Beef snorted. "It's the way he handles them. He knows his job, that chap does."

At this point Kurt slipped quickly out of the cage, and lighting a cigarette, walked slowly over towards us.

"Well," he said, "do you find it interesting?"

"Very," I said.

"Mr. Townsend here," interrupted Beef tactlessly, "thinks that those cubs are as tame as cats. What have you got to say to that?"

Kurt laughed amusedly. "Perhaps they are in some ways," he conceded. "The job's not very difficult, once you've got the hang of it. But mind you, it's always dangerous. Now those animals wouldn't attack me on purpose. But you never know what might happen."

"If they wouldn't attack you, how is it dangerous?" I asked.

Kurt seemed to be thinking for a moment. At last he said: "Well, look, it's like this. They're friendly with you, see? They don't think of you as a meal. If they were hungry it wouldn't make them attack you, although I don't say as they wouldn't be fidgety and hard to handle. But what makes them dangerous is nerves. All animals are nervous. Now suppose I was in there with them and doing a turn, and some kid threw a firework into the cage. Well, that would frighten the lions. They don't think, like you and I do. What they'd do is to take a jump out at the nearest thing to them. Might be me and it might be each other. They wouldn't think 'It was a kid's fault.' They'd just act. And then again, suppose I trod on one of them during the act. It's no good saying you're sorry to a lion. If you tread on him he bites you straight away. And a lion bite isn't something you can pretend you haven't got. Unless it's on another lion, of course."

"What do you mean by that?" I asked.

"Oh, it's just one of those funny little things about a lion. You see a lion's skin isn't fixed down like ours is, but moves about like a shirt. Then, if you stick a knife into a lion—not that I'd advise you to—the place won't bleed, because the hole in the skin doesn't often come in the same place as the hole in his flesh. Course, it festers up after a week or so, but it sometimes makes lions very touchy and you can't always find out what's the matter."

"Suppose," interrupted Beef, "that someone had something against you, and wanted to do you in without getting caught."

"Who's got something against me?" demanded Kurt truculently.

"Nobody, so far as we know," said Beef. "But just suppose that someone has."

"But if nobody has," objected Kurt. "Why suppose anything so silly?"

"Well, just for the sake of argument."

"I don't like arguments," said Kurt.

Beef looked nonplussed for a moment. "All right," he said at last. "Look at it this way. Suppose there's a lion-trainer called Smith . . ."

"You mean the one with Stirrup's Circus?" asked Kurt. "Yes, I know him. Got a good mixed act this year."

"No," said Beef patiently, "I don't mean any particular lion-trainer. This is just a story."

"Oh," said Kurt, understanding dawning at last, "why didn't you say that in the first place? Do you mean the sort of stories that Mr. Townsend writes?"

"That's right," said Beef, clutching at any straw. "Now Mr. Townsend wants to write a story about a lion-trainer who was murdered, and he doesn't know how it could be done. Can you tell us how someone might get the lions to do away with him, so that the murderer wouldn't be caught?"

"Well," said Kurt thoughtfully, "he could grease the tops of the stands, so that the lion would slip when he started to jump."

"That would be found out too easily," I said.

"Or he could fire a gun just near the cage."

"So would that."

"Well, I don't know," said Kurt in exasperation. "Strikes me it's a silly problem anyway. There are lots of ways. All he's got to do is to scare the lions when the act is on. Nobody need see him. He could hide under the seats, or even do it from outside the tent. He could easily get away before anyone saw him."

Beef had been taking all this down in his notebook, and after a brief suspicious glance, Kurt turned back to the cage again. The cubs immediately climbed on to their pedestals as soon as he entered and sat waiting. This time he was apparently going to try the same trick on the second cub which he had been practicing on the first when we came in. The second cub answered quicker than its companion, and was down off the stool almost as soon as Kurt gave the command. But as soon as it had grabbed the meat, the first cub leaped from its stool and attacked it. For a moment the two cubs rolled on the ground snarling at each other, but apparently in nothing more than a mock battle, for Kurt merely took a step back away from them and waited for the fight to finish. But at that moment the two struggling animals rolled towards him and as he moved to step out of their way he tripped and sprawled across them. Immediately, the two animals turned on him, and Beef and I leaped to our feet to run towards the cage. But before we reached it the trainer had got things in hand himself and was out of the cage, slamming the door behind him by the time we got to him.

"Are you hurt?" asked Beef.

"That blasted feeder will be when I get hold of him,"

shouted Kurt by way of an answer, and before we could say anything he had gone at a run out of the tent.

"This ought to be interesting," said Beef in an almost ghoulish voice.

"Why?" I asked.

"Well," explained Beef, "the animals' feeder, Ansell, is supposed to be here ready whenever Kurt goes in with the lions, in case there's an accident. Apparently he scarpa'd just after Kurt had started."

"Scarpa'd?" I asked.

"Yes, cleared off, skipped it. Circus palari," said Beef.

"Palari?" I asked.

"Oh, skip it," said Beef. "Let's go and see the fun."

But there was no need to go very far, because at that minute we heard the voices of the two men raised in argument just outside the opening of the tent. Beef motioned me to keep still, and we stood just inside listening to them. The argument appeared to have passed the initial stages already, for the two voices, peculiarly different, were not discussing lions at all, but generalities. Peter Ansell's suave educated voice was saying:

"My dear George, it is surprising that you can't handle a couple of baby lions. You can't even handle women."

"What do you mean by that?" shouted Kurt.

"I should have thought it was obvious," continued Ansell, who seemed to be enjoying himself. "Take Miss Jackson for example. Do you know where she is at this moment?"

"You leave Corinne out of this," shouted Kurt, "it's got nothing to do with the argument."

"Nevertheless, you don't know where she is," gibed Ansell, and it struck me that he was covering his own negligence by hitting Kurt on the raw, instead of justifying his absence from the ring.

"All right then, Mr. Clever Ansell," said Kurt, "and where is she?"

"As a matter of fact, she's gone into Hull with a certain Mr. Herbert Torrant. He called for her in his car about ten minutes ago, and asked me to tell her father that she would not be back until just before the afternoon show."

At this point, however, the two men began to walk away from the tent and Beef and I could hear no more.

"That Miss Corinne," Beef commented, "isn't half a one. Leads them all up the garden path she does."

"But there's nothing serious in that," I answered sharply. "Nothing in any case which would lead to a murder."

"You haven't seen half of it yet," chuckled Beef.

CHAPTER XIII

April 28th (continued).

THERE was no doubt about Kurt being in a rage. After a brief, but obvious, argument with his feeder, Ansell, he turned abruptly and walked across to his cabin. As he slammed the door behind him Beef said: "There you are. I told you."

"Yes," I agreed. "But you said something about Ansell. Are you sure of that?"

"Well, I don't know about sure," said Beef. "Let's go over and see him now. Soon find out."

We could see Ansell moving towards the zoo and we quickly followed him. By the time we reached him he was beginning to unload the horse-meat which had arrived that day at the station. He seemed quite pleased when Beef offered that we should help him.

"Didn't know this came in your job," I said casually, as we transferred the meat from the station lorry to the circus meat wagon.

"Bit of everything," said Ansell shortly. "Kurt looks after the supply part, works out the quantity and so on, but the actual work on it is part of my job." He threw a huge section of a carcass into the wagon with a distasteful expression. It looked as though it might have been almost any part of the horse's anatomy, hewn off with very blunt axes. The fat was a deep yellow, and the rest a dull red. It looked stale and unappetizing, even from the lion's point of view.

I realized that Ansell was not in one of his talkative moods, and that if we wanted to get anything out of him about his attitude to Corinne Jackson, we should have to wait until he had mellowed a little to our company. This was a mood in which I had not seen him before. He was abrupt in his movements, and only answered our questions in short sentences. And even these had an acid quality which had been absent from his speech at our previous interview.

"Having a good season so far?" said Beef. It was more of a statement than a question.

"There's always plenty of mugs," said Ansell.

After a slight pause Beef tried again. "You don't get on too well with Kurt?" he asked.

"I'd like to see anyone who could get on with that half-baked moron!" said Ansell bitterly.

But it seemed that this little release of feelings had placed him back in something of his normal cynical good-humor.

"You know," he said suddenly, "I've stuck this job for nearly a year. Apart from the time I spent in prison that's the longest I've ever been able to hold one down."

"And why's that?" asked Beef. "Does that mean you're thinking of staying in the circus business for good?"

"Good Lord, I hope not," answered Ansell.

"Then why do you stay?" I asked.

Peter Ansell seemed not to want to answer my question, or at least not to answer it directly, because after a pause he said:

"Well, it's not exactly the job which keeps me here. You see, sometimes as one roves around one meets a person who seems different, more interesting, than the rest of the world. Not very often, I admit, but when one does meet such a person it becomes quite sufficient reason for sticking a bit. Humanity, as a whole, rather bores me. People are such hypocrites. I don't mind a good all-round hypocrite; what I dislike is the person who thinks he's being honest and is simply deceiving himself. And in my opinion most people spend their lives doing just that. In the circus, strangely enough, that sort of person is rarer than any other place. They're cut off from all that nasty suburban littleness I suppose, and are more selfish in an obvious way instead of that pseudo-Christian pretense of concern for their fellow men which characterizes the majority of mankind."

"And this person," demanded Beef eagerly. "Who is it?"

"Corinne Jackson," answered Ansell.

"Then you're in love with her?" insisted Beef.

Ansell's mouth twisted a little bitterly. "Of course," he said, "you would put that construction on it. Brought up in an atmosphere of sickly sentiment, of Christmas decorations and popular songs, it's only natural that any interest whatever which a man takes in a woman is something to do with 'love.' Well, you may be right. Perhaps I'm running away from it, and it's I who am the hypocrite. But, so far as I know, I'm not in love with Corinne Jackson. To tell you the truth, I don't see how anybody could be, unless they were absolutely blind to her defects. No, I like her because she's honest with herself, although she manages to fool everybody else. She knows just what she wants and some day, some way, she's going to get it. Why shouldn't I give it to her? I don't want to stay in this perishing circus any more than she does. That's why I bear no resentment against the rather stupid George. If she married him there would be nothing for her but a long life in the circus; no possibility of escape."

Beef looked rather puzzled, and not a little hurt at the animal-feeder's tone. "I don't know what fancy names you put to it," he said bluntly, "but it still sounds like love to me."

"My dear Sergeant," laughed Ansell, "you have a habit of wanting to put labels on things. Put it away in its little box and everything's all right. Well, if you want to, you can call it love. I suppose it's as good a name as any. But, personally, I feel there's more to it than that. Of course, I'm not trying to kid you that the whole thing is purely platonic. But, believe me, these labels have a nasty habit of never quite answering their purpose."

When I heard Ansell talk like that, I realized in what particular sense he was *déclassé*. He had gone beyond reticence. If he had ever, as he had said, been at a public school, it was many years since its influence had died in him. A man who could stand there and discuss his petty emotional reactions was not what I understood by an educated man. I had never heard anyone so frank, and I wondered whether that frankness in itself was an elaborate façade.

"Anyway, the point is," Beef said to me afterwards, as we were walking slowly down to the local pub, "that whether he's in love with her or not, he wants to marry her and take her away from the circus. All right then. That's all we wanted to know. He can have as many fancy ideas as he likes about why he's going to do it, it still means the same to me."

On the whole, perhaps, I agreed with him. There is always something a little bogus in the man who delights in denying the obvious and universal emotions in order to replace them by vaguer and less sure definitions. But despite this, I felt a little sorry for Ansell. It was obvious that what he lacked was any anchorage; anything firm to turn to. He was alone in the world, and though it may be sentimental to feel for this particular type of orphan, I could not help attempting to give Beef some idea of my sympathy for him.

"Oh, he's all right," said Beef. "Wouldn't be happy unless he had something queer going on in that head of his. I've met chaps like that before. Make a profession of being a misfit, most of them."

The subject, apparently, did not interest Beef very much, for after a slight pause he went on: "What does strike me, though, is that Kurt. He's got a temper on him all right. The way he turned on Ansell when he had that trouble with the cubs. It just shows you. Wouldn't do no harm to keep a close eye on him."

The pub was now in sight and Beef quickened his pace noticeably. "One of the beauties of being with a circus," he said with a grin, "is the way you can get into pubs at all hours. Something I missed a bit since the days I used to be in the Force, that is."

"How do they get away with it?" I asked.

"Well, no landlord likes to turn his back on the amount of custom that a circus brings. What's a few by-laws, anyway? And then, the village policeman probably understands."

And with this he turned quickly through the door marked public bar. The bar was filled with circus people, and Beef was immediately grabbed on his entry to play a game of darts with three of the tent hands. Ginger was rubbing his hands in obvious anticipation, while Beef was elucidating a somewhat technical question on the value of feathered darts as opposed to those with paper flights.

I noticed the Darienne brothers sitting together in their usual way, alone in a corner, and went over to talk to them. Somehow or other, the conversation worked itself back to how their act had started.

"But, of course," said Christophe, "that was before we had Suzanne with us."

The elder brother merely grunted at this.

"She has made all the difference to our act," Christophe went on. "Now it's the top of the show. Before Suzanne came we had to do turns on the bars and rings and so on. We couldn't do very much on the trapeze. We knew the old tricks all right, but it needs a woman, and an expert like Suzanne, to make an act really go."

"I don't know," said Paul slowly, looking down at the table as though he felt uncomfortable, "we had good times then. Our act is better, I suppose. But we were happier then."

I thought I detected a note of resentment in Paul's voice as he said this. Christophe was looking straight at his brother, with a question in his eyes, but Paul refused to look up.

"What was Suzanne doing before she joined up with you?" I asked in an attempt to fill in the gap which Paul had made. Christophe turned to me again.

"But you must have heard of her," he said. I shook my head. "Oh, but she was famous," he went on. "*The* Suzanne. She had been with all the really big circuses. She was marvelous in those days. She is not so good now as she was then. But you must see her."

At this point a disturbance in the street outside saved me from answering, and in a few seconds the hunchback tent hand ran into the bar.

"Here," he said, holding up his long arms to the crowd in the bar and obtaining immediate silence. "Have any of you seen what's up the road?"

"What've you found, Tug?" asked Ginger. "A mermaid?"

The hunchback waved the facetiousness aside with the two words: "Bogli's Circus."

"What, in this village?"

"Where are they?"

"The dirty skunks."

Comment came fast from every occupant of the bar, so that it seemed as if the queerly named Bogli's Circus had committed some unmentionable crime against them.

"No, not here," replied Tug. "But they're playing tonight just down the road. A village about two miles out. And they're sticking their posters on top of our fly-spots. I just passed a couple as I came down."

In less than ten seconds the bar was empty except for Beef and myself, and there was a sound of shouting and footsteps in the street.

"What's bitten them?" I asked Beef. But he shook his head.

"Better follow them and see," was his suggestion, and we made our way out into the street in time to see the tail-end of the procession retreating round the corner.

But we did not have far to go. A few yards round the corner we came on them again, gathered in a group around a gatepost on which was displayed a brilliant blue poster advertising the performance that night of Bogli's Circus in the next village. The orange edging underneath showed where the fly for Jacobi's Circus was. Pete Daroga was slowly and ceremoniously peeling the new one off, and swearing to himself as he did so.

Two of the hands were immediately dispatched to tell Jackson of the occurrence and to get some new fly-bills and a pot of paste.

"There's some work for some of us before the afternoon performance," said Daroga grimly.

Beef nudged Kurt, who was spitting on his hands and rolling up his sleeves. "What's it all about?" the Sergeant asked.

Kurt looked pityingly at us. "They put their posters on top of ours," he said simply, "so we go round and put ours on top of theirs."

"But why all this fuss about it?" I asked. "Why make all this trouble?"

Kurt grinned broadly and spat on his hands once more. "No trouble at all," he said cheerfully.

CHAPTER XIV

April 28th (continued).

IN A few minutes the tent hands had returned from the circus loaded with pasting-pots and fly-bills. The group immediately divided into two, with six in each group, who agreed to take half of the village each, and set off. Beef and I were in the group which consisted of Len Waterman, who seemed to have sprung up from nowhere at the mention of trouble, the two Darienne brothers, Sid Bolton, the fat clown, Kurt the lion-trainer, and Ginger.

Sid Bolton was without doubt the most useful person we could have if we did happen to run into trouble—and from the grin on Kurt's face and the way he kept rubbing his hands together, I suspected that it was very likely we should. Sid's fists were the size of a respectable ham, and despite his size there was nothing sluggish about him.

The little cortège walked in "open formation" down the street, Ginger leading with the paste-pot and the fly-bills, and Beef and I bringing up a rather doubtful rear. Actually, Beef seemed to be enjoying the situation.

"Haven't had a decent scrap since I was set on by those poachers," he told me. "They don't like you to be mixed up in a barney when you're in the Force."

I hoped, privately, that he would have no opportunity of making up for that omission now. But I refrained from saying this aloud for fear of damping his enthusiasm. Had I not been so closely involved in this business, I might have been able to appreciate the buccaneering spirit which animated these people. As it was, the possibility of being caught up in a "bundle" of some sort, made me overwhelmingly aware of my own shortcomings as a fighter, and I was only able to see the more ludicrous side of the affair. I had even got so far as to envisage the possible headlines which might greet such an escapade. "Famous Author of Detective Fiction Arrested in Street Battle." Well, perhaps not famous, but in any case it would be most embarrassing.

But my rumination was cut short by Ginger, who had found one of the hated blue posters. With a true sense of drama he sploshed paste over the offending advertisements and covered it with one of the orange bills he was carrying. We then walked on in search of more. But after this had been done some six or seven times the whole affair began to appear rather futile. No one appeared to defend the blue fly-bills, no one offered to battle with us over the right to use this or that gatepost, and apart from a stray child, a postman, and a road-sweeper, there was nobody to see our triumph. The little group walked on in silence.

At the far side of the village we were met by the other group, and it seemed there was nothing else to do now but to return to the tober. All the available sites in the village had been reclaimed without opposition. Bogli's Circus had been vanquished without bloodshed, but it had been a barren triumph.

"Here, wait a minute," said Kurt suddenly, as they were beginning to move off. "Where does that road go to?"

His pointing finger indicated a narrow stony road, which led out of the village down into the shallow valley about a mile and a half away. The road ran straight for about half a mile, and then dipped suddenly and disappeared. But a close group of trees and houses in the distance showed where it led to.

"That's the village they're playing at," said Len Waterman.

"And there's one of their bills," concluded Ginger.

A little over half-way up the road there was the un-mistakable blue splodge which represented Bogli's fly-bill.

Without any further words the whole crowd turned and started eagerly up the road.

But we had not gone more than a hundred yards towards our objective when a group of men appeared suddenly in the distance at the far end of the road. When they saw us they stopped, and formed together as if discussing something. Kurt, who had been walking in front held up his hand, and the two groups stood facing each other over a stretch of more than a quarter of a mile of road. The blue poster was roughly half-way between us. Kurt, who seemed to have taken complete charge of the affair, signaled us to move forward with him, but as we began to walk again, the opposing group did the same. We quickened our pace, until in a few minutes both groups were running at full speed towards each other. It was like running towards a mirror. Every move we made was repeated by the men at the other end of the road. In numbers we were about equal. The road was otherwise deserted, and there was little possibility of interference. I grabbed Beef by the sleeve, but he shook me impatiently off.

"Let them fight it out between themselves," I gasped. "It's not our fight anyway."

But Beef was not to be deterred. The whole thing was utterly fantastic; like a scene out of a film. But I found it impossible to feel enthusiastic at taking part in a bad Western. Actually, none of them were concerned with the question of a blue or an orange poster, and there was little or no actual enmity in the whoop Ginger gave at that moment, as he pitched his paste-pot high in the air over our advancing opponents. The white paste sprayed out like a catherine-wheel, and the crowd ducked quickly, but did not stop their pace for it. The leader was a huge red-faced man wearing a béret on the back of his head. A smear of paste from his eyebrow to his mouth only increased his set, determined expression.

Like something in a nightmare, the two groups came together with an explosion of sound, and I found myself close behind Beef and in the center of a whirlpool of fists. Almost paralyzed, I watched the battle around me. "Tiny" Bolton was disdaining the blows which fell on his face and body, and seemed only concerned with his rhythmical delivery of hammer-like blows on the tops of the heads surrounding him. Beef, I was surprised to see, had already cleared a space around him with a series of scythe-like sweeps, and was grunting gently to himself as he prepared for the next comers. So far, no damage had been done and everybody drew back a little, on guard after the first rush.

At this point, for a short time, I entered the fight. A lanky individual, with sandy hair and protruding teeth, singled me out as a possible opponent and came towards me. There was no help for it now, I must fight. In my mind there seems little doubt that, had the fight continued fairly, I should most certainly have won. This is not said in any sense as a boast or to ameliorate the eventual result. But, nevertheless, it was obvious to me that he was an easy proposition. He had no science to speak of and came at me with his chin stuck out, ready to be hit. Unfortunately, at this moment, Beef got in my way. He had just taken on a new assailant and his peculiar windmill technique took little notice of obstacles. In any case, he drew his arm back a little carelessly and caught me under the chin with his elbow. I recovered some minutes later, to find myself lying at the side of the road in a very dusty condition, and decided under the circumstances to remain there.

The fight, however, continued for some time. From its subsequent figuring in all circus conversations, I gathered that it was an extremely good one. But not being an expert on such matters, and being no doubt a little prejudiced by my own early exclusion from it, it struck me as being nothing more nor less than a vulgar brawl.

Sitting fairly safely at some distance on a little heap of stones, I watched the progress. It soon became obvious that the adherents of Bogli's Circus were having the worst time, and that certainly Sergeant Beef had little need of my help. I therefore exercised my rights as an author and ruminated on the more literary side of the affair. It struck me that it was not unlike the street brawls of the retainers of the houses of the Montagues and the Capulets in "Romeo and Juliet." In both cases the actual fighters had little to gain by the contact, except the possibility of shed blood and bruised flesh. Some years ago a Russian production of this play had shown the two sides fraternizing before and after the conflict, and I saw now that there was something to be said for that theory. These present fighters did not dislike each other by any means. They had more in common than any of them had with the people of the surrounding villages. But both sides wanted a fight, and here it was.

One exception to this appeared to be Sid Bolton. Unlike the others, he was treating this fight as something more than a game. I watched his face from where I sat and was surprised by the ferocity and hate which was in his expression. He seemed to be always in the most active place, taking on two and sometimes more opponents at a time. I wondered if this could be explained in any way. Obviously, he had no more personal antagonism to the people he was fighting than had the rest of the men from Jacobi's Circus. Why then this viciousness? Suddenly, I remembered what he had told me in the wagon. He had once been the "fat boy" of fairgrounds and circuses, and as he had said this I had seemed to notice a faint bitterness in his voice. My memory of such exhibitions told me that the "fat boy's" tent was usually filled with giggling and chuckling people, who seemed to think that humanity was the last thing they were expected to see in the lad on show. That laughter must have rankled in Sid's mind. I could imagine him hating all the human race for the laughs he received from some senseless members of it. Could that be the reason for this unexpected violence on his part? I was inclined to think it was.

But the fight, as a fight, had begun to wane a little. Beef was surrounded by the prostrate forms of three opponents, who were either unconscious, or shamming, in order to avoid getting up to face the Sergeant's fists again. Half of the enemy had already begun to retreat the way they had come. And it probably would have fizzled out at that, had not Len Waterman and Christophe Darienne picked on the same man as a prospective partner.

"All right, Len," said Christophe calmly, "he's mine."

Len's small sturdy form seemed to bristle at that, and he attempted to elbow Christophe out of the way. But the French lad refused to be hustled.

"It would be you," shouted Len Waterman suddenly. "Always sneaking in on me."

Their opponent dropped his hands in bewilderment at this misdirection of energy, and stood watching the two men glaring at each other. Christophe was calm and assured, Len was excited and angry. Then Christophe reached his clenched hand out and tapped Len lightly, almost friendlily, on the shoulder, and in a moment the two men were fighting.

Everybody else stopped their own affairs immediately to crowd round and watch. A rough ring was made, and shouts of encouragement urged on one or other of the fighters.

"They're like a lot of babies," said Beef to me. "Like quarreling over a rattle, that's what it is. Silly, I call it. I'm going to put a stop to it."

And almost before he had finished speaking he was shoul-

[123]

dering his way through the ring as only a policeman knows how.

"Here," he said, grabbing each of them by the shoulder, "have a bit of sense. Enough's as good as a feast."

The two men looked at each other a little sheepishly, but Len Waterman did not look at all pleased that they had been interrupted.

"Oh, you mind your own business," he said, and twisting himself from Beef's grasp he walked quickly out of the ring and started off back to the tober. There was silence for a moment, and then the men started putting themselves tidy, and following Len's example.

"And mind," shouted Kurt as a parting shot to the remnants of the enemy. "Mind you keep your posters in your own village in future."

The leader of the other side shrugged his shoulders slightly. "Maybe," he said quietly.

"What did you say?" roared Kurt pugnaciously.

"Maybe," came the answer again.

For a moment it looked as though the fight might recommence there and then, but Pete Daroga pulled impatiently at Kurt's sleeve.

"Come on," he said, "we haven't got much time to wash up before the afternoon show." And slightly battered, the little group continued on its way back to the tober.

"Cor," said Beef, catching up with me, "that was a Do, all right, wasn't it?"

I thought it was probably the wrong time to tell him about his carelessness in the matter of placing blows, and so kept silent.

CHAPTER XV

WHEN we reached the tober we discovered that it was already almost time for the afternoon performance, and Jackson was raging up and down in front of his wagon.

"Where the hell have you all been?" he demanded, as the little group came through the gate. "Hurry up and get that muck off your faces and get changed for the show. There's only ten minutes or so to go."

Actually, the queue had scarcely begun to form in front of the pay-box, but no one cared about pointing out his exaggeration. In the circumstances it was probably justified.

"I like that," said Ginger, when we were out of earshot of the proprietor. "We go out and risk life and limb for the honor of his circus, and then he turns on us for being a few minutes late. Gratitude for you!"

"Don't you kid yourself, my lad," commented Beef. "You were out for a scrap and nothing more."

But there was little discussion now. All the enmities were immediately forgotten, and the artists and hands alike hurried off to get ready in time for the performance.

Anita joined Beef and me as we were strolling round the ground.

"You don't mind if I stroll with you?" she asked, and placed her hand through my arm.

"I'm still a little weak," she said, as if in explanation. And then, as a further gesture to respectability, she gave her other arm to the Sergeant, who responded with a huge boyish smile.

"Like coming home from church," he stated, "all quiet and respectable to a Sunday's dinner."

Anita laughed and squeezed my arm. I wondered if she

had also squeezed Beef's at the same time, but finding the thought a little unworthy of me I said:

"How soon do you expect to be back in the show again?"

"Only a few days now, I think," she replied. "There was nothing very serious after all, only a flesh wound. It's practically healed up already. It's mostly nerves that are the matter now. I feel frightened sometimes—especially at night —and for no reason at all."

"Frightened of who?" asked Beef.

"Of nobody. I can't explain it really. Although sometimes the way Hel . . ." She paused for a moment, and then concluded quickly: "The way Helen speaks I believe she is frightened as well."

I caught Beef's eye over the top of the girl's head and realized that he had found something suspicious in this statement. Anita had not noticed our exchange of glances. She was looking ahead with a preoccupied expression on her face.

"The trouble is," I said, "you brood too much on it."

"Oh no," she said quickly, "it's not that. I'm still a little upset, that's all." Then, hurrying on quickly, as if to prevent us returning to the subject: "You know Cora Frances is coming down to the circus tomorrow. She's coming to stay for a week or two."

"Not *the* Cora Frances?" I said in surprise. "You mean Cora Frances, the painter? The one who does those immense portraits and groups, where the people look as if they daren't move or they'll be shot?"

"That's right," Anita laughed. "She's just 'discovered' the circus and she's gone crazy about it. I told you we had all sorts of writers and artists staying with us sometimes. Now you'll be able to meet the great Cora Frances."

"It makes me feel a little nervous," I admitted. "What's she like anyway?"

"Oh, she's rather sweet really," said Anita. "You'll see when she comes." And we had to be satisfied with that.

One or two visitors, mostly children, were wandering inquisitively around the ground. The largest group were by the entrance to the Wild Animal Zoo, attempting to peer in past the canvas screen which had been drawn across the entrance. Beef and Anita and I walked slowly over towards the enclosure, and then slipping in under the canvas at the back, we surveyed the caged animals.

The only other occupants of the zoo were Ginger, who was fixing the ropes across the front of the cages, and Kurt and Ansell, who appeared to be having something of an argument.

"I said, it's a fine time to tell anyone," we heard Kurt shout at the animal-feeder.

Ansell shrugged his shoulders and turned away towards the cages.

"Well, go on. Get it done now," insisted Kurt. "We can't have the people coming in here with the tiger's cage in a mess like that. Get some of the chavvies outside to bring the tunnel in."

Still in silence, Ansell disappeared outside, and Kurt came over to us.

"Lazy good-for-nothing jail-bird," he mumbled. "Can't even be relied on to do the simplest of jobs. You have to keep your boot near his backside all the time."

Ansell reappeared as he was saying this, pulling the lion-tunnel by the shafts and assisted by half a dozen or so children, who were pushing with a will. He dragged the tunnel over towards the tiger's cage, maneuvring it until it was in a direct line with the door. He worked slowly, and apparently oblivious of the fact that we were watching. Kurt made no move to help, but stood beside us with his hands in his pockets. Ansell placed blocks under the wheels of the tunnel, to prevent it rolling back away from the cage. Then he opened the door of the tiger's cage, while Ginger, crouching on top of the tunnel, held the trap, ready to drop it into position directly the tiger was in the tunnel. The tiger refused to move.

Kurt picked up a stick and walking quickly forward, rattled it across the bars of the cage as a boy does a hoop-stick on the railings. The tiger snarled, and then slowly slunk through the door into the tunnel. Ginger quickly let the trap fall into place.

"One of these days," he commented cheerfully, as he leaped to the ground, "I shall catch his tail with that trap. Then he'll just about blow that tunnel to pieces. It rocks every time anybody leans on it now."

Ansell had climbed into the back of the tiger's cage and was sweeping out the old bedding and manure. After watching him for a moment, Anita drew our attention to the other cages.

"Why do you have all those lions?" asked Beef, when we were opposite the three-partitioned lions' cage.

"Those two," said Anita pointing, "are only half-grown. George is still training them. He wants to use them for a mixed turn later, if we can get hold of some wolves and bears. Then these three are the three you see in the ring every day. A lion and two lionesses. And this other chap," Anita moved alone to the last cage. "Well, I don't quite know what he's doing here at all. We picked him up cheap some time ago, and George started training him, but then the cubs came and so George started working on them and rather neglected this fellow. What are you going to do with him, George?" she called out to Kurt, who was at the far side of the enclosure.

"I don't know," answered the lion-tamer. "Hadn't really thought much about it, to tell you the truth. I might give it to the Sergeant as a Christmas present."

Beef chuckled. "Wouldn't half give the missus a shock if

[128]

I walked home with that on a lead," he said. "Why she created bad enough when I brought a little dog home once, when we was first married. Wouldn't have no beasts about the house, she said. Bad enough having me, I suppose." And Beef gave vent to one of his hurricane-like laughs.

As if in reaction from the sudden noise, Anita gripped hard on my arm.

"Look," she said, almost inaudibly. As she spoke there was a sudden crash as the tiger's cage-door was slammed, and I looked up in time to see the scared white face of Ansell behind the bars. At the same moment the lion-tunnel gave a slight lurch and rolled a yard or more into the center of the enclosure. There was a sudden yell from Ginger, and the striped form of the tiger slipped down between the cage and the tunnel and crouched on the ground beneath the axle.

Then I had a sudden mixed and confused impression of many things happening at once. Anita's hold tightened on my arm and I drew her behind me with some vague and heroic idea of protecting her; Kurt shouted, and Beef said the one word, "Cor."

The tiger crept forward until it lay just under the tail-board of the tunnel, looking out at us. Its tail was waving slowly from side to side, and twitching jerkily at the tip, like a bad-tempered household cat.

"Keep still, everybody," said Kurt calmly. "Keep perfectly still." And then, looking up at the animal-feeder in the cage, he said quickly: "Come out of that cage, Ansell. And leave the door open.

Peter Ansell showed his teeth in a frightened grin. "Not on your sweet life," he said. "I'm safe behind these bars, and here I'm going to stay."

"Come out of it, you blasted fool," roared Kurt in sudden anger. "Get out the back way and be quick about it."

These words seemed to have their effect upon the man, for

he slowly opened the front door of the cage, and then retreated quickly backwards and disappeared through the door at the rear. Kurt waited a moment, and then took two paces towards the crouching tiger.

"Up," he said harshly, and pointed with his outstretched arm to the open door of the cage. The tiger snarled, turning its head sideways in a worried, irritated way. For a moment the two stood there, almost statuesque. There seemed to be no sound or movement anywhere, and I had become completely oblivious of everything but that grim set-piece in front of me. Kurt, coatless and without any means of defense should the animal spring, and the tiger hesitating, a low growling snarl coming from between its open jaws.

Then it turned its eyes away from the man standing over it and carefully, almost contemptuously, began to lick one of its fore-paws. Kurt stood silent and motionless. And then, at last, the tiger moved. Almost casually, it rose from under the tunnel, hesitated, looking once more at the lion-trainer, and then leaped lightly through the open door of the cage.

As Kurt closed the door on it I became suddenly aware once more of my surroundings. In relaxing my grip around Anita, I realized how tightly I must have been grasping her shoulders. She was trembling violently, and her lips were grayish-green.

Beef blew out his mustache noisily. "Cor," he said for the second time, "that gave me a bit of a turn." He looked across at Kurt, and then at me. "I don't know about you two," he continued, "but I could do with a drop of something after that."

"So could I," said a hoarse voice behind him, and Ginger crawled guiltily from under the monkey cage.

"I'll follow you down," I said, "after I've taken Anita back to her wagon."

"See you down there, then," said Beef. And without another word the three men walked shakily out of the enclosure.

Anita, however, seemed the least shaken of us all. She seemed too impressed with Kurt's handling of the animal to feel any reactions of fear.

"You know," she said, "that tiger has never been trained. I've never seen anything like it in my life."

"It was a very unpleasant situation, though," I said, and then remembering that she had grasped me for protection, I went on: "Except, of course, that . . ."

"Except that nobody was hurt," said Anita quickly. I thought there was a very definite twinkle in her eye as she ran quickly up the steps of her wagon and left me.

As Beef had promised, I discovered the three men in the public bar of the nearest local. Peter Ansell had joined them— or had reached there before them, I'm not sure which—and the conversation had turned to animal escapes of previous years.

"You have to get them back into the cage as quickly as possible," Kurt was saying. "Or some blithering fool comes along with a shot-gun. Then all you've got left is a tiger-skin hearth-rug. I had that happen to me once. Tame as a kitten, it was—a lion I had ever since it was a cub. But somehow it got loose from the cage, and up comes this yokel with his blunderbuss, and before I had time to do anything he'd pulled the trigger and run for his life."

"But wasn't there any danger at all, really?" I asked incredulously.

"Well, in this case, yes," said Kurt. "You see, that tiger had never been trained. So in a manner of speaking, it was a bit of luck that he went back into the cage without any trouble. Yes, in this case, I should say we were lucky to get away with all our legs and arms in one piece."

Ginger shuddered expressively and emptied his glass. "Nice sort of birthday present," he commented.

"Why birthday present?" I queried. "Is it your birthday?"

"That's right," grinned Ginger. "Twenty-three today. You know I should have forgotten it if the Old Woman hadn't sent me a present. Here, you have a look at it." And after fumbling in his inner pocket, he produced a new fountain-pen for our inspection.

" 'Course," he went on, "I only write two letters in a year; one just after we start the season to say we've gone, and another just before the end to say I'm coming home. Still, it's nice to have a birthday, isn't it?"

Peter Ansell, who seemed to have been celebrating his escape from the tiger with a little too much energy, now rose shakily to his feet. "Ginger," he said, raising his glass, "Ginger, I drink to you. It is imperative that a man should not lose his life on his birthday. They say Shakespeare did, but I don't believe a word of it. Not a word. Once a year a man should be handed his life—on a plate, as it were. And that, my good friend Ginger, is what has happened to you. May you go another twenty-three years before your life is again in danger. I drink to you."

" 'Ere," said Ginger, with concern, "I think you've had a drop too much. Come on. I'll help you to get back to the tober."

"Good of you, my friend," muttered Ansell.

"I'd better help too," said Kurt, and with a knowing wink at Beef and me he grabbed Ansell's other arm, and together the three men wandered erratically out of the pub.

"And now," I said, turning to Beef as soon as they had gone, "what do you think of it?"

Beef looked at me owlishly, and I thought for a moment that he, too, had over-celebrated.

"Think about what?" he asked.

"This tiger escaping, of course," I said irritably. "Do you think it was an accident?"

"I wouldn't like to say, exactly," said Beef, with his usual maddening vagueness. "Why, what's your opinion?"

Before I had gone to meet Beef in the pub I had taken the trouble to inspect the lion-tunnel and make a few measurements, although, of course, unobserved by any of the circus people. I now presented Beef with my theory. There were, I explained, two people who might have been directly responsible for the escape; Ansell and Ginger. To take the most obvious first: Ginger was responsible for dropping the trap shut on the tunnel and might, either by accident or design, have dropped the trap in crookedly so that a slight push from the tiger would have enabled it to get loose. Peter Ansell, on the other hand, was within reach of the front of the trap, and could have opened it unobserved, quickly slamming himself in the cage directly the tiger had sprung out of the tunnel.

But, as I pointed out to Beef, there was also the possibility that the tunnel had been tampered with before the affair. In actual fact, the side runner of the trap-door had been detached, but it was impossible to tell now whether that had been done by the tiger or some time before. This possibility cast suspicion first of all on Kurt himself, who had easy access to the tunnel, but also on any other member of the circus, since anybody could have prized the runner loose without being observed.

"In other words," said Beef, with a chuckle, "you make out that we're no farther forward than we were before?"

"Exactly," I agreed. "But if we decide that this was an actual attempt at murder, then at least we have a restricted number of people at whom the murder might be aimed. I mean that, assuming this is the murder you have come up here to solve, you now have a much narrower circle of people who might be killed. That is, Ansell, Ginger, Kurt, Anita, and, of course, yourself."

"And since," said Beef thoughtfully, "there's already been an attempt to kill Anita . . ."

"Good heavens, yes," I exclaimed, "I hadn't realized that."

Beef finished his beer and stood up to go. "That's all very nice," he said, "but you still haven't proved that the whole thing was intentional, and not an accident."

CHAPTER XVI

April 29th.

IN THE afternoon Cora Frances arrived. I feel bound to give some space to this amazing woman, not only because she is nationally famous as a painter, but because of the effect she had on the whole cast of the circus from Jackson down to and including Beef himself. I had often seen her canvases in many of the London galleries, and was also familiar with her more widely known posters which were used to popularize a certain brand of tinned food, but if I had been unimpressed by her art I was bewildered by her person.

Her arrival seemed to be something of an Occasion. By the first morning post came a letter which was proudly handed round the tober, and which announced that she would be with the circus some time that day. At ten o'clock the first telegram was brought.

LEFT LONDON EIGHT FIFTEEN [it stated] HOPE TO ARRIVE FOR AFTERNOON SHOW STOP AM BRINGING BOODLE STOP LOVE TO ALL CORA.

"Boodle," explained Anita, with whom I was talking when this missive arrived, "is her dog."

At half-past ten the second telegram arrived, stating:

POSSIBILITY ARRIVE LATER THAN EXPECTED STOP BOODLE SICK ON A POLICEMAN CORA.

At eleven we learned:

MAKING GOOD TIME STOP BOODLE VERY TRYING CORA.

And at half-past eleven, more briefly:

BOODLE BETTER CORA.

After this there was a slight lull until about two o'clock, when the telegrams began to come in earnest. Not certain that I saw them in chronological order I only realized that Boodle had been sick some three or four more times and that the lady was undoubtedly drawing closer to us. By three-fifteen I noticed they were using two messengers in order to keep up with the flow, as a new message came in before the original boy had returned to the office.

And at a quarter to four Cora Frances arrived.

A magnificent pale blue saloon car drew up to the gates of the tober and gave a prolonged toot on a triple-note horn. Then a woman's head came out of the window, and a hand which waved violently two or three times. Both withdrew for an instant and then reappeared holding a bluish-gray bundle which was held up triumphantly and which raised a cheer from the artists.

"That's Boodle," was Anita's whispered comment.

Enough time had now elapsed for the whole of the circus personnel to gather at the front of the tent, and the car drove slowly through the open gates and then, like the *Queen Mary* docking at Southampton, drew round broadside to the waiting group.

A sandaled foot, with red enameled toe-nails, descended from the car, followed by its companion, and two very white legs. My eyes traveled upwards to meet first a short home-spun skirt of indeterminate greenish color, a wide peasant belt, a leather lumber-jacket, a white silk shirt and brilliant crimson tie. Her head, hatless, was cropped closely like a man's except that one long strand at the front was allowed to fall across her face and was frequently pushed back into place by her long spiky fingers.

She greeted the members of the group with effusive familiar-ity, incrusting her phrases with Romany words or circus slang.

"Ah, Anita," she said, as soon as she had worked her way around to us. "My dear, how are you?"

"This," said Anita, "is Mr. Townsend. A novelist."

"How nice," said Cora Frances coldly, and gave me a limp hand which I relinquished as soon as possible.

"My friend Sergeant Beef," I said, "who dabbles in private detection."

"But how thrilling," gushed the lady. "Perhaps you know my friend, Amer Picon. *Un tel homme. Il est vraiment magnifique.*"

"Well, yes. I have had that pleasure," mumbled Beef awkwardly. "He had a sort of an interest in one of my cases, as you might say. Hasn't he gone abroad lately?"

"I shouldn't be surprised," said Cora Frances. "How that man does get about. He never seems to grow a day older."

Before there was any chance of pursuing the subject she had turned and grasped Corinne's arm. "And *now,* my dear," she said eagerly, "you must tell me *everything* that's happened since I last saw you." And the two walked towards Jackson's wagon talking animatedly.

I had tried to observe what effect this woman had on the majority of the circus artists, whether they liked her or just pretended to. But strangely enough, the only people un-affected by her arrival seemed to be Anita, Beef and myself; and even then I was not sure of Beef, who was gazing after the painter with a bewildered expression. I waited impatiently for his first pronouncement on her.

"You know," he said at last, "I had a sister that went to an art school once. But she came home at the end of the first week because she didn't like drawing people what hadn't any clothes on. Indecent, she said it was."

"Cora was jealous of you," said Anita astutely.

"Jealous," I echoed. "But why?"

"She hardly ever takes any notice of me. But this time,

[137]

when she saw you were talking to me, she made quite a fuss. Didn't you notice? And then when I said you were a novelist she just froze up."

"Perhaps she's got a grudge against novelists," I suggested.

"No, it's not that. She hates anybody else being here when she's on a visit. Competition's always bad for patronage."

But this was by no means the end of Cora Frances. During the days that followed her presence was continually to be felt in the circus. Her voice, harsh and emphatic like a circular saw, was nearly always to be heard about the tober, and there was no escaping it. She appeared to do very little painting, and when occasionally she did decide to get some work done, it took the major part of the day for her to get her easel set up and a suitable position found. Then, before an admiring group, she would begin to execute a new masterpiece of circus life. But it was her voice which chiefly bothered me.

That very afternoon, before the afternoon show, it drew Beef and me out of our wagon to find that she was half-way across the tober seated on the steps of the Dariennes' wagon.

"She doesn't seem to mind who hears what she says," commented Beef, as her voice suddenly rose in its high-pitched but controlled laugh.

"Why, Christophe," she was saying. "You didn't tell me you had a new costume. Let me see. Oh, *c'est formidable.*"

There followed a low mumble of words from inside the wagon, and then she replied:

"No, no. I promise I won't look. Let me stay here. See, I've covered my eyes." And with an exaggerated gesture she pressed her hand over her eyes and sat crouched on the steps like one of the Three Wise Monkeys.

"Look at the window of Suzanne's wagon," said Beef quietly. The curtain was pulled to one side as though some-one were looking out. Then it fell back into place, and after a brief pause the door opened and Suzanne came slowly down the steps.

"Chris," she called, as she walked over the grass towards the Dariennes' wagon, "Chris, did I leave my hair-brush in your wagon?"

Cora Frances looked disconcerted, and quickly drew her hands away from her face. She bridled slightly as she saw Suzanne approaching and gave a nervous smile.

"But my dear," she said loudly, "how very compromising."

"Only if people like to think that way," said Suzanne shortly. "The boys always borrow my hair-brush to clean their jackets with."

Christophe thrust his head through the door. "Catch," he shouted cheerfully, and tossed the brush over Cora Frances's head. Suzanne caught it neatly, and turned back to her own wagon.

"Don't need no clues for a case like that," Beef muttered to me. "Nor none of that pie—psy-chology neither."

"Why, what do you mean?" I asked accommodatingly.

Beef sucked his teeth in disgust. "You don't half ask some silly questions sometimes," he said. "She didn't want that brush. Her hair was done perfect, and she had one of them bandeau things on. Just wanted to put her spoke in, she did."

"You mean she was jealous?" I asked.

"The trouble with you," said Beef bitterly, "is you haven't got any subtlety. That's what's the matter with your books. You ought to let the readers work it out for themselves sometimes. Like a cross-word puzzle."

"Subtlety," I choked. *"I have no subtlety?"*

"That's right," Beef calmly assured me. "You go at things like a bull at a gate. How can I be a Man of Mystery and a Great Detective when you go about asking me downright silly questions the way you do? All I can say is, after all the detective stories you read you ought to know better."

I had no reply ready for a frontal attack of this kind, but fortunately at this point our conversation was interrupted by the reappearance of Cora Frances.

"Oh, Mr.—er—I didn't quite catch your name," she said brightly, approaching me. "Do tell me about the novels you write. What sort of novels are they exactly? There are so many different sorts nowadays, aren't there?"

"Detective novels," I answered briefly.

"But so many people are doing that," she said. "Why, a young friend of mine does two or three a year—and all in her spare time. But still, it's a way of earning a living, I suppose, like anything else."

"I had rather wondered myself," I said in what was, I hoped, a sarcastic voice, "why such an original artist as yourself should come to a circus for subject-matter. But I suppose it is only a fashion."

She was unmoved. "You know," she said, pouting slightly and pressing the tip of her finger into the side of her cheek, "I *did* rather wonder once whether Dame Laura Knight had not done all there was to be done with the circus. But then I said to myself: 'No. The artist must be a free agent. Must be able to paint anything and everything he or she fancies.' And then I discovered this divine circus—and what else could I do but paint it? I mean, the color, the movement, the splendid fitness of everybody, so tremendously alive, so vital. Just crying for a painter's brush. But, of course, Sergeant, you don't see it that way, do you? You see everything from its darkest side. You only see people who might commit a crime. We ordinary ones are uninteresting to you."

"I don't know about 'ordinary'," said Beef. "As a matter of fact, this circus interests me very much. I'm up here on a sort of a case, you see. Not the usual case you read about, but one that hasn't exactly come off yet, if you see what I mean?"

"Oh, perfectly," said Cora Frances. "As a matter of a fact,

I've been told *all* about you. I think it's a divine idea. You must let me help you over it. And all on account of something that old Gypsy Margot said, wasn't it? It's terribly original. I don't think any of the other detectives take very much notice of what gypsies say. But as I always say, unless you get out of the rut, you're doomed. What does it matter if you find there's no case—at least, you'll have got out of the rut."

"Don't you think there's going to be a murder, then?" asked Beef.

Cora Frances laughed. It was a very cultivated laugh, based, I thought, on the novelist's statement that a woman could laugh like a tinkling of bells. He may have been right about some women, but Cora Frances was not one of them. "Oh, but my dear," she said. "Of *course* there's going to be a murder. Some time or other it's bound to happen. With all these animals around, and the way they drink milk out of tins . . ."

"Who drinks milk out of tins?" asked Beef.

"Why, everybody in the circus does."

"And what's that got to do with a murder?"

"Well," said Cora Frances, "I think I read somewhere that if you kept stuff in a tin after you'd opened it, you'd get ptomaine poisoning. What could be better for a murder?"

"Hadn't thought of that," said Beef. Fortunately the artist did not notice the wink the Sergeant gave me, but swept on.

"Why, the most likely person to be murdered is myself. I know two or three who would like to get me out of the way."

"You?" asked Beef incredulously. "Why should anyone want to do you in?"

"Jealousy," said Cora Frances in a slightly softer voice. "Jealousy. Simply mad with jealousy some of them are. Now there's Suzanne," she ticked them off on her fingers, "who's frightened I'll take the Dariennes away from her. And there's

Anita, who likes to think herself the most popular person in the show and would like to get me out of the way. Then there's Mrs. Jackson, who thinks I might steal her husband from her. She hates me like poison."

"How about Gypsy Margot?" asked Beef. "Isn't she jealous in case you take her fortune-telling business away from her?"

Cora Frances laughed again. "You know," she said, "I have theories about Margot. She's an astonishing old dear. I think she's probably the best-read woman I've ever met."

"Never heard her talk about books," commented Beef.

"Oh, but neither have I," said Cora blandly. "It's just an idea I have."

"Any other idea about who might be murdered?" asked Beef.

"Well, there's yourself, Sergeant," said Cora. "We mustn't forget you. In all good murder cases the criminals always have a shot at the detective when they find he's a little too hot on the scent."

"Here," said Beef, "we don't want nothing on those lines. I'm a peaceful sort of chap, I am. Don't want no shootings and that going on."

"We shall see, anyway," said Cora in her "tinkling" voice. "Well. I must go off and get dressed for the evening show now."

"Why? Are you going in the ring?" asked Beef.

"Oh, no," said Cora. "I meant *dressed,* not dressed. See you in the tent." And waving a hand at us she walked away.

CHAPTER XVII

April 29th (continued).

It was odd that Beef and I had never seen a complete performance of the circus. We had seen bits of it, a turn here and there, but never the whole show. Something had always happened to interrupt us. Sooner or later, for some reason or another, we always had to leave the tent before the show was ended.

That night, when we took our places in the tent, we intended to see the whole show, and it was therefore with some misgivings that I realized that we were seated next to the young man whom we had seen talking to Corinne Jackson a village or so back; a young man called Herbert Torrant.

During the first of the turns he leaned forward in his seat watching the ring with close attention, and for some time did not notice us. Then he turned round and stared at Beef.

"Aren't you Sergeant Beef?" he asked suddenly.

Beef grinned with obvious pleasure, as he always did when he was recognized. "How did you know that?" he asked. "I didn't know you'd seen me here before."

"No, not here," answered Torrant. "I used to know you in Wraxham—I was there for a short time when you were solving that second big mystery of yours. I was in the Ordnance Survey. Get about a bit, you know. But it's funny meeting you here."

"Ordnance Survey?" said Beef. "I don't seem to remember that. Was it the one just past the station? The one where the landlord never quite filled the glasses? I never went there but the once."

Torrant laughed. "No, Ordnance Survey," he said. "You know, we make maps and things."

Beef must have thought a change of subject the best way out of this situation, for he asked, after a slight pause: "And what, might I ask, would you be doing following this show around?"

"Well . . ." said the young man, turning slightly pink, and stuttering, went on to say that he was "interested in the show business."

"Oh, I see." Beef nodded wisely. " 'Course, this is no holiday for me," he went on. "I'm working."

"On a case?" asked Torrant, lowering his voice and looking round suspiciously.

"Murder," said Beef, with a brief decisive nod.

Torrant appeared to jump slightly in his seat at this simple word, and he stared at the Sergeant incredulously with slightly open mouth.

"Hasn't happened yet," went on Beef, "but it will do, all right. I got my eye on quite a number of people."

Torrant's hands began to stray unaccountably up the buttons of his waistcoat towards his tie, until he noticed them and stuffed them quickly in his coat pockets.

Frankly, I found this attitude surprising. I had always imagined that a generation brought up on "thrillers" and "shockers" would find little to make them nervous in a murder in real life. Perhaps the fact that the crime had not actually been committed made this difference. Solving a murder when it had been done was rather like a cross-word puzzle, but when, as in this case, the possibility of a crime lay in the future, then perhaps it was not quite so commonplace. At any rate, Torrant's nerviness seemed to hint this.

At this point Paul Darienne, still in his ring clothes after his act, came through the opening of the tent and sat down next to me. Beef and Torrant continued their conversation in low voices.

"Have you seen Christophe?" asked Paul.

"Oh, he's always in a hurry," said Beef. "Come on. Let's ask him."

Jackson did not seem too pleased to see us, but he stopped when Beef called out to him.

"Well, Sergeant," he said briskly, "what's worrying you now? I haven't been seeing very much of you since you first arrived. I'd like to know how your little investigation has been going on. Have you found anything suspicious?"

"It's easy to find suspicious things," said Beef quietly, "because people nearly always have something to hide." It seemed to me that Jackson looked up suddenly as Beef said this, but I could not be sure of it.

"Yes, I suppose they have," he said in a casual voice. "But then, of course, that's not what you're looking for, Sergeant, is it? I mean, dirty washing and family skeletons and all that are of little interest in this particular case?"

"Well, you can get too much of them," said Beef, "but a little scandal, as you might say, is sometimes a great help to an investigator."

"Is that what you've come to me for?" asked Jackson sharply. "Because if so, I'm afraid you're going to be disappointed."

"Oh no," said Beef. "Nothing like that. I was only speaking generally. I just wanted a little bit of information about the circus, and I thought you would be the right person to come to, that's all."

"Perhaps it would be better if you came into the wagon," said Jackson, and led us up the steps. After offering us cigarettes he lit one himself, and then, carefully seating himself in an arm-chair, he looked expectantly at Beef.

"All right. Fire away, Sergeant," he said.

"How long has the circus been going?" asked Beef.

"Well, actually my father started Jacobi's Circus in nineteen-nine, but we reckon that the circus is twenty-five years old this season."

"How's that?" asked Beef after a pause, during which he had been doing rather obvious mental arithmetic.

"We had to stop for four years during the war. Transport was very difficult, and often it was next to impossible to get food for the animals. And, of course, many of the men went to fight. Almost all the traveling circuses shut down during that time, you know."

"So that makes you twenty-five this year. Jubilee year, eh?" said Beef with a grin.

"Yes," answered Jackson. "We have a special show every year on the birthday of the circus, but this one is the twenty-fifth, and a special Jubilee performance. I hope you'll be here to see it."

"Oh yes, of course," said Beef, remembering. "Anita told us something about that. It should be good, eh?"

"It should be the best show we've given," said Jackson.

"Have all the artists been with you since the war?" I asked, in order to give Beef time to think out his next question.

"Apart from one or two, yes," replied Jackson. "Of course, some of them were only children, and didn't start showing until later—like my daughter and Eric, and the Concinis. The only ones who have joined the show since are, let me see, the two Darienne brothers, Clem Gail, and Peter Ansell. I think that's all."

"What about Suzanne?" Beef asked.

"Suzanne joined just after we'd started—in the second season to be precise. We wanted a trapeze act, and Len Waterman said he thought he knew someone he could get, and recommended Suzanne."

"I see," said Beef. "So he must have known Suzanne before she came here?"

"Unless he saw her picture in the papers," said Jackson sarcastically.

"Anything between them?" continued Beef, unperturbed.

CHAPTER XIX

April 29th (continued).

"Do you remember which day they said the Jubilee performance was to be?" I asked Beef when we had returned to our
wagon.

"Saturday, wasn't it," said Beef. "Saturday, May the third?"

I made a quick calculation. "That's strange," I commented.
"Do you realize that May the third is the time limit?"

"Time limit? I don't know what you're talking about.
Why can't you say something sensible instead of making it
into a mystery?"

"Gypsy Margot," I pointed out, "gave a certain time limit
within which, she said, the murder would be committed. And
the last day of that prediction happens to be the day of the
Jubilee performance. What do you think of that?"

"Might be an accident," said Beef, "or she might have
thought it was a good date to pick on, or, on the other hand,
she might have known something we don't. How should I
know?"

"I don't know *how*," I said coldly, "but I think you ought
to."

"Oh, I don't think there's much in that," said Beef carelessly, and began to prepare himself for bed.

"And another thing," I persisted. "That button. What was
the point of that? Just when it looked like turning into something interesting you let Jackson snatch it away from you."

"Well, it was his, wasn't it?" demanded Beef. "And, anyway, I took a copy of what was written on it. Doesn't seem
to make sense to me, but see what you can make of it."

He handed me his notebook opened at a page on which
were printed the letters A.P.T.N.C..T.

"What do you suppose they stand for?" I asked. "They might mean almost anything."

"Can't make out what they mean at all," said Beef as I looked at them. "Perhaps it's a trade union or something. They're fond of having long strings of letters—like the A.U.B.T.W. or the N.U.W.M., and all the rest of them. Never could make out what they were all about."

"Well," I said, "the A probably stands for Association, the N for National, and the T for Trades."

"Like the Association of Pipe-Turners and National Carving Trades," suggested Beef.

"Good Lord, of course," I said.

"Only," said Beef, "there's probably no such union. I just made it up as I went along. And, anyway, Jackson's not a pipe-turner, is he?"

"Still," I said, "we can find out about that later. The point now is to discover something about the relationship between Suzanne and Len Waterman. Jackson told us that she joined the circus before the Darienne brothers, and that she was here nearly ten years before they came. Time enough for her to give that photograph to Len Waterman—and mean what she wrote on it, too."

"That's something we've got to find out about," stated Beef. "Trouble is these circus people are like oysters. They never tell you anything about themselves unless it's by accident."

"What about Gypsy Margot?" I asked. "She doesn't seem to be in love with the circus. Perhaps she might tell us something."

"That's the one," said Beef. "And we'll see her tomorrow morning. I'm going to turn in now."

The show was just coming to an end in the big tent, and the lights and people made me feel that bed was the last place I wanted to go to just then.

"I think I'll take a turn outside first," I said. "You get some sleep, if you like. I'll try not to wake you as I come back."

Beef had already drawn his shirt over his shoulders, and as I left the wagon his voice came indistinctly through the linen shrouding his head.

"Gmyloveta," he seemed to say.

"What did you say?" I queried, with my foot already on the top step.

Beef's face, red with exertion and wreathed with a wide grin, emerged from the shirt. "I said: 'Give my love to Anita'," he said.

As I wandered around the ground I thought how little of the country one really saw from a traveling circus. Perhaps it was our own fault. The circus people themselves seemed to know every corner of England, however remote, and could remember places even ten and twelve years after. But I had traveled with the circus through some half a dozen villages, and I found it impossible to even name them in the order in which we had passed through them. Today, I knew, we were at Beverley. But that was only because the Minster stood right next to the tober as a constant reminder. The moon lit its intricately carved exterior, and the tower with its overhanging gargoyles seemed to lean right across the big top. It was a fine night for a walk, with everything brightly lit and quiet. As if echoing my thoughts, a voice said at my ear:

"A lovely night for a walk," and I turned to find Anita smiling not more than a yard away from me.

"Beef's gone to bed," I said. "He's not affected by the moon."

Anita gave a cry of dismay. "Our watchdog gone to sleep?" she said. "Why, we might all be murdered in our beds."

"Honestly, though," I said quickly, taking advantage of the subject. "I feel very nervous about you."

"Me? Why me?"

I went on to tell her of the discussion which Beef and I had

had about the possible murder, and the discovery that she had been present in both attempts so far. Anita seemed, however, unaffected by this.

"I think that is just chance," she said. "Why should anyone want to kill me?"

"That's what we're trying to find out," I said grimly. "But the fact remains that you're in possible danger. Personally I think you're perfectly safe as long as you don't appear in the ring. But as soon as you begin performing, I think—provided it is you who are in danger—that another attempt will be made."

Anita laughed. "Then you'll have to come and watch very carefully," she said. "So that if I am killed you will know who did it."

"Actually," I said, with difficulty, "I'm much more concerned about keeping you out of this than I am with the Sergeant's new case. I mean . . ." but the words would not come in consecutive order and I broke off.

Anita's eyes had a peculiar twinkle in them as she looked up at me. "I think," she said gently, "that we'd better start walking back now. It's time I was in bed, anyway."

I felt extremely foolish as we walked back to the tober, but Anita kept up a string of light remarks which served to cover my embarrassment. In my ears I seemed to hear Beef's caustic comments on my "romantic nature" and squirmed inwardly at the thought of them.

"Good night," said Anita quietly as we reached her wagon. She spoke almost as if she were saying good-by to an invalid in a hospital, and pressing my hand quickly she ran up the steps and disappeared into the wagon.

I felt that I could not bear to return to the wagon under the sceptical eyes of the Sergeant, so I walked over to the clowns' wagon, which was, I knew, often used as a sort of meeting-place for the artists after the show. It was almost full of human beings, and with the minimum of fuss I was greeted, given a mug of beer, and settled in a corner. Next to me was Pete Daroga, who merely grunted a greeting at me and then seemed to retire into his thoughts.

The conversation which was being tossed backwards and forwards across my head was mostly concerned with the show, and I soon lost interest and began to study Pete, who had taken a letter from his pocket and was studying it with concentration.

Noticing my interest, he held the letter out to me with a grin. "It's an invitation to join a European circus," he said, with obvious enthusiasm. "It's a big show that is touring the Soviet Union just now. I wrote to the manager at Leningrad, and he's replied that they would be glad to have me next season."

The letter was typed in a language that I could not understand. In fact, the alphabet itself was beyond me, although many of the letters were similar to our own.

"That's Russian," said Daroga. "Listen, I'll translate it for you."

He held the sheet between us and read out in English while his finger followed the Russian words.

"Comrade artist Daroga," he translated, "the management committee have great pleasure . . ."

But I did not hear the rest of the letter. The second word on the typescript sheet—the word which Pete had translated as "artist," was written APTNCT, except that the center stroke of the N was written in the reverse direction to the usual English letter.

As soon as I could I congratulated Peter Daroga and got away from the wagon. This was obviously the solution of the problem of the mysterious lettering on the button. I ran quickly to the wagon and shook Beef into consciousness.

The Sergeant was not, at first, very enthusiastic.

"You remember that button?" I said. "Well, I think I've

found something out about it. Quick, where did you put your notebook? I want to see the letters you copied down."

"What are you shouting about?" demanded Beef. "You gone crackers, or something?"

After a time I managed to impress upon him that I had important news, and he staggered out of bed and threw his overcoat round his shoulders.

"Well," he said doubtingly, "here it is. What's the idea you've got?"

"Look," I said, pointing, "the N on this is backwards."

"Very interesting, I'm sure," said Beef sarcastically. "I'm very pleased you woke me up to tell me. Now I suppose I can go back to bed."

"Don't be a fool, Beef," I said sharply. "Listen to what I've got to say. These letters aren't English letters, they're part of the Russian alphabet. They happen to be the same as ours, but they're pronounced differently. You see, APTNCT is pronounced Arteest—Artist, see?"

"Trust those Bolshevists to do something silly like that," grumbled Beef. "But where does that get us?"

"The point is," I pointed out, "why was Jackson so excited about it? Why should he not want people to know he had a Russian button in his possession?"

"Something to do with Daroga," suggested the Sergeant. "He's a Russian, isn't he?"

"But how does Jackson come into it?" I said.

"Here," said Beef suddenly, "I don't like the look of this at all. I don't want to be mixed up in no politics. Might be a Trotskyist or something. Perhaps they're going to liquidate Jackson."

"Don't be absurd, Beef," I said. "This may lead to something."

"It may do," said Beef. "But not till tomorrow it won't. I'm going back to bed."

Obviously there was nothing to be got out of Beef until the next morning, so I, too, proceeded to undress and climb into my bunk. But somehow I could not sleep. The clock in the tower of Beverley Minster, just near the tober, sonorously marked off the half-hours one after the other, and I found myself waiting impatiently for it to strike again. At last I got out of bed, and throwing on an overcoat I walked out on to the tober.

It had turned cold and the grass was like wet silver where the dew was on it. The air tingled in the back of my throat as if I had been eating peppermints. Not many hours ago I had stood on this spot struck by the contrast made by the white face of the Minster, and the white circus tent beneath it. The building had seemed flattened in the sunshine, leaning backwards like a cardboard cut-out as the clouds moved slowly away behind it. Men's hands had placed stone on stone of a building which would stand for centuries, and not fifty yards away men's hands had driven the iron pegs and pulled on the ropes of something which they themselves would undo just as carefully in a few hours' time. In the afternoon sunshine the tent had shone as whitely as the Minster.

Now, as the bells chimed away the time with something of triumph in their tone, the Minster was alone in the moonlight, and where the circus tent had been was a dark open patch across which one or two of the horses moved, grazing as they went.

There was nothing of sacrilege in bringing them together, these two. If anything, the contrast gave each back some of its old meaning. It would be difficult to prove the debt which the clowning in the sawdust ring owed to the old miracle plays which had been performed probably in the shadow of this very Minster. Religion and drama, though they went their separate ways, could neither of them be cut out of people's lives, and

[167]

the pitching of the tent under the very eaves of the Minster seemed to me something of acknowledgment.

I shivered suddenly. The camp was completely asleep and the only sounds were the faint munchings from the grazing animals. The wagons looked small and remote in the clear white light of the moon. And I wondered in how many of those wagons the tenants were asleep.

CHAPTER XX

April 30th.

As soon as the new tober had been reached next morning, and the tents set up, Beef and I strolled round to attempt to see Gypsy Margot. We found her sitting in her little tent laying out the peculiar paraphernalia of her trade, mumbling indistinctly to herself all the time.

"Good morning," said Beef pleasantly. "I wonder if we could have another little talk with you. That is, of course, if you're not too busy."

The old woman looked up at us suspiciously without anwering.

"I said," began Beef in a considerably louder voice, "I wonder if we could . . ."

"All right, I'm not deaf," said old Margot sharply. "You don't need to shout at me."

Beef took a seat and leaned towards her. "You've been with the circus a long time," he said in what I had learned was his "humoring" voice.

"What if I have?" demanded the old woman truculently.

"Oh, I didn't mean anything," said Beef pacifically. "I was just making a statement, that's all."

"Well, if you didn't mean anything," said Margot, "why do you trouble to say it?"

Beef looked abashed, and it was some seconds before he was able to return to the attack.

"Now, there's nothing to be gained by you getting cross with us," he said, as if admonishing a small boy who was playing with a loaded gun. "We only came in a friendly way, like."

The old gypsy sank back into her chair and folded her arms.

Her bright eyes flicked quickly from Beef to myself as if assessing the forces which were against her.

"What do you want to know?" she demanded at last.

"You joined this circus just after the war—that's right, isn't it?" asked Beef.

The old woman snorted. "A good deal before that, young man," she said.

"Then perhaps you were with the original show before Jackson took it over? Perhaps you were with it in nineteen-hundred and nine, when Jackson's father started it?"

"It started in nineteen-nine," she stated. "But it wasn't Jackson's father. This circus belonged to my brother, and Jackson bought it off him when he was too ill to carry on by himself. You don't think Jackson would let me hang around the gates unless it was in the contract, do you?"

"Well, that's certainly news to us," I said.

"Who was Jackson's father?" asked Beef. "Was he in the show then, or something?"

"By the look of him," said the old woman sourly, "I shouldn't be surprised if he hadn't got a father. Anyway, I've never seen him."

Beef pulled out his notebook. "You don't mind if I make a few notes, do you?" he asked.

"Anything but take my finger-prints," said the old woman grimly.

It struck me as I listened to this interview that the old gypsy woman was showing far more intelligence and coherence than she had done in our previous interview. At that time I had thought she was mad, but now I began to wonder whether that might not have been simulated in order to avoid giving us information.

"What's this about Christophe and Suzanne using your tent in the evenings?" asked Beef suddenly, and the question seemed to take the old woman off her guard. She looked accusingly at me before she spoke, but I avoided her glance and looked as innocently as I could at the ground.

"I suppose that stupid young man told you," she said, and I felt that she was glaring at me. "But there is so much of which you know nothing that the stars would still count you ignorant."

"Never mind about the stars," said Beef. "How long has it been going on?"

"Perhaps a year, perhaps a day," said the old woman. "When love has entered a man's heart he takes little count of ticking wheels and the numbers on the sheets of a calendar. His clock is then the green of the hedges and the soft feathered heads of the dandelion."

"Did anybody else but you know about it?" asked Beef.

"The measurement of a man's foolishness," said Margot, looking venomously at me, "is often the number of times he opens his mouth to no useful purpose."

"So he didn't tell anybody?" said Beef. "Not even Paul? Didn't he tell his own brother?"

"There were days," said the old gypsy vaguely, "long gone now, when Christophe was as a mother to his brother. In those days when the bed of sickness was tighter around them than the bindweed around the stem of a young ash sapling, Paul grew to learn his own weakness. He learned that there would never be a day when he could live without his brother's constant presence. And because he has understood that lesson well, he might do much to follow it."

"You mean, to keep Christophe away from Suzanne?" I asked, but Margot merely shrugged her shoulders and refused to answer.

"And what about this affair Suzanne had with Len Waterman?" demanded Beef.

It struck me that this question was unexpected. The old woman did not answer immediately, but drew her shawl tighter about her shoulders, plucking nervously at the tasseled fringe. "These things pass," she said at last in a low, almost inaudible voice. "You think no less of the summer's warmth because an east wind blew there in the winter. The mistakes of a schoolboy are no criticism of the man he will one day become. So it is with a woman, perhaps. It is best to remember only the warm wind and the sun, the small darting lizard disturbed by your foot, and the dry brittle rock under your hand, which seems to have known no other. In its day the ice was powerful enough no doubt, but it has no claim on the future. The cold dead hand of the past is nowhere so strong as when warm living minds recreate it."

I felt once again that there was something in this old woman which defied one to classify her as a charlatan. If she were trying to elude Beef's questionings, she was doing so in a way far cleverer than her ragged clothes and appearance would suggest. There was something like beauty in her speech, even if she meant it to bewilder us.

"I can't say as I can follow all of that," said Beef with honesty, "but at any rate I think I know what you're driving at."

"Some men," said the gypsy condescendingly, "hide the baseness of their metal under the red sheen of gold. But it cracks and shrivels in the strong sun and they are discovered. But you need not fear, for though the powerful beams pierce you through and other men pretend to detect a flaw in order to divert attention from their shortcomings, yet finally they will shrink when they find you are so much more than you pretend to be, while they themselves are only so much less."

"Well, that's very nice of you, I must say," said Beef and I thought he looked slightly embarrassed by this speech.

"I think there's little more we can learn," I interrupted them coldly. "Don't you think it would be better if we got on with some real work?"

"Like all city men," said Margot, and her voice had taken

that peculiar droning quality which I remembered from the last meeting we had had with her. "Like all city men, you are in too much of a hurry. You should watch your footsteps. You should watch behind and before like a man walking in the snow who can only tell by looking behind how deep the snow is getting around him. You must not leap ahead without cry or warning, or you will bring more trouble than you cure. Be less rash, young men, and you will succeed."

Beef's mouth was slightly open, and he looked startled. "Here," he said, "wait a minute. I believe you know something."

The old woman went on as if she had not heard the interruption.

"There is a day already chosen," she went on, "on which that which you seek will come about. When men are happy, and the curled paper of their happiness litters the grass; when their cries are louder and less self-watching; that is the time to look for death. For it lurks in the twisted shell of happiness and endeavor; the brightest flame casts the blackest shadow. Even the moon is dark on the farther side. On that day will occur that which you set out to find. You may not both see it, but be assured it will happen. I only warn you not to be too precipitate in your lack of knowledge. It will fall into your hands in its own good time and the scarce-dried blood of a murdered person will turn to a golden crown."

"What do you mean by all that?" asked Beef, as soon as he could get a word in.

The old gypsy seemed to grow taller, and pointing a thin bony hand through the tent flap, said:

"I have spoken. Go, young man, and be cautious."

"She's been reading too many Wild West stories," was Beef's comment as soon as we had left the tent. "Why, she was speaking like Big Chief Sitting Cow or something."

"I wonder if there's anything in it?" I said thoughtfully.

"Of course there is," said Beef. "It means that none of what she tells us is much good. Because if we got her in a witness-box to swear to it and she talked like that to the judge her evidence would be dismissed."

"But she seems to know something," I persisted.

"She knows a thing or two all right," agreed Beef. "But you have to take all she says with a grain of salt. I think she's crackers. But you ought to ask Anita next time you take her for a little walk, and see if her mother's all there."

CHAPTER XXI

April 30th (continued).

As WE left Gypsy Margot's tent we noticed a small group talking animatedly by the gate. Ginger, and Tug the hunchback, were talking to a small shabby man whom I had not seen before. Ginger waved us over towards them, and said, as we approached:

"Here you are. This is the man you want."

The stranger turned his attention to Beef and touched his cap briefly with one finger.

" 'Morning, sir," he mumbled. "I heard word that you might be needing an elephant man here, so I come along to see if you would give me the job. I've been with Jill's for a couple of seasons, and before that I was with Twanger's, and I've done some of the larger tenting shows like Josaire's and Mott's and . . ."

Beef looked with amazement at the man. "I think there must be some mistake," he said heavily. "Who was it you thought I was?"

The man turned to Ginger for support. "I was told you was the boss," he said. "Please give me a job, guv'nor."

I could see that Ginger was trying very hard to suppress laughter and realized that this was his way of playing a joke on my friend. Beef, however, was not in a mood to perceive the joke, for he turned to the man with some concern.

"Couldn't have meant me," he said. "I'm not the boss here no more than he is. Must be some mistake."

The man looked at Ginger, but was met by a blank stare.

"Well, I don't know," he muttered. "Someone's a bit cracked around here, and it's not me." He looked defiantly around at the four of us, but no comment greeted this, so he commenced to walk away towards the main tent, where he could see one or two hands working. One of them pointed to Daroga's wagon and the man approached it, knocked on the door, and in a few seconds was admitted.

"Now there'll be trouble," commented Ginger.

"Why?" I asked.

"Well, Jackson's the only one who's supposed to take hands on, and he gets a bit riled when anybody else is consulted first. You watch Jackson's wagon."

For a few minutes nothing happened, and then Daroga's door opened and he and the stranger walked down the steps together. They were what is happily known as an ill-assorted pair. Daroga, tall, loose-jointed, with his long easy stride and dark-tanned face, which seldom seemed to alter its expression; the stranger a slight, underfed little man, one shoulder higher than the other, so that he seemed to walk sideways, a dingy bowler jammed down to his ears and faint wisps of uncut hair hanging down at the back and resting on the frayed collar of his mackintosh. He must have walked many miles in the last few days, for he placed his feet down at every step with a respect usually accorded to broken glass.

The couple were obviously making for the elephant tent, but before they had got half-way there the door of Jackson's wagon opened and the proprietor himself emerged.

"Daroga," he shouted.

The wire-walker turned sharply at the voice, and after a slight hesitation began to retrace his steps. The new hand trailed along two or three paces behind him.

"I've just engaged a new elephant man, Mr. Jackson," said Daroga loudly.

Ginger nudged me painfully.

Jackson walked up to the new man and inspected him with cold interest. "Do you think he's capable of handling the animals?" he asked.

Daroga's eyes were like beads. "If you doubt whether I know what's good for the elephants . . ." he began.

"I have no doubt at all about that, Daroga," replied the proprietor, "but this . . . man does not impress me as a desirable addition to the circus." ·

Both men were talking over the head of the new hand as if he did not exist, and his whining voice, in which he began to repeat his previously-claimed experience with other circuses, was over-ridden by their argument as a bus goes over a dirty newspaper in the streets.

". . . The point raised is whether you or I am the proprietor of this circus," Jackson was saying.

"I think I ought to be capable of finding the men I want to do *my* work," retorted Daroga with some heat.

Beef and I stood uncomfortably by as this quarrel proceeded to its conclusion. The others were obviously enjoying the whole affair, either out of their dislike for the proprietor, or because they could appreciate any disturbance of the routine of the morning's work.

At last, however, Jackson gave in with a very bad grace. It was the kind of defeat, however, which is often called a strategic withdrawal. Daroga began to lead the new hand towards the elephant tent. I had noticed this particular characteristic about nearly all the circus quarrels which I had heard; they never seemed to be solved. In a few cases, when they actually developed into a bout of fisticuffs, I suppose the matter might generally be considered settled, but the normal argument always seemed to leave quite sufficient material for beginning it again at the slightest opportunity.

Beef and I followed the two men to the elephant tent.

"Might as well see what's going on," Beef said.

As far as I could see it was difficult to discover which were the real antagonisms in the circus, and which were the ordinary "routine" quarreling. It was bad enough in any case attempting to find the basis of the real ones. I saw Beef's case becoming more and more complicated at every turn.

The elephant tent was the scene of unusual activity. Cora Frances seemed to be in charge, leaning against one of the poles, her pale legs crossed and a long cigarette-holder stuck in one corner of her mouth.

"Wash them in warm water first," she said to the negro who was crouching at the feet of one of the elephants with a small paint-brush in his hand.

"Yes ma'am," replied the negro brightly, "it sure does make them animals look pretty."

Strange explosive noises from the other side of the tent attracted our attention, and we saw Daroga walking in wide circles around the second elephant, looking at the animal's feet in sheer bewilderment.

"Don't you think it's an improvement?" asked Cora Frances coyly.

"Cor," breathed Beef in my ear, "look what she's done."

His wide forefinger was pointing at the elephant's feet and I noticed for the first time that the toe-nails of this creature were enameled a bright scarlet.

"I'm sorry it had to be red," went on the irrepressible artist. "Of course they should be lacquered with gold, but none of the shops had gold enamel, so I thought red would do. More modern really."

"What's it for?" spluttered Daroga furiously. "Who's been tampering with my elephants, that's what I want to know?"

"Oh, but it's not tampering," said Cora, waving her cigarette-holder at him. "In India they decorate the elephants' toe-nails whenever there's a great ceremony. They did it in the London Zoo for the Coronation, you know. I think it would make quite an impression, don't you?"

"Impression?" Daroga was almost speechless.

"Yes. I mean, it's rather a clever amalgamation of the

ancient royal custom, and the modern fashion. The audience will be thrilled to bits."

Daroga recovered himself with an effort. "Here, you," he shouted to the new hand. "Here's your first job. Get a bucket of water and a scrubbing-brush and see that all that colored muck is off before the afternoon performance."

"I'm afraid it won't come off as easily as that," said Cora. "You see, it's enamel."

"I don't care if you have to sand-paper it off," was the elephant-trainer's parting shot. "But get it off before I see those animals again."

"Dear me," said Cora Frances with concern, as soon as he had left the tent. "I seem to be creating quite a disturbance here, don't I?"

For a moment she seemed different from her usual self, and I felt a passing pity for her. She seemed to be lonely and deflated, and I thought that perhaps her whole manner was only a gigantic mask to cover just that. I could visualize her, solitary, after the crowd of "admiring" people had gone, suddenly allowing her expression to fall into more natural and less vivacious folds. I could see her aging. Perhaps it was fanciful; perhaps even to herself she was the over-blown, self-opinionated person she was to others. In any case, the one remark which I made, and which was an attempt to be friendly, was not well received.

I said: "Perhaps you don't understand circus people thoroughly, Miss Frances."

"Oh, but I do," she said immediately, recovering her normal manner in a flash. "They simply adore me here. Why, I really don't think the circus would be able to go on if I stopped coming."

I felt that the tragedy, if there was one, lay in the fact that she really did believe this fantastic statement. The three of us walked slowly back across the field to the wagons, Cora

Frances chatting brightly to Beef all the way and receiving grunts and monosyllables in exchange. Anita, who was standing in front of the big top, waved to us and walked to meet us.

"I really feel we are not wanted," said Cora to Beef. "Shall we leave the two young people alone?"

But before he could answer this outrageous statement, I said quickly: "Let's all go down the road for a drink," and gathering Anita on the way out I shepherded the little group, almost by brute force, out of the gate.

CHAPTER XXII

April 30th (continued).

THAT afternoon Beef and I managed to get Suzanne alone and talk to her about Chris and Len Waterman. Looking back I think that it was probably the most uncomfortable interview I witnessed during the whole of the case, for it became clear after a time that Suzanne was not only nervous about telling us anything, but when Beef broached the subject of the old affair with the electrician, she seemed to be really frightened of something.

"I'd rather not talk about it," she said. "Everything's so terribly mixed and muddled."

But Beef managed to persuade her that we were only trying to help, and at last she gave us something of a story. It was very incoherent and breathless, and Beef had to ask many questions on each point before she would give us a complete answer.

There really had been, she told us, a love affair between herself and the electrician Len Waterman. It had started a few years after she had joined the circus. Len had known her before then, and had been the cause of her getting the job. Actually, he had been the friend of her late husband, and when an accident on the trapeze had made her a widow, Len had tried to persuade her to marry him.

But Suzanne had wanted to give up circus life, and had refused and run away. It was only by an accident that Len had found her again. She was unhappy, and eventually he got her to take up her old job, this time with Jacobi's Circus.

Perhaps she had been very lonely, she said, perhaps it was Len's continued, quiet kindness to her. She didn't know how it happened, but slowly, almost unnoticed, she discovered that she was falling in love with him. Although she felt that there was something wrong with this, that it was false, she was too tired to talk the position over with Len. And so it had gone on, almost like a dream for her, until the Dariennes arrived.

It had been, Suzanne told us, like coming out of a thick misty valley into the sunshine on a hill. The two French boys had been so kind to her, and the younger one was so full of life and an almost irresponsible gayety, that the whole atmosphere of the circus seemed to change. And she had fallen in love with Christophe.

Len must have guessed that this was happening, because he chose this particular time to ask Suzanne if she would marry him. But he had left it too late. Suzanne refused him. There had been a terrible quarrel, which somehow Suzanne had kept from the two brothers. She was frightened that Chris would find out about Len.

"What did Len Waterman say?" asked Beef. "Did he threaten you at all?"

"He didn't exactly threaten me," said Suzanne. "I can remember some of the things he said, though. You see, I didn't dare tell him that I was in love with Chris—I was frightened he might quarrel with him if he knew—so that Len only suspected. He said: 'You're in love with somebody else, that's what it is.' And though I told him that was not true, he went on, 'Whoever it is, I'll get even some day. I can wait,' he said, 'I'm a very patient sort of a chap. But one day I'll get even with you both.' "

"You're in a bit of a fix," commented Beef thoughtfully. "And do you think he ever found out about Chris?"

"I don't know," said Suzanne shaking her head. "Just lately I've thought that perhaps he does know something. He's been acting very strangely—very friendly to Chris and Paul. And then, in that fight the other day with Bogli's Circus, I heard that Chris and Len started to fight each other."

"And what do you think he might do if he did find out?"
I asked.

"He might do anything. Len's such a queer fellow. He
keeps very quiet for weeks and weeks and nobody knows
what he's thinking, and then suddenly he'll do something that
nobody suspects."

"But that's not all the trouble, is it?" said Beef. "You have
to keep it from Paul as well. That's a bit queer."

"It's all a terrible muddle," said Suzanne. "I think sometimes it would be easier for everybody if I just ran away and
never let anybody know where I'd gone to. You see, Paul is
so dependent on his brother, and he hates me, I think. We
can't let him know about our being in love—he's so violent
when he's cross."

"Violent, is he?" said Beef. "How do you mean, violent?"

"Over all sorts of silly little things. There was one time
when we were in the ring and the band played the wrong
music by mistake. Paul was terrible. He climbed down from
the trapeze and walked across to the band and began to tear
the instruments out of their hands. Of course, the audience
thought it was part of the clowning and clapped and laughed.
But he was serious about it. He wouldn't appear in the ring
again for two or three days. And yet generally he's so quiet
and good-natured. It's just every now and again that he
seems to become another man; someone fierce and violent,
who likes hurting for the sake of hurting. I can't describe it
any better than that I'm afraid."

Beef closed his notebook slowly, and got up to go.

"But you won't tell anybody what I've been saying, will
you?" said Suzanne suddenly. "I'm so frightened that something terrible might happen if Len or Paul got to know about
this. You mustn't let anybody know, Sergeant."

Beef smiled, and I thought for a moment that he was going
to pat Suzanne on the head. "That's all right," he said

reassuringly. "I'm not going to tell nobody until you give me your permission."

"But do you think it will ever be cleared up?" asked Suzanne.

"There's a lot of things in this circus that want clearing up," said Beef pompously. "I don't say as I've got the hang of them all yet, but I soon will have. And then you'll see. What you want to do, Miss Suzanne," he said, laying a wide and kindly paw on the woman's shoulder, "is to keep a stiff upper lip. Everything will come all right in the end. Mr. Townsend will see to that."

"Poor kid," he said, as soon as we were out in the open again. "She seems really scared of something. I wonder if there's anything in it?"

I did not answer because I was thinking. I had never been involved in a case with so many tangled threads of emotion as this one. Somehow or other I had come to think of murder mysteries as being fairly straightforward affairs, in which one looked for typical and rather common motives, such as revenge, greed, jealousy, madness; something quite simple once you had put all the clues in the right order. But with this case there were no clues to speak of, and the emotions were mixed and muddled to such an extent that it would be hard to say whether any of them constituted a motive for murder. It was altogether too lifelike. Murder stories were better when they remained simple, and did not get mixed up with real people and real feelings. Murder was no doubt a profound crime, but a story about murder, I felt, should be anything but that. Quite beyond my own wishes I was being drawn into a case in which there was scarcely a clue. It would hardly make, I thought, a detective story at all.

"You know," said Beef, breaking in on my reflections, "this may be a very unusual case, but I can't help saying that I'm enjoying it. Change from the old routine."

"I wish," I said, all my bitterness welling up, "that you'd get on with a little more of the *routine* investigation. That would be a change all right. What am I going to make of this case if you don't get on with something active? Here we are, after days of wasted time in the circus, and simply nothing to show for it. You know, the trouble with you, Beef, is that you're too lazy. If you'd been almost any other detective you'd have been clubbed insensible four or five times, pushed over a precipice, shot, kidnaped, run over, caught in a burning building, blown up by a bomb, and a hundred other unpleasant but exciting things. If you had a little more respect for tradition you'd see what I mean. Every other detective of any standing at all is threatened half a dozen times a day. Have you ever been threatened?"

"Yes," said Beef triumphantly after a moment's thought. "How about that time I got an anomalous letter?"

"I never heard about that," I said skeptically.

"That's right," said Beef. "Someone wrote to me and threatened to tell the inspector about how I used to go round the back of the 'Blue Dragon' and get a drink after hours, when I was on duty."

"And did they?" I asked.

"I don't know," said Beef. "But the funny thing was that a day or two after that the inspector dropped round and had a drink with me. So I suppose they must have done."

"I can't help feeling," I persisted, "that you ought to be attacked or something. It's hardly respectable to have an investigator who lives in the lap of safety the way you do."

"Here, you lay off that stuff," said Beef becoming a little alarmed. "Didn't I risk being knocked over the head when we had that scrap with the other circus people? What more do you want for your money? Anyway, I'm not supposed to be a hero. I solve my cases by brain-work, that's what I do. There's no call to drag in a lot of violence."

[185]

"Brain-work!" I said. I felt that Beef was rather overreaching himself, but I could think of nothing to say in reply.

"And what's more," went on Beef, thoroughly aroused now, "you seem to forget that tiger escaping. Why I might have been eaten alive, or something. That's never happened before in my other cases, and I don't want it to happen again. No, those were the sort of cases I like. Nice quiet ones, with no danger or discomfort. And if you did your work proper and found jobs for me I shouldn't have had to come all the way up to Yorkshire."

This was, without doubt, the last word. And we walked the rest of the way to our wagon in silence.

CHAPTER XXIII

April 30th (continued).

CALLING for Anita some time during the afternoon to take her for a stroll had now become something of an established custom of mine, and although her wound had completely healed she still took my arm as we walked. To be perfectly honest, I think she would have got more exercise had she gone by herself, but I somewhat weakly refrained from suggesting this to her.

For me these walks had become small tours of exploration of the district we passed through, and although this was not a very impressive part of Yorkshire, there was a sort of lazy comfort to be obtained from the wide sun-warmed fields and lanes. On this particular day we went a little farther than usual. The surrounding fields were a patch-work of different shades of green, and the tiny footpaths through them stretched their straight lines in a network far away from the tober.

As we walked in single file along one of these footpaths the drills of pale-green wheat-blades seemed to curve towards us, straighten themselves, and then curve away again behind.

"It has a sort of hypnotic effect," I said to Anita, after a few minutes. "The sun flickering through a spile fence does much the same thing."

"That reminds me," I added, when she did not answer, "that you told us your mother was a hypnotist."

"Yes, that's right. You had a theory that she had something to do with Helen stabbing me, didn't you? Do you still believe that?"

"Well," I said awkwardly. "I only thought of it as a possibility, you know. In this sort of business, detection I mean, you have to take every single factor into consideration."

"I see," said Anita, "so you haven't really made up your mind. Is that it?"

"That's it," I said gratefully. "We can only know things like that for certain when the case is over. If it ever is over," I added with a sigh.

"You know," went on Anita thoughtfully, "you have quite the wrong idea about hypnotism. Most writers have I think. It's quite a simple thing really—you can hypnotize yourself, if you care to. But I don't think it would get you anywhere. You see, the sort of hypnotism that my mother dabbles in is quite harmless. She can't make people *do* anything. She just sends them into a trance, that's all. You can get rid of a headache that way sometimes."

"Do you mean to say," I exclaimed, "that it is impossible to make people perform certain actions of which they know nothing when they wake up again?"

"Oh, I don't know about that," said Anita. "But what I meant was that I had never seen my mother do anything like that."

I left the subject there, and when in a little while we turned back towards the tober, the conversation passed easily on to other matters of little interest to anybody else but Anita and myself.

We emerged, unexpectedly, on a lane which ran behind the tober, sunk lowdown like the bed of a spring stream and hidden from the tober itself by a high brambly hedge. No one seemed to be moving in the field. It was nearly time for the afternoon show, but the only person visible from where we stood was the groom, who was leisurely applying whiting to the mane of one of the ring horses and sissing gently and soothingly. It was the sort of afternoon which, had it been a Sunday in a London suburb, called for the harsh repetitive whirr of a lawn-mower or perhaps the very distant cry of a hawker. The leveling heat seemed to demand only sounds which were familiar; continuous, recurring sounds. Anything else would have been like a knife slashing suddenly through the center of the heavy blanket of the sky.

And suddenly, inevitably, the disturbing sound came. It was the high-pitched scream of an angry elephant, and then, rushing quickly into the silence behind it, the violent sound of a man swearing. It was the voice of a frightened man, made brave by the loudness of his own voice.

Without comment of any sort Anita and I scrambled quickly up the bank out of the lane and crawled through the hedge into the tober. One or two people had already appeared on the field and were moving towards the elephant tent, but before any of us could reach it the elephant trumpeted again, and this time the body of a man was hurled through the tent flap and landed limply and heavily on the grass. Anita ran over to him and knelt on the ground.

"It's the new elephant man," she said, as her fingers quickly set about undoing his shirt-collar.

The man's face was a gray mud color, and from the corner of his nostril ran a thin dark trickle of blood. He seemed soft and yielding, like a piece of clay; scarcely a man at all. Then, slowly, he opened his eyes and moved his head. He stared at us for a moment with an incredulous, hurt expression, and then slowly, one by one, he began to move his arms and legs, watching them doubtfully.

"Seems all right," he said at last.

"Try and stand," said Anita, and together we helped him on to his feet. He swayed for a moment, and then, shaking his head with a queer worried movement, he grinned shakily at us, as if to show he was all right.

By this time most of the others had gathered round and were waiting for some sort of an explanation.

"What happened?" said Beef, pushing his way through the group, as only a trained policeman can.

Hesitantly, the man told us. It was quite brief. Apparently, he had been cleaning one of the elephants for the afternoon show, when it had screamed at him. He stepped up close to it to show that he was not to be intimidated, but the animal began to wind its trunk round his body. For a moment he had struggled, striking the elephant with the back of the heavy brush he had in his hand, but the squeeze of the trunk had tightened until he was no longer able to breathe and he lost consciousness before the animal threw him out of the tent.

I was surprised to find everybody taking the affair quite coldly. It was nothing very new to have a man attacked by an elephant it seemed. Daroga, directly he had heard the man's story, walked straight into the elephant tent and we could hear his voice talking to the elephant in a low, soothing tone.

"They do that sometimes," said Daroga to Beef. "One of the elephants takes it into his head that he doesn't like one of the men. After that it's best for the chap to go home if he wants to do it all in one piece."

The new hand looked at Daroga and gave a grin. "I never ran away from an elephant yet," he said, "and I don't mean to start now. I'll have him eating out of my hand in a couple of days, you see if I don't."

"As long as he doesn't eat your hand," said Daroga. "Still, that's your business."

That seemed to be the opinion of the others, and slowly they drifted away from the tent and went back to their wagons. One or two, however, remained, and Beef and I noticed that they seemed discontented. It was Sid Bolton, the fat clown, who voiced the reason for this.

"It's not only his safety that's concerned in this," he said. "Those elephants are not safe for anybody if there's someone about they've taken a dislike to."

"How do you mean?" I asked. "Does it disturb them, or something?"

"Well, look at us in the ring. Clem and I have to roll about under the elephants' feet as part of the clowning—that's all right when the animals are in their right minds, but I don't go much on it if they're nervous."

"You see," joined in Clem Gail, "it makes them restless. Maybe they wouldn't hurt anybody else on purpose, but when they get like that they might do damage to anybody who was near them. It's too dangerous to play about with animals that way. If they don't like someone, then you ought to get rid of him straight away. What an elephant says, goes."

They were not the only ones who were feeling uncomfortable about the affair. I noticed one or two of the others discussing the affair in various parts of the field, mostly those artists who appeared in the ring with the elephants at one time or another.

"There's only one thing to do," said Anita. "And that is to go and see Jackson about it. He's the boss."

"He's also ring-master," said Clem, "so he won't like the risk any more than we do."

With the usual amount of talk and argument, the artists at last decided to go straight to the proprietor and tell him what they thought. Beef and I watched the little procession lining up before the wagon, while Sid Bolton knocked on the door.

"You know," said Beef thoughtfully, "this is a funny do."

"What do you mean?" I asked. "Do you think the new man is purposely annoying the elephants for some reason? I should think it was a rather dangerous thing to do."

"I didn't say as I thought anything of the kind," said Beef. "All I said was as it was a funny do. You always exaggerate everything."

We saw Jackson open the door at Sid Bolton's knock and went across to hear what he had to say about it. There was actually little necessity for this, as his voice was loud enough to be heard almost all over the tober.

"Well, you know my feelings about the affair," he said to the crowd gathered at his wagon steps. "I didn't like it in the first place. But it's Daroga you want to see about it, not me."

"But you can sack the man, can't you?" said Sid Bolton. "He's a danger to the show, that's what he is. Better for all of us if he went. He doesn't know Fanny Anny about elephants, and he'll only go and kill himself, and maybe us too, if someone doesn't tell him to clear off."

But Jackson merely shrugged his shoulders at this. "Daroga put the man on," he said coldly, "so if anyone's got to sack him you'd better go and persuade Daroga to do it." And with that he shut his door on the disgruntled and murmuring group.

It seemed perfectly clear to me who had the whip-hand between these two men, Daroga and the proprietor. Jackson, I felt, would have been only too pleased to sack the new elephant man. But something stopped him from trying. What was it?

I turned to Beef. "You know," I said, "I think Daroga's probably got something on Jackson, and is blackmailing him."

"Go on," said Beef derisively with a broad grin. "You don't say!"

CHAPTER XXIV

April 30th (continued).

AFTER a few days with the circus, the show in the ring had begun to take on a new significance. Some of the turns seemed more and more brilliant, and some of them seemed just boring. One turn especially I enjoyed was the wire-walking act, and I went into the tent during the evening performance in time to see that only, and then came out again. I left Beef watching the show, and wandered slowly round the tent.

The evening was warm and lovely. Hardly any moon, but a sort of soft light blurred the edges of the trees and made them seem half-human, standing round the side of the field like parents waiting to collect their children from a party which was going on inside the tent. The lorry which fed electricity to the tents was purring softly, and as I walked slowly by it I noticed Len Waterman seated hunched up on the step with his head in his hands. He did not seem to notice me. I wondered if he were feeling ill, but I was too nervous to approach him and ask if he were all right. His fingers were sunk deeply into his hair, and he sat still, almost without breathing it seemed.

Anita was on the steps of her wagon, trying to read by the thin yellow light which came over her shoulder, and I stopped to talk to her. From the inside of the wagon came rattling and clattering, as if old Margot were beginning to get the supper ready. Even the fact that neither of the twins had been appearing in the ring now for a week, could not break the circus routine of exceedingly late supper. Like the artists who had been performing, Anita and Helen would not sit down to the last meal of the day until nearly midnight.

As I approached the wagon steps Anita looked up and

smiled at me, and then, closing the book she was reading, she held the back of the cover up to me for me to see the title. It was *Case With No Conclusion,* the story of Beef's last case, and I felt childishly flattered. To me, Anita was an unusual sort of person altogether. Most people, on discovering that I wrote detective novels for a living, take up one of two attitudes. Either they think "thrillers" are the perigee of degradation and look at me as though I were something which had slipped out of a hole in the wainscoting, or else they gush at length about writing in general and tell me how they have a cousin who "writes," and have I ever heard of him. I seldom have, by the way, and it gives me pleasure to say so.

But the point about Anita was that she did neither of these things, and yet was genuinely interested in me. She had not, perhaps, been delivered up to "middle-class morality," as Shaw's dustman would have phrased it.

"What do you think of it?" I asked.

"I don't think you're quite fair to the Sergeant," was her comment.

The circus band had begun to play the "Skaters' Waltz."

"That's the trapeze act starting," said Anita.

The crowd in the tent had become now completely silent. I could imagine the row on row of strained white faces, the unanimous turning of heads, the bright lights reflected in the widely-staring eyes. By now I knew the turns off by heart, and when the first burst of applause came I could visualize Paul and Christophe bowing from the center of the ring after their introduction of the act. Once more the band struck up— slow, soft music, which was the only sound to be heard from the big top.

"What would happen," I asked Anita, "if the band played the wrong music?"

"I don't know," she laughed. "We're all like circus horses really. Some of us have routine acts which we've been doing for years. And with the same music. If the music went wrong, you know, I think the act would just crack up. But it's never happened yet."

A fresh burst of applause from the tent made me look up. Sharp brilliant flashes of light came through the small gaps which the wind opened now and again in the canvas. From the dynamo-lorry stretched the two wires which carried the current to the lighting in the tent top. I had often noticed the rough joints and knots in these wires, and even now, in the dark, it seemed only an act of fortune that the current ever reached the lamps.

There was a prolonged roll on the drums. The finale had started. In perfect silence—there was no band now—the lithe figures of Suzanne and the two Dariennes were swinging slowly on the high trapezes. A gasp, bitten off sharply, as from one gigantic man rather than from a crowd of three hundred people, told us that Suzanne had slipped backwards on her trapeze and was hanging by her feet. The drums again. I seemed to feel the tension in the air as she prepared to hurl herself across the ring to where Paul was already swinging gently with his arms ready to catch her. My mind seemed to time it so that with my eyes shut I could see the somersaulting figure pass through the steady white light in the center. And then, as Paul's arms would be stretching out to catch her hands, instead of the usual mass sigh of relief, came the piercing scream of one woman.

But before the sound had ended, the tent seemed to quiver with excited shouts and cries from the audience. Anita and I leaped to our feet, and as we did so I noticed that the guide-bulb over the lorry had gone out.

"The lights must have fused," Anita managed to say, as we ran toward the tent entrance.

Inside the tent we could see nothing. Some of the crowd were attempting to find the exit, and their angry, frightened voices, gave us no clue to what had happened. I could hear Jackson's voice rising powerfully above the clamor:

"Keep perfectly calm, ladies and gentlemen. Keep in your seats. A small technical hitch . . ."

At first the crowd seemed to take no notice, but his voice went on and on in the darkness, and it must have seemed to the frightened people, the only thing to which they could cling.

"Those of you who have left your seats, please remain exactly where you are. The lights will be repaired in a few minutes. No one will be hurt so long as they keep still."

The people in the tent seemed to have obeyed Jackson's commands, for the noise subsided to a low but steady murmur. Some genius in the bandstand began to play "Daisy, Daisy," as a solo on his saxophone, and by the second bar everyone was singing.

"Good God," I said to Anita, "have they no imagination at all? Why, at this moment Suzanne may be lying on the ground with her . . ."

The dim red flickers of matches struck here and there in the crowd only served to illuminate the staring faces of those who struck them. But at that moment the lights came suddenly on. My eyes immediately sought the trapeze. At one end sat the two Dariennes, staring into the crowd below; and the other, empty, swung with sickening slowness, with the white sweat-handkerchief dangling from one corner. The scene below was in unutterable confusion. The ring was half-filled with standing and seated members of the audience.

As Anita and I rushed forward I glanced upward and saw the still figure of Suzanne lying in the net. Paul and Christophe were descending as fast as they could, and in a few moments they were lifting Suzanne out of the net and handing her carefully down to Jackson and Clem Gail, who stood ready at the side of the ring. Christophe sprang out of the net and bent over the still form when they placed her on the ground. "Suzanne," he almost shouted at her, "speak to me."

He raised his head and looked swiftly round the circle of faces. His jaw muscles were set, and his eyes looked hard and rock-like, almost unseeing. Then suddenly he seemed to shrivel, and pitching forward on to the pale figure in his arms, he pressed his face against her breast. His slow rhythmical sobbing increased, until it had become almost animal-like in its intensity. His fingers twitched, nervously pulling at the spangles on Suzanne's costume.

The thin querulous face of a woman in the crowd poked suddenly between Jackson and myself. "Why doesn't someone get a doctor for the poor thing?" she said shrilly. I became conscious of the people around us.

"Where's Beef?" I said.

Almost as if I had called him up from some smoky depth, a stir in the crowd proclaimed the appearance of the Sergeant.

"Here, what's all this?" his disembodied voice was saying. And the round anxious face of my old friend appeared over the heads of the crowd.

I felt a sense of relief when Beef bent down briskly and shook the hysterical Christophe by the shoulders.

"Come on, young fellow," he said kindly, "that sort of thing won't get you nowhere. Pull yourself together." And after lifting the boy bodily away, he expertly raised Suzanne in his arms and walked with her to the entrance of the tent. The crowd stood back in silence and made way for us as we followed Beef to Suzanne's wagon.

Beef laid the still figure on the bed, and after a brief examination reassured us:

"She'll be all right in a minute or two. Doesn't seem to be nothing broken."

"Are you sure?" asked Christophe anxiously.

Beef nodded, and bending down, began to rub the unconscious girl's hands. "Look," he said, after a minute or two, "she's coming round now."

Suzanne moved uneasily on the bed, and then drew a deep breath through her parted lips. "What happened?" she said in a dazed voice.

"That's what we want to know," said Beef. "You gave us a scare, you did, young lady. How are you feeling?"

Suzanne sat up. "I don't know," she said. "Did I fall into the net?"

"That's where we found you," said Beef.

Suzanne pressed her hands across her eyes. "All I can remember," she said, "was seeing Paul's arms for a second as I came out of a somersault. And then, suddenly, I couldn't see anything. It was just blackness. I caught Paul by one hand, but I slipped. Then I think I must have hit the edge of the net with my shoulder."

She touched her neck gingerly with the tips of her fingers, and I noticed for the first time a long red weal which was gradually turning blue.

"That's where it caught you all right," said Beef. "Knocked you out, it must have, and thrown you back into the net. Lucky it wasn't the other way or you would have broken your neck."

"I seemed to go blind," said Suzanne, "I felt . . ."

"That's all right," said Beef. "It was the lights went out. And that's what I'm going to see about now."

The Sergeant looked at the two trapeze artists for a minute, and then turned to Paul. "What exactly did happen?" he asked him.

"I saw her coming towards me," burst out Paul suddenly. "I saw her coming, and then, suddenly, the lights went out and I tried to catch her. But I was only able to seize one arm, and she slipped."

I felt there was something strained and artificial in the way

Paul was speaking. He seemed to be justifying himself. I looked quickly at Beef to see if he shared my suspicion.

"And then what happened?" said Beef.

Paul shrugged. "I don't know. She should have fallen into the net—it was just underneath us—but I suppose she twisted and missed it. There was just the scream, and it was too dark to see anything."

"I see," said Beef. "Then the man I want to see is the electrician, isn't it?"

"Well," I said to Beef as we walked across towards the dynamo-lorry, "have you got your case ready?"

"Case?" said Beef. "Not going anywhere, are we?"

"Evidence," I said with exasperation; "clues."

"Oh," said Beef, "that. Well, I wouldn't say as I'd exactly got a case."

"But Beef . . ." I protested.

"The matter with you," said Beef, "is that you're in too much of a hurry."

"Hurry," I said, "but you've had three attempted murders already. What are you waiting for?"

"As I've said before," Beef pointed out patiently, "you jump to conclusions. We've had nothing to show that this was anything more than an accident."

"But the tiger," I said.

"Tiger!" Beef was scornful. "Tigers are always escaping. You want to read your Sunday papers."

"But in this last case," I pointed out, "we do know that Christophe was frightened of his brother finding out about the affair with Suzanne."

Beef interrupted sarcastically. "I suppose your theory is," he grunted, "that Paul blew the lights out and then dropped Suzanne to the ground. Ver-y interesting."

"Nothing of the sort," I snapped. "You forget Len Waterman. What about the photograph we found in his wagon?

We know that there was an affair between him and Suzanne some years ago. And he was in charge of the lights, wasn't he?"

"Well?" said Beef.

"Then he might have done it," I said.

"So might Father Christmas," said Beef.

After which example of what Beef would no doubt have called humor, we walked in silence. We found Len Waterman sitting on the running-board of the lorry coiling a length of fuse-wire.

"Nasty turn out," he greeted us. "Always did think something like that would happen. Now perhaps they'll take my advice about having a double circuit."

"What difference would that make?" asked Beef.

"Well then, if one circuit failed," said Len, "the other one would be all right. Couldn't have all the lights going out at the same time then."

"Is that what happened this time?" asked Beef, in his "casual" voice, which would not have deceived a child.

"What do you think did then?" demanded Len Waterman, in a belligerent tone.

"I just wondered," said Beef. "I mean I don't know nothing about this electricity stuff."

"Nothing at all?" said Len.

Beef shook his head. Whereupon, rather, I felt, like the doctor in *Le Médecin Malgré Lui,* Len proceeded to give a technical discourse, of which not more than one in five words was comprehensible to us.

"Oh," said Beef, when it was finished, "so that's what happened. Now you don't mind if I ask you a few personal questions, do you?"

"Depends how personal," said Len.

"Well, what was this affair you had with Suzanne? I mean,

wasn't there something between you two? You know, walking out and that?"

I felt that if ever there was an example of an elephant trampling through tissue-paper, this was one. I was a little disappointed however in Len's reaction.

"Well," he said slowly, "there *was* a sort of an arrangement."

"Marriage?" said Beef.

"Her husband was still alive."

"Oh," Beef nodded. "Like that, was it?"

"I don't know what you're driving at," said Len angrily. "She wasn't in love with her husband. It was sort of understood that she'd marry me when she could get a divorce or something."

"But," I interrupted, "I understood her husband was dead before she joined the show."

Beef's large and heavy toe seemed to be attempting to break my shin.

"Who told you that?" asked Len suspiciously.

"I think it was Jackson," I replied.

"Oh, him," said Len. "Well, anyway, as far as I knew he was still alive."

"But it didn't come off?" queried Beef. "What happened?"

"Oh, you know," said Len. "We had a bit of a quarrel, and then those Dariennes joined the circus."

"What had they got to do with it?" asked Beef sharply.

"Nothing, nothing," said Len quickly. "Sort of drifted apart, we did then."

"I see," said Beef in an understanding voice. "Happens like that sometimes, doesn't it. I remember my first girl. It was all a question of cork-tipped cigarettes . . . Still you don't want to hear about that. I suppose you've got to get these lights down. We'd better be going. I'm sorry about all these questions." And grasping me firmly by the arm he led me away.

"But Beef," I protested as soon as we had left the electrician, "you were just getting on to something important then."

"You mean he knows about Christophe and Suzanne?" said Beef.

I nodded.

"Well, if we'd have asked any more questions he'd have got suspicious. You have to be tactful with chaps like that."

"Oh," I said caustically, "is that what you were doing?"

CHAPTER XXV

May 1st.

IT WAS drizzling with rain when we moved on to South Cave. Rain, I had noticed, often acts as a sort of poultice on the circus people; that is, it brings out their petty irritations and animosities. This is not difficult to understand, since there can be no more dismal job than building up the big top when it is a mass of sodden canvas in a field where the long grass quickly soaks your shoes and feet.

And besides this, I thought to myself, the accident of last night had made a sudden difference to the whole personnel of the circus. It had been noticeable to some extent in the manner in which they had treated Beef. Up till now everybody had been inclined to take the Sergeant's presence as something of a joke, but last night, when he took control of the situation, they had given way to him immediately. Could it mean that many of them were taking the murder idea seriously?

An important by-product of Suzanne's fall was the revealing of some "understanding" between her and Christophe. Paul would hardly take his brother's hysterics as an instance of ordinary friendship. I felt that anything might come of that situation. Paul knew that his brother was in love with Suzanne, and Len Waterman appeared to already have some inkling of this. Would either of them take any action about it?

At any rate, as I wandered casually around the ground on this particular morning, I had the feeling that something was very definitely drawing to a head. It was not something I could lay my hand on like a concrete clue or piece of evidence; it was something in the way the men spoke to each other, in the way they seemed to avoid me. Anita was the only person who was not affected.

"I'm going into the ring again on Saturday," was her cheerful greeting to me when I strolled past her wagon.

"The day after tomorow?" I asked. "Are you sure you're well enough?"

"I couldn't miss the Jubilee show," she said with a laugh.

I had almost forgotten this Jubilee show, but I felt a sudden return of anxiety now, when Anita mentioned it. It would be a great day for the circus people; more their own show than the audience's. It was something they had all looked forward to throughout the whole year. It seemed to have a special significance to them, like a bank-holiday, or May Day to the Labor Movement. Two more days! I had a premonition that those two days would show us the end of this strange case—if there was to be an end to it at all.

Beef was cooking the breakfast when I returned to our wagon, and I told him my feelings.

"Nice bit of liver, this is," he said, poking at the frying-pan with his fork. "Wish I'd bought a bit more now."

This, I knew, was Beef's way of telling me that he thought I was talking nonsense, so we began breakfast in silence. Outside the rain had stopped and a thin watery sun was showing through. The big top steamed gently, and from the farm at the bottom of the tober came the clear sound of milk-pails clinking and a girl's voice calling monotonously. Beef demolished his breakfast in silence; or perhaps I should be more accurate in saying that he did not speak while he was eating.

"That's starting early in the morning," he commented suddenly, pointing his loaded fork out of the window.

At the rear of the big top, out of sight of the rest of the wagons, I saw two figures in a prolonged embrace.

"Who are they?" I asked.

"Better wait till they sort themselves out," said Beef dryly.

As he spoke the two people looked up suddenly in the direction of our wagon, almost as if they had realized they were being observed. And I was able to recognize Corinne Jackson and Peter Ansell, the animal-feeder.

"Platonic, he called it, didn't he?" Beef said sarcastically. "Funny way of showing it, I must say."

For a moment the two stood looking at each other, and then they separated quickly, and Corinne disappeared round the far side of the tent, while Peter Ansell came around towards us, walking casually, with his hands in his pockets.

"Nice organization," commented Beef, and returned to his plate.

"You know," the Sergeant said a few moments later, as he wiped a piece of bread carefully round his plate, "I think I ought to go back on our tracks a bit, one of these days."

"What do you mean, back on our tracks?"

"Well, the chief trouble with this traveling circus as the scene of a crime, is that any sort of evidence or clues and such, are left behind every day when we move on. I mean, in an ordinary case you find things that have been lost in the garden or thrown down a well; or maybe there's something a tramp saw, or the butcher's boy. But in this case you don't get any of that because we move around so quickly."

"And you think," I asked eagerly, "that if you went back to some of the old tobers, you might be able to find someone who knew something which would help solve the whole case? The only trouble so far," I added ruefully, "is that there's no case as yet to solve."

"Nor I wouldn't say," said Beef carefully, "that anything would come of it if I did have a look around. But you never know what you might come across."

I felt very strongly—and in fact I had been feeling this for some time now—that this present affair showed the Sergeant in his worst light. It seemed to reveal the complete lack of any scientific method in all he did. Perhaps in his previous cases that had not mattered so much, but here, where the whole affair was of the most tenuous sort, it seemed to me that he was only playing with the case. However, I knew from experience, that nothing is ever obtained by arguing with Beef, so, as usual, I waited for him to make the next move.

"All right," he said at last, "let's go and have a mooch round for a bit."

The sun was shining warmly now, and all the early rain had dried off the grass. We had built up in a very small tober, so small that the ropes from the big top were in some cases pegged down under the hedge on either side, leaving no room for the wagons to pass by until the tent was pulled down again. It was very quiet too. There were no visitors today, since it was not a large village, and the tober was on the very edge, some way from the center of population. This silence seemed to me to emphasize the peculiar difference in the circus, the slight strained atmosphere.

Pete Daroga was sitting in his customary position on the steps of his wagon bending intently over a small yellow book.

"Dobroye ootro," he greeted us, with a wide grin.

"I don't know what you mean," said Beef cheerfully. "But the same to you, anyway."

"It's Russian for 'Good morning'," said Daroga, and held out the book to us. It was one of those little Self-Tutor volumes.

"If I take that contract," he added, "I shall want to be able to speak the language a bit, shan't I?"

"But I thought," said Beef, bewildered, "that you were a Russian, anyway."

"So I am. But I left the country before I could walk, let alone talk. My parents were Jews and they thought things would be more comfortable in America than in Russia in those days. But that was a long time ago. I was too young to remember anything. My mother used to tell me that the Tsar had half a dozen Jewish babies for his breakfast every morning."

"So you've never been able to speak Russian?" asked Beef. "And you've never been there since you were a baby?"

"That's right," said Daroga. "Seems funny, doesn't it, learning your own language in middle age." He smiled again, rather boyishly, and opened his book again, moving his lips silently as he followed the words.

"Dosvedanya," he called after us as we began to walk away, and I guessed that it meant good-by.

"Well, that's funny," said Beef slowly. "What about that theory of yours about the button? It can't have been nothing to do with him, can it? That means someone else in the troupe has been to Russia."

"Not necessarily," I said. "After all, it may be something—like a souvenir—which Jackson has had given to him. Or he might have relations in Russia. Or for that matter, Daroga might still be the owner. It might be something his mother gave him."

"This is getting too complicated for me," said Beef. "I don't suppose it matters much, anyway. Let's go and have a drink."

CHAPTER XXVI

May 1st (continued).

ALTHOUGH I had been constantly aware of Cora Frances being with the circus—her voice was inescapable—yet I had seen very little of her during the past day or so. I was rather surprised, therefore, when she sought me out quite late in the morning to ask me if Beef and I would have lunch with her.

"Just a little luncheon-party," she told me. "One feels the need, don't you think, of *civilization* now and again. Of course, the poor dears here have not time for such luxuries, they must eat where and when they can."

The place arranged for this little party appeared to be the largest hotel in the district, and I felt flattered that Cora Frances should take such trouble on our account.

"Oh, and do bring the Sergeant, won't you?" she went on. "He's so quaint. I can't imagine how you manage to spend so much of your time with him, but in small doses you know . . ." and she laughed girlishly.

"I find the Sergeant's company very pleasant indeed," I said coldly.

"But how loyal," she said, staring straight into my face. "How I admire you for that. But really, you must admit that he can be a little trying, mustn't you? I mean, my dear, there's something so *barbaric* about him." Then, seeing my expression, she hurried on: "Of course, I find it perfectly charming. Such a change from the society I'm used to. Like a breath of fresh air."

"We should be very pleased to come," I said quickly, hoping to stem the flood.

"Good," she cooed. "Now I must go and tell Clem. I think this is going to be rather difficult, because I don't want the others to think of it as favoritism. One has to be so diplomatic over these things, you know, otherwise one causes so much trouble."

"In that case," I suggested, "it would surely be best to invite the others too."

"Oh, no. That would never do," said Cora, raising her eyebrows in an exaggeration of shocked surprise. "There are such *depths* in Clem which you'd never dream of if you'd only seen him in company. He's a most unusual man. And such a darling. Do you know," she leaned forward and laid the tinted tips of her fingers lightly on my sleeve, "do you know I think he's the most handsome man I've *ever* seen?"

I gave the incredulous-surprised expression which I imagined she expected of me. "I can't say that I've noticed it," I said, "but now I come to think of it . . ."

"Just look at him carefully next time," she said, rather as if I might find something concealed behind his ear. "Well, see you at one o'clock then. At the 'Dog and Gun'." And with a coy flutter of her hand she was gone.

Beef received the news of our luncheon arrangements with rather more good humor than I had anticipated.

"Save us a bit of cooking, anyway," he said, "and you never know but what it might put us on to something."

We arrived punctually at one o'clock to find Cora Frances alone.

"He has such a will of his own," she fluttered in explanation of Clem Gail's absence. "He simply refused to let me bring him down in the car. I tried to walk with him, but he wouldn't let me. He almost lifted me into the car. Such charming independence. The dear boy doesn't like to feel that he's *beholden* to anybody. So naïve, don't you think?"

Beef merely grinned without answering, and I searched quickly for some subject of conversation. I need not have bothered, for Cora Frances was not the sort of person who expects others to make conversation for her. She swept on:

"Don't you think these flowers are lovely? I had them sent up specially."

I glanced at the huge bowls of lilac which were arranged in the center of the table and massed around the room. Flowers in such quantities, I thought, became more than decorations. They were almost indecent in their profusion, hampering one's movements about the room and leaving little space on the table for anything but themselves.

"Circus people do so adore flowers," went on Cora, "and yet they have such little opportunities to see them."

"Course, they might see one or two growing in the hedges," said Beef, with heavy sarcasm.

"But that's so different," said Cora. "I always feel that flowers only give themselves up to you when they have been picked and brought indoors. But perhaps that's my civilized mind."

Fortunately we were interrupted by the arrival of Clem Gail, so that there was no need to worry any further about Cora's original theories on flowers.

"Crumbs," said Clem directly he got into the room. "Has somebody died or something?"

I glanced quickly at the artist to see how she would take this blow, but she was almost purring with pleasure. "How priceless," she said. " 'Has somebody died'? Really, I must remember that."

For a considerable part of the meal Beef and I played a very small part in the conversation. The Sergeant, in any case, was concentrating, as usual, on his food.

"Oh, Clem," said Cora suddenly, "before I forget. Who *was* that girl you had with you last night? What a *frightful* little piece she was, my dear."

Clem gave a smug smile. "I don't know who she was," he said carelessly. "She came up to me, and after that I simply couldn't get rid of her."

"I didn't notice you trying terribly hard," said Cora. "I mean, your arm, my dear."

"That!" said Clem, with scorn. "I didn't like to hurt her feelings, that's all."

"Really, Clem, you're incurable."

"Got a way with him, hasn't he?" said Beef suddenly, and gave the unembarrassed clown a broad grin.

Eventually, however, the luncheon came to its end, and Cora suggested that we go downstairs for a drink before we left.

"Sergeant," she said as soon as we were in the bar, "I've heard so much about the way you play darts. Do show me, will you?"

"Same way as anybody else," mumbled Beef.

"But they said you were awfully good at it. Couldn't you have a game with Mr. Townsend so that I could see with my own eyes?"

"What does she think I am," mumbled Beef to me as we walked over to the dart-board, "a performing monkey or something? The *way* I play darts! Anybody would think I threw them with my toes."

This must have put Beef a little off his game, for his first dart for the center landed in the treble sixteen.

"What a wonderfully straight eye," said Cora Frances rapturously.

Beef merely grunted, and the game went on. But Cora appeared to take no more interest. She sat in a corner with Clem, and the regular cadence of her voice went on almost without interruption. It was fortunately impossible to hear the words, so Beef and I continued our game without further interruption.

"You know," said Beef quietly to me after a while, "I don't like the way things are going over there," and he jerked his head in the direction of the corner. "I think that lad's drinking a drop too much."

"Nonsense," I said. "He's got to go into the ring this afternoon. He wouldn't be such a fool as to get himself drunk."

"I didn't exactly say drunk," said Beef. "Take a look for yourself."

Cora was still talking, but she now had her hand on the clown's knee, and Clem's face wore a faintly smiling expression as he leaned towards her.

"Anyway," said Beef, "I think we'd better do something about it," and he walked straight across to the couple before I had time to answer him.

"It's about time we were getting back," he said bluntly to them. "There's only an hour before the show starts."

Clem looked up at him and waved his hand. "The show?" he said, "yes, let's go and see the show."

"You're in it, darling," said Cora.

"In it? 'Course I'm in it. Come on then, let's go," and he jumped to his feet, and dragging Cora after him made for the door. Beef and I followed at a little more sober speed.

"I wouldn't say as he was rocky," said Beef as we drove slowly back to the tober, "but all the same, I think he's had a drop too much."

When we arrived back at the ground I decided that I would see the show. The least I could do, I thought, was to see if Clem performed as usual, or whether he was affected by his condition. Cora apparently had the same idea, for she was already seated in her place when I went into the tent and she beckoned me over to her immediately.

"Do you think it was wicked of me?" she asked.

I pretended not to understand what she was talking about.

"Why, giving Clem just a tiny drop too much to drink. I have a feeling that it may lead to something. It would never do for the others to find out that he had had lunch with me. My dear, you've no idea how terrible they would be over it. Jealousy isn't in it. Why, if Eric—he's a dear boy but so flippant. He hasn't the depth of character that Clem has—if Eric found out he'd be simply *livid*. And Sid Bolton too. You've no idea what children they all are really. Sometimes they squabble over me as though I had no say in the matter at all. But that's so like circus men. So masterful."

But the show had started, and at last Cora Frances turned her attention away from me and towards the ring. I waited impatiently for the first appearance of the clowns, which was after the first turn.

It was quite a small appearance, in which the three clowns came on and attempted to clear the ring of the previous properties and set up the apparatus for the next turn. They ran in now, Sid Bolton in front trailing a length of sacking on which the other two kept stepping and losing their balance to fall flat on the ground. They conspired together, with Sid blissfully unaware of them pretending to talk to the crowd, and then, their scheme hatched, they began to creep up on him. Meanwhile Sid had rolled the sacking up into a large bundle and was trying to auction it to the audience. "All right," he said in despair when no one would bid for it, "if you don't want it I'll throw it away," and with these words he pitched the bundle suddenly behind him, catching the two approaching clowns full in the face. A roar of laughter filled the tent as Clem and Eric fell once more on the ground.

Sid seemed to be overcome with remose, and ran quickly from one to the other helping them to stand and brushing the sawdust off them. "All I was doing," he explained to Eric, "was to throw the old sack away like *this*," and he flung his hand back in imitation of his action. Clem, who was in the way, seemed to catch the blow on the side of his cheek, although actually he clapped his hands together to make the sound of an imaginary blow. The laughter roared out again.

And now the quick climax of the act came. Each clown

began to slap the next one, shouting as if he himself were hit, until finally all three should lie prone on the ground to be moved roughly aside by the Dariennes when they came in for their act. The rolling laughter of the audience filled the tent as the slapping grew louder and the actions of the clowns more and more vigorous. Then suddenly Cora gripped my arm.

"My God," she said, "those slaps are real."

"Real?" I stared at the figures in the ring. They were no longer clapping their hands to imitate the sound of the face-slapping, but were actually hitting each other. Even as I realized this the audience seemed to feel that something was wrong and their laughter dwindled quickly to silence. One loud individual laughed persistently for a moment and then broke off in the middle. Amid a deadly silence from the crowd the three clowns faced each other on the sawdust and struck out. The heavy sound of the open-handed slaps echoed horribly.

Then slowly a murmuring spread over the audience, swelling into a continuous buzz, and I noticed the heads turning restlessly from side to side as people spoke to this or that neighbor.

"I must put a stop to this," whispered Cora in my ear, and giving her jacket a quick, almost masculine tug, she stood up and walked towards the ring. The audience was immediately silent again, watching her stepping briskly out under the hard lights to the center of the ring. When she reached the clowns she tugged at Clem's shoulder and said something which was inaudible to the audience.

"Don't you come poking your nose into our affairs," shouted Clem loudly, and then before she could move he brought his hand down in an immense whack on her behind. "Go on, get out," he said. The crowd, satisfied that is was a gag after all, roared louder than before and began to applaud the act enthusiastically.

The curtain at the end of the ring parted immediately and

the Darienne brothers, dressed ready for their trapeze act, ran quickly into the center of the ring and grabbed each of the clowns by an ear to lead them away. For a moment it looked as though they would be resisted, and then the clowns suddenly seemed to become aware of the huge applause coming from the house, and the effect was too great for them. With a few characteristic clowning tricks they were led from the ring.

Cora, however, made straight for the exit, and I followed as unobtrusively as possible and caught her up before she had gone very far.

"How terrible for you," I sympathized. "It was awfully brave of you, but really you ought not to have tried it."

To my surprise the face she turned to me was beaming. "Oh, but my dear," she said, "you don't know . . . it was too marvelous for words . . . doesn't it just show how much they think of me . . . right out there in the ring. And turning it into a joke too."

"But I thought he slapped you," I gasped.

"And how like these adorable creatures that was," gurgled Cora Frances. "So boisterous, so healthy. I've never been so excited in all my life. Right out there in front of the whole audience . . ."

"It was a little public," I admitted.

"But don't you see," she said, "that only proves how much they adore me. To make me one of themselves. You just can't imagine how pleased I am about it."

And to be quite honest, I don't think I could. Yet neither could I help seeing, in that display in the ring, something far less casual than Cora seemed to suspect. The venom which had been obvious to me could not be explained away by some little theory of petty jealousy. I felt that there was some antagonism much more fundamental at the root of it all.

CHAPTER XXVII

May 2nd.

THE next day's tober after South Cave was only a few miles along the road, so the circus did not need to start off as early as usual in the morning. The sun was already warm and the dew gone from the grass as the king-poles were hoisted into position. Ginger passed the wagon singing raucously with the heavy hammer balanced on his shoulder.

"How I love to hear the organ," he bellowed, with complete insincerity. And then, as he caught sight of me he stopped in mid-song to shout: "You want to go and have a look at old Kurt. Swinging the lead this morning, he is, the lazy beggar."

"What's the matter with him?" I asked.

"Miking," said Ginger briefly. "Never heard such a lot of fuss about nothing. Go and have a chat with him." And he jerked his thumb in the direction of the lion-trainer's wagon.

"What's up with him, then?" asked Beef, looking over my shoulder and wiping the remains of his shaving lather out of his ears.

"He *says*," answered Ginger, with fine scorn, "that he's ill. 'Orrible pains."

"Come on," said Beef, "let's go and see what's up."

We walked over towards Kurt's wagon, and even before we had reached it the sound of his voice raised in a shout could be heard.

"I tell you I want to see a doctor," he was demanding. "There's no good you looking like that. I'm not crazy. I want to see a doctor, that's all."

The door of the wagon opened and Jackson came down the steps shaking his head. When he saw us he beckoned Beef over.

"I don't know what's the matter with Kurt," he said. "It's either something serious, or else he's just trying to fool us."

"You mean about wanting a doctor?" asked Beef, and then added quickly: "We couldn't hardly help hearing what he was shouting the odds about."

"Yes," said Jackson. "It's just that. You know, of course, the almost superstitious dislike all circus people have of the medical profession. I have it myself, although I'm quite aware of the illogicality of it. But in all the years I've been in the circus I've never known a person actually *want* to see a doctor. And now Kurt is shouting that he must see one. Really I find it a little odd."

"We'll go and have a talk to him," said Beef. "Sounds as if he might be interesting."

Jackson waved his hand vaguely as if to say that he delivered the peculiarities of the lion-trainer over to us, and Beef approached the wagon and rapped sharply on the door.

"Come in," Kurt's voice invited. "Come in."

His eyes stared brightly and hopefully at us as Beef opened the door, and then, seeing who it was, he quickly pulled the bed-covers tightly up to his chin and shut his eyes determinedly.

"Now then," said Beef, "what's all this I hear? How are you feeling?"

"Considerably worse than I did two minutes ago," said Kurt pointedly.

Beef laughed. "Like that, is it?" he said. "Is there anything I can do for you?"

Kurt grunted and then leaned up on his elbow and looked at the Sergeant. "Look here," he said. "I only want one thing —and that is to see a doctor. The idiots round here seem to think that I'm playing a game on them and they won't help me."

"What do you think's the matter with you, then?" asked Beef.

Kurt stared at him for a second, and then said slowly: "I think I've been poisoned."

"Poisoned?" I gasped. "Who by? Have you got any idea who might have done it?"

"Here, wait a minute," said Beef. "Who's running this case, I'd like to know? You stick to your side of the business and I'll attend to mine." Then turning again to the lion-trainer, he went on: "What makes you think you've been poisoned?"

"I feel sick," said Kurt abruptly.

"Might have been something you had for supper," said Beef. "Lots of people get like that. I mean, do you think there's anybody who might want to do you in?"

I felt somehow that Beef was being over-flippant with what might possibly, even probably, be a genuine case, but he seemed also to realize this, for his next question was far more serious.

"No," he said, "all joking aside, can you tell me what you've been eating for the last twenty-four hours or so? I mean who cooks your meals and that?"

"I cook all my own food," said Kurt.

"Haven't eaten nothing but what passes through your own hands?" queried the Sergeant.

"Nothing," said Kurt decisively. Then: "No, wait a minute, that's a lie. I had a cup of tea yesterday afternoon that I didn't make myself. That's right, I forgot all about that."

"And where did you get that from?" asked Beef.

"Mrs. Jackson."

Beef suddenly became alert and brisk in his manner. "All right, Kurt," he said, standing up and moving towards the door, "I'll have a doctor up to see you just as fast as I can. Don't you worry now. It's probably not very serious, but there's no sense in taking risks."

When we were outside, and Beef had sent one of the hands off to fetch a doctor, I asked him if he really thought what he had told the lion-trainer.

"Well," he said, "you know how it is. Best thing to do with these nervy people is to make them feel it's going to get better. Worry never did anybody any good."

"Then you think it might be poisoning?" I asked.

"I don't waste my time thinking about things like that," said Beef. "There's a doctor coming along soon, and then we shall *know*. That's what's important."

"Then there's nothing for us to do but to wait?" I said.

"Well," said the Sergeant, "there's one or two little jobs I'd like to get off. You might give me a call when the doctor arrives. I'm going back to the wagon."

This seemed to me an obvious hint that I was not required, so I looked around for something to occupy myself with while Beef went back to our wagon. The big top always attracted me at this time of the day. The loneliness of its huge empty interior with the warm sun shining dully through the roof, the hot smell of crushed grass and canvas, the effect of being indoors and outdoors at the same time, all produced in me a peculiar sensation of a deep past knowledge of these things which now was forgotten. Perhaps it was the flower-shows I used to visit with my uncle at which the exhibits were seldom so exciting as the thick heavy atmosphere of the tent, somehow mixed up with the brassy music from the energetic local band playing outside, which had left in me some faint and almost untraceable remembrance rising again as a feeling of unease whenever I entered the deserted circus tent. There was, I felt, something uncanny and denaturalized in the presence of living grass in such a place, sprouting like a panache out of the center of the ring.

Instead of walking straight in through the normal front entrance of the tent, I lifted the side wall and slipped in under it. I was behind the tier of seats, but as I glanced between the boards I saw Jackson enter the ring and walk across it. For some reason I did not move or attempt to attract his attention, but stood perfectly still and watched him. He seemed preoccupied with his own thoughts, and his eyes never raised themselves from the ground just in front of his feet. When he reached the edge of the ring he bent down and hauled at the wire support of Daroga's wire-walking apparatus, walking backwards and so pulling it roughly into the correct position across the side of the ring. Then he fastened the end he had been holding loosely to one of the quarter-poles and began to examine the tightening screw half-way up the wire.

I began to feel slightly embarrassed in case he should glance up and see me. I was not hidden by the planks of the seating, and should he happen to turn his eyes in my direction he was bound to notice me. But I dared not move. As far as I could see, there appeared to be nothing suspicious about his action so far, and yet I had a feeling that it would be better somehow not to be discovered spying on him.

After a few minutes, apparently satisfied with his scrutiny, he returned the apparatus to its normal position between acts, and quickly left the tent. I waited a little while until he should get clear, and then left by the way I had entered, and went to find Beef to tell him what I had just witnessed.

Beef, however, as usual, was unimpressed when I told him

"That's right," he said. "As ring-master he's supposed to inspect all the apparatus before it's used."

"Perhaps so," I said a little damped, "but not necessarily at this time of the day. There's another three or four hours to the afternoon performance, so why was he sneaking around in there just now?"

"Shouldn't think there's very much in that," commented Beef. "Perhaps he wanted to save a bit of time, or perhaps it just struck him that something might be getting a bit worn somewhere. You know how, when you think of a thing, it's best to go and do it straight away. Perhaps . . ."

"Perhaps, perhaps, perhaps," I said, with exasperation. "It doesn't strike me that's a very good foundation on which to base one's investigation into a murder."

Beef grinned at me. "No, it isn't much of a way of doing things, is it?" he said, and shrugged his shoulders. "But there you are."

Beef in this sort of mood infuriated me, and I walked to the window in an attempt to conceal my feelings. A long black car was driving through the gate of the tober, and after stopping by one of the hands who was apparently giving information, it moved on toward Kurt's wagon.

"Here's the doctor, anyway," I told Beef, with a sense of relief, and he immediately jumped to his feet.

"Nice car," he commented, glancing out of the window. "Does well for himself. Come on, let's hear what he's got to say."

Actually the doctor had very little to say. There was no doubt that Kurt was ill, but the doctor seemed to think that it was nothing more than a slight breakdown. Kurt had been overworking for some time. On no account, the doctor said, must Kurt get up or do anything energetic for three or four days.

"If you can," he went on, "stay in bed for a week. But I know you people. You'll be up long before you should and working as usual. With a constitution like yours, of course, that's not very serious. But take my advice and rest as long as you can. If anything further develops, let me know straight away."

To Beef and me privately he confessed that he could not tell for sure whether the breakdown might not have been brought on by some sort of poisoning. But he doubted anything so romantic, and seemed to think the Sergeant was trying to pull his leg. He was a very prosaic little man and his imagination fitted his stature. Beef watched him walk fussily away, and then gave me a grin.

"I bet he was the sort of boy," he said, "that never read Sexton Blake because it was too 'far-fetched.' Just shows you, doesn't it?"

Beef did a great deal of writing and pondering in the wagon that night. He would sit in his chair staring blankly at the wall for long periods, and then suddenly grin at me. After one of these long periods of intense thought I could stand it no longer.

"What are you thinking about?" I asked.

"What, just then?" he said. "Well, I was just wondering what would happen to my window-boxes. I told Mrs. Beef to give them a look over now and again to see they was doing all right. But I bet she forgets all about them. Wouldn't like anything to happen to them."

"Great heavens!" I exclaimed, "I thought you were working on the case."

"Oh, you don't want to get yourself worried over that," said Beef comfortingly.

"Do you think you know everything now?" I asked eagerly.

Beef grinned boyishly. "I'm going to arrest Cora Frances tomorrow," he said.

"Cora Frances!" I gasped, with amazement. "Do you mean that . . ." And then something in the Sergeant's eye made me realize that I was having my leg pulled. "Beef, you're impossible," I said.

"That's what the missus says," agreed Beef.

At last I could stand it no longer and left the wagon. The last sound I heard as I closed the door behind me was Beef's derisive chuckle. The evening show had nearly finished, so I waited about the grounds until the people had crowded out and the big top began to come down.

I saw Ginger and Tug Wilson talking together, and wandered slowly across to them. They did not notice my approach, and I heard a few scraps of their conversation before I reached them.

"And that Bogli's Circus," Ginger was saying, "been trailing along after us for the last three or four days. Do you know they're going to be in the next village to us tomorrow?"

"Looking forward to another barney with them?" asked Tug.

"I reckon we've got enough on our hands without them," replied Ginger. "This circus is no bed of roses."

Tug leaned forward and put his hand on Ginger's sleeve. His face, turned sideways to me, was deeply shadowed and the hump on his back seemed to stand out more than usual against the canvas of the zoo behind them. "You want to remember one thing, though," he said.

"What's that?" asked Ginger.

"The ghost walks tomorrow night," answered Tug.

At this moment they both looked up and noticed me approaching and stopped their conversation immediately. We talked for a few minutes rather inconsequentially, and I left them as quickly as I could to return to the wagon.

"Here," I said as I burst into the wagon, "I just heard something very queer."

"Shut the door," said Beef, who was undressing for bed. "I'm not a peep-show."

I told him what I had heard pass between Tug Wilson and Ginger.

"The ghost walks, does it?" said Beef, struggling into his pajamas. "Well, I hope it keeps fine for it."

"Now, Beef," I began. But the Sergeant pulled the covers over his head and appeared to be paying no attention. "Good night," came his muffled voice from under the blankets.

CHAPTER XXVIII

May 2nd (continued).

As I commenced slowly to undress I thought briefly over the part I had so far played in this case. Surely I had done all that could be expected of an investigator's chronicler? I could think of no time when I had not lived up to my traditional role, nothing I had left undone which I ought to have done, or done that which I ought not to have done. At times had I not been the abject fool? I had asked all the right questions, showed excitement over every single piece of evidence, no doubt missing all that was really important; I had allowed Beef to snub every suggestion I had made, and yet shown no rancor or bitterness in reporting his suggestions. I had even, I thought mournfully, attempted to provide "interest" with what I was still not sure was not a real love-affair with Anita. Now, traditionally again, all that was left to me was to wait patiently for Beef to clarify the puzzle. The Sergeant appeared to have made up his mind.

But, I thought suddenly, if Beef had made up his mind, why should not I make up mine? There was nothing revolutionary in a chronicler having a theory. But why, for once, should not the chronicler's theory be correct? With this resolution I drew out paper and pen and ink, turned the lamp higher, and sat down at the table.

In the first place it seemed to me that if there was to be an attempt at murder in the circus, it must occur on the next day. Not only because Gypsy Margot had given a time limit in her prediction, and tomorrow was the last day of that period, but for other more immediate reasons. Tomorrow was the Jubilee performance. The circus had been running for twenty-five years, and this was, in a sense, a personal celebration of the artists. But it was still a public show, and because of the unusual feeling in the show about the importance of the event, I realized that all the artists would be keyed up for the performance. It should have been the best show the circus had ever given, we had been told, but so also, it might be the most tragic. An intending murderer could scarcely choose a time when the circus folk's attention would be less acute, less likely to notice small irregularities. And this gave the murderer the biggest chance of getting away with it.

I proceeded to run through the circus people, trying to assess them, and take into consideration all that we had learned of them since we had been with the show. Somewhere among them, we had to suppose, was a murderer, and somewhere was a person on whose life there was going to be an attempt. Only tomorrow's show would tell us for sure which of them fitted into these roles.

I felt as I wrote that there was something unreal about considering people as possible murderers, but that was the only possible way of producing a case.

Jackson was obviously the man to begin with. That cold, cynical face was like a mask on the real man, a mask which looked at the circus he was running as if it were no more than some halfpenny peep-show. Did he really think all people were fools? Or was it some inadequacy in him which required cynicism and sarcasm as a defense against a world a little too big for him? In this particular case, I felt, it was the characters themselves which were the clues, and their actions, thoughts, behavior, which made up the evidence. It was as important to decide what sort of a man Jackson really was, as to discover why he had been so agitated about the button Beef discovered in his wagon.

The button seemed, in some way, to link him with the wire-walker. Of all the people in the circus there was only Daroga who was not afraid of the proprietor. Even Corinne, with her defiance and ostentatious selfishness, was nervous with her father. She lost, as everybody else did in his presence, her self-complacent scorn for anything outside herself. Mrs. Jackson had shown her own feelings only too clearly on that day when Anita had been stabbed; she had scuttled back to the wagon to get her husband's supper not in the way some wives do—to keep peace in the house—but because of Jackson himself. Eric, perhaps, was harder to understand. He seemed to keep well out of his father's way as much as possible, but whether from fear or because he simply disliked trouble was difficult to decide. And yet Daroga, in every meeting between the two, had shown complete self-confidence. What was there between the two men which always gave Daroga the whip hand? When the circus had pitched into the wrong tober it had been Jackson who scurried off to change the booking with the landlord. When there had been trouble over a new elephant-man, it had been Daroga who triumphed, and the man still worked in the show, despite Jackson's obvious disapproval.

Was Jackson the sort of man who could stand this belittling of his dignity? And if he could not, what would his action be? It seemed fairly clear that he was being blackmailed by the wire-walker; it was almost certain that Daroga knew something about Jackson which the proprietor wished to keep quiet. Suppose the way he chose out of this difficulty were the way of murder. There had been the small incident in the empty tent when I had watched Jackson inspecting the wire-walking apparatus. Perhaps that had its significance here. But if Jackson were in some way to make the apparatus unsafe, surely there was little chance of his doing more than disabling Daroga? There could be no point in that. Daroga must have had many accidents on the wire in his time. They were often serious enough, though never likely to prove fatal. But perhaps there was some way Jackson has discovered of making the wire a death-trap; some way which Daroga would not be able to foresee.

Before leaving Jackson I tried to think for a moment if there was anybody else he might possibly kill. Gypsy Margot seemed to be trying to break up the show; at least, we had Jackson's own word that he suspected her of that. Might he not try to murder her in an attempt to stop her influence over the others? There was even a third possibility. Jackson might be nothing more than the traditional father jealous of his daughter's honor. If it seemed to him likely that Corinne would compromise herself with young Torrant, and so leave the show, would Jackson stop at mere words in order to prevent it? Of course, looked at coldly, this made the whole thing appear fantastic, but I had to start with the supposition of murder in order to draw up something of a case, so that I must face even the most fanciful of possibilities.

One of the only factual clues we had been lucky enough to find had been the button picked up by Beef in the proprietor's wagon. Did that in some way link Jackson with Daroga? The proprietor had claimed the button as his own, and yet the wording on it had been in Russian, from which country the wire-walker had originally come. How did it fit into the relationship between the two men, and what part was it likely to play in tomorrow's show? It might possibly be the clue on which many things hung.

Of Daroga himself we seemed to know even less than we knew about Jackson. Quiet, experienced, apparently well-liked by the rest of the artists, he had the sort of frank, open manner which only left one more intrigued. Born in Russia, he had lived the life of an exile since his earliest infancy. In that life there must have been much suffering, hunger, occasionally, perhaps, fits of desperation against circumstances which had been inexplicably harder for him than for others. One could imagine such a life souring a man, making him hate the rest of humanity. But Daroga, if he hated anyone at all, appeared only to hate Jackson. And in this there seemed to be more contempt than real hatred. If, as we suspected, Daroga was blackmailing the proprietor, what had he to gain by murdering him? A blackmailer seldom murders his victim. And besides, there had been no incident which pointed to this desire. But on the other hand, it must be remembered that Daroga was in charge of the elephants, one of which had already attempted to kill a man. These animals could be made to do very curious things, as we had seen in the incident when Albert Stiles had been ducked in the village pond. Could Daroga have some scheme in which the elephants themselves played the part of murderers? Jackson was the ring-master and had to be present during the elephant act. There seemed to be no other person against whom Daroga bore the slightest animosity.

If one were looking for people with a grouch against the world there was no better example in the show than Peter Ansell. His cynicism was far more deep-rooted than Jackson's because it had behind it a kind of developed philosophic anarchism. He was more impersonal in his dislike of people. It seemed that it was not so much that they had done wrong to him, or given him a too slender chance in life, as that they were ant-like and remote. I did not agree with his conclusions in the least, but I could appreciate his detachment.

The only part he played in the life of the circus was in his love for Corinne, but we had no knowledge of how strong that love could be. He had shown no jealousy as far as I had noticed, but he might have been given no cause yet. He had, moreover, been one of the five present when the tiger had escaped. Had he been the one responsible for that incident? And if so, what had been the intention behind it? During the actual performance, however, he did not appear in the ring and it was difficult to foresee what action he could take.

It was clear that the only motive he might have would be centered in Corinne. He disliked the circus and would not be worried at leaving it. In fact, he probably would have done so before now had it not been for Corinne Jackson.

But Corinne herself wanted to be free of the circus. Anita had told us this, and it was easily visible in the girl's manner. When she appeared in the ring it was with an air that she was conferring benefits on an audience who should be overjoyed by her condescension. She had, as they say, other ideas, and those ideas were concentrated outside the influence of the saw-dust ring. She would never be content to follow the age-old traditions of circus families, training their children to continue with the act or start out with new ones. She might not be happy away from the circus, but there was no doubt that she wanted to get away. These affairs she had with young men were only one aspect of this desire. From what Herbert Torrant had said to Beef, it did not seem that she looked to any of these ephemeral suitors as an actual means of leaving the circus, but each of them did show where her sympathies lay. And yet when she was performing in the ring she seemed to be a different person altogether. I remembered once, as she rode round the ring, watching her face. She was doing a turn I had never seen before—an equestrian act which had replaced the Concinis for a while after the stabbing affair. She did not seem to notice the audience very much, but it was not the scornful disregard of her normal appearances. It was rather as if she had been caught up in the act and was thrilled by it. She and the horse performed perfectly together, as if through long habit. Yet I had never seen her rehearsing the act at any time. She was a very clever and daring rider. Why did she only show the horses and the absurd Eustace? It seemed that she was consciously limiting her part in the show as a gesture of her dislike. No other theory could reconcile her obvious enjoyment of the riding act, and the fact that normally she never rode for the show.

Corinne was deliberately flaunting young Herbert Torrant in front of the other members of the troupe. She had led him into a pub where she most probably knew they would be collected, and at that point had insisted on holding his arm, an act which had apparently never been repeated. Who was she trying to impress? Kurt? But she took the trouble to calm any suspicions he might have, and, in any case, had never treated him as anything else but a friend, despite his obvious love for her. It was hardly the way to make him jealous. Ansell? But why should she try to make Ansell jealous in public, when whatever affair she was having with him was being conducted in private? It was a relationship of which, I believed, only Beef and I had any knowledge. But in this light there seemed to be no reason why she should attempt to keep Kurt in love with her by friendly words and gestures.

To think of Corinne as a murderess seemed completely far-fetched. She was selfish to an extreme degree no doubt, but so far as I could see, she had no motive for such an act. We had seen her almost feline exasperation with Eric when he had been teasing her, but that did not seem important enough to note as a likely reason for murder. Her fear of her father might at some point become fruitful, but even so, it was difficult to see the girl as a murderess.

Kurt was slow, stodgy perhaps, but he was not a fool. He had a streak of solid obstinacy common to people who have had to make themselves fit to undertake a certain sort of job despite personal handicaps. Illiterate, short-tempered, Kurt had taken up lion-training much in the way, if he had lived in South Wales, he might have taken up coal-mining. Lion-training was to him a normal sort of way of earning one's living. As in most other jobs, you were all right so long as you did not make mistakes. After that came pride in doing it well.

Kurt was proud of his act, even thinking sometimes that it was too good for Jacobi's Circus. But in most things he was honest and straightforward. He was in love with Corinne Jackson and did not try to hide it. Neither did he try to hide the jealousy he felt when Corinne picked up stray young men. But would he be quite so outright and honest if he discovered there was something between her and the animal-feeder, Peter Ansell?

When the tiger had escaped from its cage Kurt had shown immense personal courage in dealing with the untrained beast, and it had only been his sureness which had saved what might have been a very nasty situation. But at other times he had shown an unreasonable surliness to Beef and myself, and there was no denying his jealous disposition. I felt that in some respects Kurt was dangerous. It was not easy to define precisely why, but I had a clear picture of his enthusiastic hand-rubbing when the fight with Bogli's Circus had been pending. And Bogli's Circus was still in the district. If Kurt were likely to commit the murder, it was Torrant and Ansell who stood in his way over Corinne.

Since, however, he was ill, he would not be appearing in the show tomorrow. What was this strange sudden illness? Could he really have been poisoned, as he seemed to suspect? Who did he suspect of wanting to poison him? Or could it possibly be something more underhand and cunning than that? He might not be sick at all, but pretending illness for a special reason of his own.

As the personnel of the circus ran through my mind I tried to find what it was which made all these people alike in some way. It was not that they were all circus people, but, strangely enough, that they all had some grudge or other against the circus itself. Even Jackson, the proprietor, seemed to share this with them. Were all the others the same? And if so, what was the cause of it?

Sid Bolton was surely an exception. But the memory of the street fight we had with Bogli's Circus made me think of Sid in a new light. I had noticed then the peculiar venom in the way he had attacked people he not only did not know, but against whom he had no personal enmity at all. I had come to the conclusion then that it must have been a sense of personal wrong done to him by the whole world, a bitterness left in him from those days when he had sat in a booth on the fair-ground to be laughed at by unthinking people for being the "fat boy." And again in the ring this afternoon he had shown the same attitude. When the three clowns had been striking at each other in dead earnest I had no doubt that, as far as Sid Bolton was concerned, it was no personal grudge he felt against the other two, but a general feeling which somehow was only able to express itself in violence of a personal kind. But would he always choose his fists as the best weapon of striking back at a world he hated?

For Eric Jackson and Clem Gail, again, the fight had meant something entirely different. Eric was the most brilliant clown I had seen in the ring for a long time; he had nothing to envy the others; and yet the intensity which he, like the others, had shown, proved there was something behind it. Perhaps the clue lay in his treatment of his sister. I suspected that his bantering, flippant behavior with her, showed a sympathy with her ideas. That he, too, perhaps, felt cramped and dwarfed in the circus and would not be sorry to leave it. But he had far less chance than she, so that it would have been foolish to hope for much in that direction. If that were true, then to a certain extent the other actions followed. But although he felt frustrated as the clown in his father's circus, he might not be quite so antagonistic had he been in his own.

Neither could that fight have arisen entirely from Clem's drunkenness. Perhaps the clue lay in Clem himself. When we had first met Clem we had become aware of a dual personality; the extremely handsome young man who resented his anonymity in the ring. He was vain, and more than a little proud of his success with women, but those qualities did not necessarily constitute a murderer. In what way, then, could he be considered as one? Although the fight in the circus ring had shown what bitterness each of the clowns could feel, it did not necessarily show against whom it might be directed. Had Clem's treatment of Cora Frances been a gesture of sudden disgust, of loathing for the painter, or had it been simply the heat of the moment? At the little luncheon-party Clem had been on his guard against Cora Frances. She had bored him, but had that boredom turned suddenly, with her intrusion into the ring, into nausea? Or was the whole thing the revealing of a concealed hate for the two other clowns?

Neither could one assume that Cora was "above suspicion." Foolishness had, before now, been used in a murder case as a stalking-horse. Her apparent simple pleasure with everything the circus people did might, in reality, conceal her deeply wounded vanity. It was difficult to believe that she could actually enjoy being humiliated before the entire audience of the circus, and it would be foolish to take her own statement to this effect on its face value. Already she had angered Daroga by tampering with the elephants, and although it had only been in order to paint their toe-nails, there might be something much more serious behind it. The clowns were in the ring at the same time as the elephants, and in case of trouble would be the people most likely to be hurt. Was it possible that Cora would retaliate on Clem through the elephants?

Four people, bound close together in this case, were the Darinne brothers, Suzanne, and Len Waterman. In the first place there had been an affair between Len and Suzanne, so much was clear from the photograph in Len's wagon, and from what we had been told by Margot. But equally clear now was the fact that Suzanne was in love with Christophe. What would Len do about that? The lights had fused in the middle of their act under very peculiar circumstances, when Len alone had been responsible for the lights. If Len had been trying to kill Suzanne, or one of the Dariennes, then, would he not try again? And next time such an accident might prove fatal. On the other hand, did Christophe know of the previous affair between Suzanne and Len Waterman? If so, must there not be some resentment against the electrician; even against Suzanne herself? The relation between Paul and his brother complicated this even further. From the first I had felt there was something uncanny in Paul's dependence on his brother, something which defied a clear analysis. But the emotion Paul must undoubtedly feel would be very close to jealousy. That he knew nothing about the affair between his brother and Suzanne was doubtful. He had not known a few days ago when the little incident about Suzanne learning French had occurred. But there had been time for him to suspect much since then. Margot might have spoken to him, or even Len Waterman. There was no doubt that he feared the loss of his brother more than anything else in the world. But Suzanne herself must be considered in this light. Paul stood in her way. Without him she would be able to love Christophe openly. And there were many things which might happen on the high trapeze without arousing people's suspicions. Could it be possible that one of those three was at this minute planning the death of another? Some little slip of the hand, a miscalculation in leaping, and it would be difficult even for a detective to say whether it had been an accident or not.

Tug Wilson was a character I had almost forgotten to include in the possible murderers. Yet in some ways he seemed the most sinister of them all. What had he meant by the phrase: "The ghost walks tomorrow"? If he had a scene for tomorrow night's performance, this must include Ginger, since it was to this lad that the words had been addressed. Were there more than just those two in it? Many of the other tent hands were surly, and were often treated by the proprietor as less than human beings. Could it be possible that it was against Jackson that this plot was aimed? The phrase in itself was no proof, but if looks revealed intentions, there were many among the hands who would be glad to get even with Jackson for some of his biting words. Tug himself was almost too villainous to be a villain, with his dark face and loosely hanging hands. But he was an unknown quantity. Ginger I knew and liked, and I did not feel that he could easily be suspected of a murder. But a group of men banded together will often do things which none of them singly would have wished. I felt we had neglected the tent hands in our investigations.

But what of the old woman who was behind this case? It was Gypsy Margot who had first predicted the murder, and whose daughters had given us the first hint that there might be something in her prediction. Jackson himself seemed to think that she would be pleased to see the circus break up. That might be true, but would she go to the length of committing a murder to achieve her end? She was a strange person, and it was not fantastic to suppose that she knew much more than her peculiar talk revealed. She might, in a sense, be daring us. The sort of challenge which had been issued enough times before in detective stories, by the intending murderer to the detective. Suppose she meant to commit the crime herself and was getting a strange satisfaction out of watching Beef and me turning our attention away from her to the other members of the circus. She hated Jackson because he had taken over the circus from her brother years before, and would now be glad to see Jackson broken. She might try to kill Jackson himself, or, what would be far cleverer, murder any other member of the troupe. Her end would probably be achieved in either case, but the latter would be far more difficult to prove. A murder without a motive would be almost impossible to trace in the conditions under which the circus worked.

And then, was there anything at all in the theory of hypnosis? Anita admitted that her mother was a hypnotist, but insisted that it could not be used to do harm. But Anita had also admitted that she was a bad subject, so that if Margot had been using her powers evilly she would scarcely have used Anita, or even told her about it. If Helen had been hypnotized when she stabbed her sister, the same method might be used again. But if even the first stabbing had been quite simply a sudden revulsion from the likeness between the twins, there was still a possibility of it occurring again. This time it might be successful. Could it have been that Gypsy Margot had foreseen the outbreak between her two daughters? I wished suddenly that Anita had not decided to appear in the ring again tomorrow. If only she could have rested for another day or two, I felt the danger-point would have passed. But now she was placing herself in danger unnecessarily, and the thought sickened me.

Well, there they were. All the people connected with the circus. Two or more of them would be mixed up in an attempted murder by this time tomorrow night, and it was impossible still to do more than guess which ones it would be. There must be some way, I thought to myself, of limiting the possible murderers to some two or three. Then it would make the Jubilee show much less nerve-racking. Perhaps if I ran over the salient points once again I might get some clue. But as I turned the sheets, Beef's voice suddenly startled me.

"Have you got it all worked out nice?" he asked. I had thought him asleep, but I suppose he had been watching all this time, smiling to himself over my attempts to get the whole case clear.

"At least, I've got the evidence in order," I said abruptly.

"Do you know who's going to murder who?" went on Beef relentlessly.

"Well, not exactly," I replied. "But I do know who might commit the murder, and who might be killed."

Beef chuckled. "So do I," he said, "if you don't put that light out and come to bed."

CHAPTER XXIX

May 3rd.

I SHALL never forget that day. The quick succession of events, the feeling of an almost unbearably hastening time, made me feel that I was being pitched forward into something of which my powers of observation were too slow to take full account. Actually there was no particular rush in the early morning. It had been decided, because of this day of the Jubilee performance, to cut out the afternoon matinée show altogether. We moved on to the next tober more than an hour after the usual time, and by the time we arrived there the Sergeant was up and dressed, a fact which by itself denoted the lateness of the hour. Beef was in a silent mood, and made no reference to the previous night. We ate without speaking, while he glanced cursorily over the newspaper. At last he wiped his mouth, and taking a long and noisy gulp from his tea-cup he turned to me.

"Well," he said, "nearly time I was off."

"Off?" I was aghast. "Surely you're not going anywhere today?" I asked.

"That's right," he said complacently.

"But what about the murder?" I demanded. "There's the Jubilee show tonight. You're not going to miss that, are you?"

"I might be back in time," said the Sergeant. "But I can't be sure. There might be more to do than I bargained for."

"But this is madness," I said. "We've been collecting evidence all this time, and then on just the one day that the murder is bound to happen, you decide to go away somewhere. Surely it's not as important as all that? It can wait a few days."

"Who told you there was going to be a murder today?" asked Beef.

"Well, nobody told me," I admitted. "But it's obvious. And I thought you knew who was going to commit it. You've been behaving as if you knew."

"I know what somebody's going to try on," said Beef, "and I'm going to stop it."

"And how are you going to stop it?" I asked.

"I'm going to get the one who means business before anything can come of it."

"So you're going off for the day?" I asked sarcastically.

"That's right," agreed Beef. "There's a bit more evidence I need before I can lay my hands on the one I want, and I'm going to get it. Take a run round some of the old tobers and see what I can find out."

"What in heaven's name can you get from the places we've left?" I demanded. "When the circus leaves a village it's finished with. You might get a little pub gossip, but what do you expect to find in the way of evidence?"

"You leave that to me," said Beef reassuringly.

"But do you mean just the tober we've left this morning, or farther back?" I asked.

Beef shrugged. "Can't hardly say," he said. "Might be six, might be seven, might be as much as eight tobers back."

"It doesn't make sense," I said despairingly. "You say you're going to stop the murderer, and yet today is the day the thing is most likely to happen, and you go away. I don't care if you get enough evidence to hang the murderer fifteen times over—I still can't understand why you must go off today."

"Now don't you worry about that," said Beef. "I know what I'm doing. Can I take the car?"

But I could not be persuaded as easily as that. I felt that Beef was behaving with unexampled stupidity. Almost anything might happen at this Jubilee show, and yet he calmly told me not to worry, and wanted to borrow the car for the day as if he were going off on a little spree. Was this an admission of defeat? If anything went wrong this would be the end of Beef. I perceived only too clearly that the Sergeant might, after all, know no more than I about the possible murderer. Perhaps he knew even less, and my list of the previous night might be more useful in the end than his investigations. At least, it was a complete summary of all we had found out.

But was it? Suddenly I realized, with a clarity that sickened me, that there was one name I had forgotten to add to the list of possible victims; and that name was my own. I had been taking my role as chronicler too much for granted, had imagined that I stood securely outside the whole affair. And yet the opposite was true, as I saw now. There was hardly an incident of importance at which I had not been present. I had been one of those whose lives were threatened by the escaped tiger, I had taken part in the street fight with Bogli's Circus, Anita and I had been approaching the elephant-tent when the new hand had been thrown out, I had been present at Cora Frances's luncheon-party and later sat beside her during that frightening exhibition in the ring.

In fact, I was linked to the circus much more closely than Beef himself was. Why had I not seen this before? Until now I had seen the curious affair with Anita as having only a purely personal importance. But these few days had shown us that the circus was riddled by jealousy and suspicion, and quite unconsciously I had been dragged into the center of the danger. Which way should I look for my possible attacker? From Helen? From Old Margot? Or from some unexpected direction, one of the other men who envied my success with the quiet, lovely Anita?

It might even be that one of the women was jealous. All false modesty aside, it was quite possible that a young successful writer like myself, good-looking, cultured, with easy, pleasant manners, might cause some stir among the feminine element in Jacobi's Circus. Perhaps I had been too absorbed in Anita and in the murder case to notice anything of this sort. But there was no excuse for not realizing that my monopoly of the young equestrienne might cause trouble. This was no time for self-congratulation, however. I must think of some way of placing myself out of this danger.

My first instinct was to offer to go off with Beef for the day, but I saw quickly that this would be absurd. One of us at least must remain with the circus, and since the Sergeant had already made his plans to leave, then I, despite the personal danger, must remain. It would do no harm, though, to take some measures to defend myself.

"What happened to your revolver?" I asked as casually as I could.

Beef grinned. "Getting the wind up?" he asked.

"Well, at least," I said a little irritated by his manner, "I ought to be prepared in case there's any sort of attempt. And since you've taken it into your head . . ."

"All right, all right," said Beef. "If it'll make you feel any the more comfortable I'll tell you this. Nobody's going to try anything on tonight."

"How can you possibly say a thing like that?" I demanded. "How do you know there won't be a murder?"

"I'll tell you after, how I know," replied the Sergeant, "but there won't be one. I shall be back here all right before any attempt is made, just remember that."

"I should feel far safer if I had the revolver," I said.

"You don't want that," coaxed Beef, as if he were trying to persuade a child not to eat some obnoxious sweet. "Might do yourself no end of harm mucking about with a loaded revolver."

"Don't be absurd," I said indignantly. "I'm not a child. I know how to look after myself. I'd just like to have it in case of emergencies."

"All right," said Beef at last. "I'll lend you my gun if you let me borrow your car."

"If you're determined to proceed with this 'investigation'," I said sourly, "I suppose I can't stop you. And in that case you may as well take the car."

"Fine," said Beef. "Now I'm just going over to see Kurt, and then I'll be off."

He was not with the lion-trainer more than a few minutes, and when he returned he looked a little worried. "He seems in a pretty bad way, poor fellow," he said. "Wouldn't do no harm for you to take a look at him later on and see if he wants anything."

As the Sergeant climbed heavily into the driving-seat of my car about half an hour later, he leaned over and said to me: "Now look after yourself. Keep your eyes open and don't let nothing escape you. I'll be back as soon as I've got what I want."

"That's all very well," I said bitterly, "but it would be far better if you weren't going at all."

"Nonsense," said Beef, pressing his foot on the starter. "Everything's going to be all right." And with that the car moved forward towards the gate of the tober, and I turned a little wearily back to the wagon.

Beef's revolver, which he had so amusedly left with me, turned out to be one of very ancient and unbusiness-like design. With a memory of George Raft I tried to stuff it into my hip pocket, but the end projected awkwardly, and contrived to pinch me when I sat down. Neither would it fit into any of my pockets except those in my overcoat. I could scarcely walk about the grounds in the boiling sunshine wearing an overcoat, so that I was forced to compromise and leave the thing near the door of the wagon hidden under a towel. Anyway, it was, as Beef would have said, "handy" in case I needed it.

It was significant that other people beside myself were concerned at Beef's absence on this particular day. Even Ginger seemed to have a feeling that it was a serious mistake on the Sergeant's part.

"What's he done that for?" he asked. "Suppose something happens?"

"He had very important business to attend to," I said loyally, and not knowing how much of the Sergeant's movements he wanted known among the rest of the circus.

Ginger shook his head. "He's a card, he is," he commented. "Still, I expect he knows what he's doing. Hope there's no trouble, that's all."

"Are you expecting any?" I asked quickly.

"Haven't you heard?" Ginger looked amazed.

"Heard what?"

"Them Bogli's Circus people are coming over," answered Ginger. "Coming over to see the show."

"How can they?" I protested. "They have their own performance to run. Do you mean they'll be coming over afterwards?"

"No, that's what's funny," explained Ginger. "They're not giving one. Never heard of such a thing before. But that's what I was told. They said that seeing as how this was such an important show for us, and seeing as how they were in the district themselves, they'd cut their own gate, so that more people would come to see us. Then they said they'd be coming themselves, *and* they'd pay. Queer, I call it." Ginger shook his head. "Whoever heard of circus people paying to go to see another circus? Fishy, if you ask me."

"And you think they may give some trouble?" I asked.

"Well, there's no harm in being ready in case they do," said Ginger, and gave me a broad wink, which I interpreted as meaning that preparations had already been made for the followers of Bogli's Circus.

In the afternoon I decided to look in on Kurt to see how he was feeling. As I crossed the tober I noticed a familiar car drawn up in front of the proprietor's wagon. It was Herbert Torrant's, and he himself was standing by the steps of Jackson's wagon, talking earnestly to Corinne. He did not see me, but in a few moments turned and walked down towards the village, accompanied by the girl. It must have been a good seventy miles drive for him, and I wondered what had made him come so far. Corinne's young men, I had learned, were not usually so persistent.

Kurt, I realized directly I saw him, was very ill. His face was white and looked thinner than only a day before. When I entered his wagon he leaned up on his elbow to greet me. The sickness did not seem to have sapped his strength much, but he was nervous, and his fingers fidgeted on the sheet. After a few ordinary questions about the routine of the circus he led the conversation round to Corinne, and asked me if I had seen her that day.

"As a matter of fact," I said incautiously, "I saw her just as I was coming over here. She was talking to that young Torrant chap."

Kurt seemed immediately interested. "When did he come over?" he asked.

"I don't really know," I confessed. "I only noticed his car a few minutes ago. Some time this afternoon I suppose it must have been."

"A long way to come," said Kurt. "What do you think made him come all that way?"

"I suppose," I said, "he's got some idea about the circus being terribly romantic and so on. Most people outside the show see you people in a rather rosy glow, you know."

This seemed to comfort him a little and he lay back in bed without speaking for several minutes.

"Is there anything you'd like me to get for you?" I asked.

He shook his head impatiently, and it was obvious he was still thinking about Corinne and Herbert Torrant. "You don't think, then," he said after a moment, "that he's come across just to see Corinne? You don't think there's anything in it?"

"Who?" I asked, pretending not to know what he was talking about.

"Corinne and young Torrant, of course," he said. "Of course, she's picked up all sorts of young men before, but they've always drifted away. I expect she feels a bit hemmed in in the circus. You can understand that. She isn't the sort of person for this life. She ought to have something better."

I decided that it was best not to answer his question and merely grunted non-committally.

"I know what she wants," he went on, "she's told me often enough. Comfort, and clothes, and people to call on her, something a bit more steady than this forever moving along, as if there was a policeman behind you all the time. I think I'd like to settle down myself sometimes—but what could I do?"

I let him talk himself out of it, and then, when he was calmer, I left the wagon quietly, with a promise to call in again at the first opportunity. I did not want to stay in his wagon while everybody else was getting ready for the show.

There was still an hour or two before the performance and I decided to spend it around the tober. The few people who had come along early, either not knowing that the afternoon show had been cut, or because they expected something special from the Jubilee, were being entertained for the most part in the Wild Animal Zoo. Quite a large crowd was in the enclosure when I entered, spread fairly evenly around the cages. Something, however, began to occur in the monkey cage, and the crowd moved quickly over towards it, so that I had some difficulty in seeing over their heads. One of the smallest monkeys had been stretching out of the cage to grab a banana from a visitor, and had succeeded in getting his head right through one of the holes in the cage. But there it had stuck, and the crowd's amusement was caused by his frantic efforts to get himself loose and at the same time retain the banana, with which his pouches were already stuffed.

"Laugh," said a voice behind me. "Go on, laugh, you ignorant lot of blighters. Laugh!"

I turned, to discover Sid Bolton close at my elbow. "You sound very bitter," I commented.

"Well, look at them," he said, indicating the crowd in front of the cage. "They're all like that. They don't know what they're laughing at, they don't think, they just laugh. Open their great mouths and roar at the slightest chance."

"I suppose the basis of most humor is the discomfort of others," I observed.

"Humor," Sid was scornful. "People don't laugh like that at humor. That sort of laugh is hate. People hating anything a little bit like themselves. Everybody has some small fear, some stupidity or ugliness he wants to hide. And when he sees it in others he laughs, he roars, because he hates seeing himself so clearly. That little monkey, frightened and greedy, is like a mirror for most of the people here. Somewhere, they're all frightened and greedy. So they laugh. Listen to them. Aren't they horrible?"

Without waiting for my answer Sid Bolton turned away in disgust and left the enclosure. How bitter he had sounded. I realized afresh how deeply this aversion for human beings had sunk. It must have sprung from those early days on the fair-ground, when people had paid to laugh at him because he was fat. But it had grown and blossomed into a loathing which now seemed almost to dominate his life.

I wandered round the zoo until I noticed Peter Ansell beside the lions' cages. He appeared to have noticed me some time before, for when I looked up he had a quiet smile on his lips, as if I amused him. Perhaps my nervousness was noticeable. I had not thought of it before, but I must have been pacing along with an intensely worried expression on my face, altogether unusual in me.

"Don't you ever do any work?" I asked, with an attempt at cheerfulness.

Ansell slowly removed the cigarette from his lower lip and looked at me. "I seem to have the night off tonight," he said with a smile. "I shall be able to come in and watch the show with the big nobs."

"Why, aren't you . . ." I began, and then realized what he was talking about. "Oh, of course, there can't be a lion act while Kurt is ill, can there? I'd forgotten about that."

"Oh, I could have handled them," said Ansell airily, "but nobody asked me, so why should I put myself out? As a matter of fact, Clem Gail's going to do a little tumbling act of his own to fill in the program."

"Tumbling? I didn't know he was an acrobat!"

"Good heavens," Ansell was amused. "Clem's a damn good little acrobat. That's what's such a shame about it. Jackson will never let him do anything but clowning, and Clem just sits there and says nothing. I know what I'd do in his place. I'd made a stink about it. Jackson seems to think he owns the world. It would do him good for someone to take him up on that sometime. But they're like a lot of poodles when it comes to sticking up for themselves."

"How right you are," said a familiar voice behind us, and there was no need to turn round to recognize Cora Frances. "Isn't that just what I've been telling you all?" she went on. "Anything for a quiet life, that's what's the matter with most of the people here. I hate a quiet life."

"Be a bit late to start trying it," said Ansell quietly to me.

"What I say is," swept on Cora Frances, "if everybody insisted on getting their own way, like I do, the world would be a far happier place. Why, if everybody got their own way there'd be no such things as unemployment, or Mussolini, or football coupons, or pedestrian crossings, or . . ."

"In fact," said Ansell, "there'd be hardly anything at all."

"Not a thing," agreed Cora. "That's the beauty of the scheme. But, of course, it's too Utopian. We can only do our best in little things, that's what I believe in. Now tonight, for instance, I've just had my own way about those elephants."

"The elephants?" I asked, with a strange suspicion of what was coming.

"Yes," cooed Cora Frances. "I managed to persuade the new hand to let me enamel their toe-nails. I said to myself, if the elephants can have gilded toe-nails for the Coronation, I see no reason why they should not be painted for the Jubilee."

"Does Daroga know?" asked Ansell.

"But of course not. It will be such a surprise to him."

"But he'll be furious," I said in amazement. "You know what he was like last time."

"Oh, my dear, this traditionalism," said Cora. "He'll get used to it in time. There has to be a first time for everything. I think he'll be thrilled to bits really."

Personally, I doubted this, but there was no point in arguing the matter further. There was simply no limit to the way Daroga would behave when he found Cora had been tampering with his elephants. The trick she had played was so stupid that it seemed diabolically clever. I looked closely at the artist, and it struck me that her face looked tired and the lines around her eyes could not be completely hidden, however made-up she was. Had there been a shade of strain in her voice too? It was so difficult to tell in this woman, who was putting on an act all her life, whether she was acting for a different reason.

"Oh, by the way," she said coyly, just as she was about to

leave us, "Anita asked me to give you a message." She came close to me, with the exaggerated pretense of whispering in my ear, although when she spoke Ansell must have heard quite clearly.

"She said she'd like to speak to you when you have a moment to spare," she said. "She'll be over by her wagon."

Whatever had possessed Anita to use Cora Frances as a messenger I did not know, but it seemed the height of foolishness to me. If there was any jealousy about us, Cora would be bound to spread the news of our meeting and the message, it would only exaggerate any danger I already stood in. I wished Anita might have been a little more thoughtful over it.

It was with a pleasant anticipation, however, that I walked over to see what she wanted. She was seated on the foot of the wagon-steps, in the attitude in which I had first seen her reading one of my books. Strangely enough, she had it in her hands now.

"I've just finished your book," she said, as soon as I had approached.

"And what did you think of it?" I asked expectantly.

"I think," she said, "that I never want to speak to you again."

"Good heavens, what are you talking about?" I asked with surprise.

"I've only just realized what you've been doing in this case of yours," she said vehemently. "I'm just a 'love interest,' that's all I am. You've been using me for your next book, and you've been pretending to like me because it might be useful to you, because it might help to sell the book."

"But Anita," I tried to interrupt.

"You're not a human being at all," she stormed. "You're just a poking prying writer, who only wants to know people's affairs to make money out of them. All right then. This time

it's not going to work out the way you want it to. You want
the reader to go on to the end of the book, in case anything
happens between you and me. Well, I can tell them now,
that it won't. I'm not going to have anything more to do
with you. This is the end of the love interest as far as I'm
concerned, so you'd better hurry up and find someone else,
while there's still time." And with that she ran quickly up
the steps of the wagon, and slammed the door behind her
before I had a chance to say anything.

There was no doubt that she had reason enough for what
she had said. On the surface it did look as though I was
behaving in a peculiarly cold-blooded way. But she might
have given me a chance to clear myself—or did I want to clear
myself? I was not quite sure on that point, even now. In
any case, I thought ruefully as I walked away from the wagon,
she had been extremely violent over the affair. Had she
actually been in love with me, or was there something else
behind it? Had not there been something just a little
exaggerated in her anger? I could find nothing to completely
explain her attitude.

By the time I had wandered back to the box-office, there was
a long queue already formed there. I had a strange feeling
that I was looking at the audience for the last show Jacobi's
Circus would ever give. Could there be anything in that feeling? And yet, when one realized that the whole case so far
had been built up on a series of predictions and presentiments,
it was not impossible that what I felt now had some validity.
I could think of no reason why it should come true, I just
felt it to be so. Somehow, during tonight's performance, I
was certain that a murder would take place.

And what was more surprising was that the artists felt it too.

In contrast, I remembered the day, not much more than
a week ago, when Albert Stiles had hushed us for mention-
ing the word "murder." He had been afraid then that the

[250]

others might laugh. But now there was no laughing. Everybody knew why Beef was with the circus, and they still did not laugh. That was, perhaps, the most terrifying aspect of them all; that the idea of murder had been accepted by these people, they believed in it, and thought it would happen tonight.

And I believed with them. Even my confidence in the Sergeant would not allow me to think that I was making a mistake. Though he had seemed so sure that a murder would not be attempted while he was away, I still could not shake off the feeling of horrible certainty. What was it that Beef had said? "I shall be back here before any attempt is made, just remember that."

But perhaps he was back. Perhaps, in fact, he had not really gone away at all. What would be more like Beef than to pretend such a thing? That stolid ex-constable had imagined that the attempt at murder would not be made so long as he was in the circus. And so he had pretended to go away. He was trying to force the murderer's hand. That must have been the evidence he wanted. He was going to stop the whole thing in the open—with five hundred witnesses. What could be better? But where could he be? Why had he not taken me into his confidence? Surely I was to be trusted with a scheme like that. Somehow, the idea gave me relief. I had been worried all day with the possibility of myself being present alone when the murder was attempted, and not knowing what to do about it. Now I felt happier.

I was brought abruptly out of my brown study by the sound of shouting by the gate. The queue was beginning to file slowly into the tent, and looked back with vague curiosity to see what the noise was about. It was Gypsy Margot, trying to clear half a dozen children away from the front of her tent. But what was amazing about it was the change in her voice. It was no longer the distant dreamy voice of the seer which we knew so well, but the harsh and strident screaming of a harridan. Not even in London had I ever heard such blasphemous and obscene language in my life. The queue went suddenly quiet when they realized the words she was shouting. It was too horrible even to giggle at, and for a long time after she had ceased the people continued to file into the tent in complete silence.

CHAPTER XXX

May 3rd (continued).

IT MUST have been about a quarter of an hour before the Jubilee Performance was due to begin that the rain started. It came suddenly, with only the slight warning of a few heavy drops falling sullenly on the canvas of the big top. The clouds must have gathered without my noticing them, for when I looked up into the sky now I was surprised at the torn ragged edges of gray which hurried across, and below them the swollen black bellies of the coming storm. The canvas walls of the big tent flopped suddenly against the poles, as if all the air had been withdrawn from the interior, or as if the tent itself were gasping for breath. The queue fell silent, huddling closer and pressing towards the box-office. Then the rain swept across them and I heard women's cries, and the short exclamations of the men as they tried to hurry Mrs. Jackson to issue the tickets faster.

Neither did the wagons around the big tent do anything to cheer the evening. With their curtained windows showing only a dull glow of the lights inside, or the occasional slit of yellow, they seemed to be hiding themselves away from the rain. One felt that, in contrast to this wet, shelterless field, the interior of each wagon was warm and comfortable.

I felt there was something macabre about the evening itself. This preternatural darkness, which had crept up suddenly and unobserved, the figures which hurried past with collar turned up, more as if they were hiding something than shielding themselves against the rain, made me feel that the circus was being isolated from the rest of the village, shut away like a plague-spot by the walls of water and darkness. Still distant was the dull roll of thunder, like a far-away shuddering, which one felt rather than heard. The exasperated cries of men rose above it, angry and short-tempered, as they tried to catch the horses. And then the swift rush of hoofs and the eerie sound of a horse neighing invisibly in the darkness. I could imagine no more unfortunate setting for the Jubilee Performance. Despite the threatening possibility of a murder, I had thought it would be a cheerful, personal affair. However, with the last of the queue, I entered the tent.

Although we were getting towards the back-end of the season, quite a lot had been done to make the tent appear brighter. Some of the apparatus had been repainted, and the quarter-poles decorated with long bindings of ribbon in the circus colors. Yet the atmosphere was anything but festive. The audience was dull and quiet, without the usual chaff and shouted conversation. Here and there in the crowd an umbrella had been opened where the rain was coming through a hole in the tent, giving the gloomy look of forced but impatient waiting to the silent audience. Somehow, there always seemed to me to be that air of despondency in an organized "occasion" of this sort, and it would seem that when you expected people to be gay and light-hearted, then was the time when they chose to be depressed by the very means you had used to cheer them.

There was a moment when I wondered whether the strain and anxiety of the cast had communicated itself to the audience; whether they too felt, in some dim way, that they had left their comfortable firesides for the enacting of a tragedy. But I realized almost immediately that it was probably nothing more than the suddenness of the storm and the fact that they were waiting for the show to begin. Somehow, they all seemed yellow and unreal. The lighting of the tent was itself unfamiliar. Possibly Len had been trying to make it stronger by adding new lamps. I could not recognize them, but the whole arrangement looked different. It seemed to transform everything in the tent, so that people's faces were yellow and dismal.

Cora Frances was already in her seat, talking animatedly with Herbert Torrant. They both greeted me as I sat next to them, Torrant with obvious relief, and Cora with a pleasure which showed she had some news.

"My dear," she said immediately. "Do look at those extraordinary people from Bogli's Circus. Really, they look quite a menace, don't they? Whatever have they come for? When I saw them trooping in, one after the other, I said to Mr. Torrant here—didn't I, Mr. Torrant?—that they all looked as though they had bombs in their pockets."

"Hardly likely," I said mildly. "Although, as you say, there does seem to be something rather threatening about them."

"And yet," said Cora, "there's something rather stirring in their manner, don't you think? I mean those scowls, my dear. Really, they might be eighteenth-century sailors. A sort of foreboding expression, 'coming events cast their shadows before,' and all that. I wonder if, perhaps, I ought to have gone to them this year? For my pictures, of course," she added quickly as she caught my eye. "I think I shall go across to them soon and see how they react to the idea. I really don't feel that I shall want to come tenting with Jacobi's next season. Such an atmosphere of crime is really too much for me."

It was easy to pick the circus people out of that crowd of stolid Yorkshire faces. Seventeen or eighteen of the men and women from the rival circus were seated just across the ring from us, making a clearly-defined island. Every now and again one of them would point to some fitting of the tent or ring, and the others would follow his finger with their eyes. Immediately a discussion would arise. I thought their whole attitude seemed both expectant and hostile.

I wondered whether Beef might have come in as an ordinary member of the audience. He had, I remembered, a boyish admiration for disguises, and although I had always persuaded him against them up to now, this might have seemed a golden opportunity to him. His was not the sort of face which could be changed much by nose-putty and grease-paint. I began to run my eyes over the audience, row by row, in the hope of being able to pick him out.

Not far from me sat a man with a close-clipped beard, whose eyes were almost hidden by the soft brim of his hat. He sat perfectly still, apparently absorbed in reading a newspaper, but every now and again his large red hand would creep up to his chin and scratch gently at the edge of the beard. I knew the irritation of spirit-gum, and it seemed impossible that the man I was watching was not in reality the Sergeant in disguise. There was no doubt that he was playing the game cleverly enough. His seat was on the edge of a row, just opposite a gangway. If anything had happened in the ring, he could have been there in little more than a second or two.

I began to realize now that if this were Beef's plan, it really might be effective. It was, perhaps, a little melodramatic, but it might be the only measure likely to succeed. Perhaps I had laughed at the Sergeant a little too soon.

On the pretext of going to buy some cigarettes, I went over close to where the bearded man was sitting. He seemed to hide himself even deeper behind his paper as I approached. But, luckily, the man next to him jogged his arm, and he lowered the paper for a moment to stare with mournful brown eyes at his neighbor. I returned to my seat. However clever the Sergeant might be, he could not change his pale-blue eyes for brown ones. But because that particular man had turned out not to be Beef, it did not mean that the Sergeant was not somewhere in the tent. It made me feel quite creepy to realize that any one of these people might be Beef concealing himself under a disguise. Any one of these people might suddenly leap into the ring and stop the performance in time to save a man or woman's life. It was absurd that I did not know for sure exactly what the Sergeant had planned for this evening. I could only sit and wait.

When the band struck up with a march, its liveliness, somehow, fell a little flat on the wet and dispirited audience. I could see quite clearly that the bandsmen had worked themselves up for the occasion, probably with a few drinks down at the local before the show, and were doing their best to cheer the people. But, somehow, it did not come off. There is nothing more depressing than synthetic gayety. The people only wanted the show to commence, so that they could forget the storm outside and the wet walk home ahead of them. As if to emphasize the dismalness of the whole affair, there was a sudden heavy crash of thunder almost overhead, which quite drowned the band, making it sound tinny and small.

Until now both Beef and I had neglected the band. It consisted of half a dozen of the tent hands, who were paid extra for this part of their activities, and who packed away their instruments after the show and helped to pull down with the rest. But what I had not realized fully before was that they actually took part in the performance. Anita had confessed that she did not know what would happen if the band played the wrong tune during an act. What would happen? Ginger was one of the members of the band. Could there be any connection between this and the sentence I had overheard from Tug about the ghost walking? It was too late to worry now, but at least I could keep my eyes open, hoping not to miss anything.

My reflections were cut short by the entry of Jackson into the center of the ring. He bowed gravely to the audience and there was an uncertain burst of clapping. He was obviously going to make a speech. I felt that the truth about Jackson, as I saw him standing there, was something I had never until then fully realized. He was a very lonely man. As he stood under the hard lights he looked small and slim, and his voice sounded tired, as though he had undergone some frightful strain, as if, perhaps, he were at the end of his tether. It was not that the distance or the lights gave this impression, but they seemed to bring it out, make it apparent for the first time.

"Ladies and gentlemen," he was saying, "for the performers in this circus, tonight's show is one of great importance. Twenty-five years ago today this circus was giving its first performances in a tent which held only a hundred people at the most. Since that day . . ."

I realized more than ever, as this speech went on, that this particular show was the circus people's own evening. As an experienced showman, Jackson must have known that an audience does not like a long "speech before the curtain." And yet he was not hurrying himself over the history of the circus. The only people who were listening eagerly were those from Bogli's Circus, and the artists and hands behind the scenes.

". . . Tribute to him now because he was the founder of this circus. We are very fortunate to have with us still, his sister, Gypsy Margot. Although she no longer actually appears in the ring, you must all have noticed her name as you came into the grounds this evening . . ."

A slight movement at the entrance of the tent made me turn round. Old Margot was standing perfectly still, watching the proprietor as he mentioned her. Her face was expressionless, but her eyes showed vividly what she was feeling. Closed, almost to slits, they looked straight at Jackson, and then, as she turned to go, the lines from her nose to the corners of her mouth, seemed to deepen into a faint sneer. But she disappeared before I could be sure.

One by one, Jackson called the artists into the ring and introduced them to the audience, and then, with them standing behind him in a semicircle, he concluded his talk with the hope that we should all enjoy the performance. Then the band struck up with a lively tune, and the Concinis galloped straight into the ring.

CHAPTER XXXI

May 3rd (continued).

THE twins slipped from the backs of the two white horses and stood for a moment in the center of the ring, making the traditional introductory bow to the audience. Two attendants came forward to take their cloaks, and the girls were revealed in the silver riding costumes they used for this act.

With their slippered feet bouncing lightly on the cruppers of the horses, Helen and Anita followed each other round the ring. Once round, lightly, easily, as though they had been standing on a solid table, and then Anita caught a skipping-rope tossed to her by the attendant. Helen sat her horse so as not to divert attention from her sister, who commenced what could only be called an intricate dance on the trotting horse. The rope flashed under her feet as they traced an invisible pattern on the moving white back. She seemed to be pointing, emphasizing, exaggerating the steady rhythmical motion of the horse, so that there was a peculiar harmony between the rather heavy circumspect animal and its deliberate circling, and the slender girl on its back. She did not seem to be performing on the horse, so much as dancing with it.

The horses now drew level, running side by side and in step. Anita passed one end of the rope to her sister and the two riders did a variation together of the skipping dance. Then Anita passed across to the inside horse and they finished that part of their act with a fast gallop round the ring, hands raised to the clapping audience. Until then, I had been so occupied with watching the swift movements of each girl that I had scarcely noticed their faces. They were both smiling, as they must have been smiling all through the act, with broad set creases of their faces. For a moment I was horrified with the mask-like effect this had. It was as if those expressions had been painted on their lips. I saw the two, one behind the other one, the horse, leaning inward with the speed at which it was running, and Helen's face just visible over her sister's shoulder, like a reproachful other-self in a mirror. For a moment it seemed that there were not two girls, but only one. And it was exactly in that that Anita's chief danger lay. I had a sudden realization of fear, fear of something almost unknown, that the closer the two girls approached to each other the greater was the danger. It was rather like two similar poles of two magnets which exert a violent repulsion if their magnetic fields happen to overlap.

But at that moment the twins leaped down from the horse, which ran straight out of the ring, and were bowing gracefully to the full applause of the house. A pure black horse ran in and began to canter round the ring, and the attendant came forward with a long lance and a whip, which he handed to Anita. Helen leaped into the saddle, seeming to reach it in one bound from the center of the ring. Both girls appeared to be giving the sort of performance which I had imagined only men could have given.

Meanwhile, the attendants had been placing small white wooden pegs in the ground at intervals around the ring. The horse cantered round for a while, slipping a little and breathing heavily through its nose, then it changed to a gallop. Helen grasped the lance which Anita handed her as she passed, and placed it at the "rest" position against her thigh. I realized that the next part of the act was going to be a display of "tent-pegging" fairly familiar with cavalry exhibitions, but which I had never seen in the restricted space of a circus-ring. The idea was to pierce each of the small wooden pegs with the steel tip of the lance as the horse galloped past them. It needed a supple and accurately-timed stroke to avoid a broken wrist or the unseating of the rider.

Then, with a feeling of horror, I watched Anita flick the horse once with the whip-lash and walk in behind it, so that she was standing astride one of the pegs. Was it possible that Helen was going to pick up the little white thing from between her sister's legs? It looked almost suicidal to me. Only the slightest slip of the horse, or an unsteady aim, and Anita would be pierced by the lance. I heard Cora Frances gasping beside me as the horse raced around, and Helen lowered the lance ready. With the horse going at that speed it would need an exceedingly strong wrist to raise the lance in time to avoid the waiting girl's body. Anita's face was expressionless. Had she no fear at all that her sister might not try once again to complete that which she had set out to do a few days ago?

As horse and rider approached Anita turned slightly sideways to them and then held her left foot about an inch above the peg. From where I sat it looked as though she had covered it. Helen rode past. There was a faint whistle and the flash of the lance over her shoulder, and Anita turned, almost casually, and walked to the next peg. The first one was impaled on the tip of the lance. I could not draw my eyes away from the ring, although I hated the whole thing. Somehow it fascinated me. As I looked from one sister to the other, I saw the same set, hard expression, almost as though they had not heard the violent applause which had greeted this act. The applause burst out again for the second peg, and the third and the fourth. There was only one more to be picked up.

But instead of standing over it, this time Anita lay down beside the peg and spread her arm, so that the peg shone whitely in the crook, not more than an inch from her side—and not more than six from her heart. The audience were completely silent now. They might have been holding their breaths, there was so little noise. I could hear the dull thumps of the horse's hoofs. Again the horse flashed by, and the lance was waved in the air with all five pegs on the tip. Helen leaped from the horse and held the lance out to the audience, as if in proof that there was no trick, and then held out her other hand to her sister, who had got slowly to her feet. I sat back in my seat, to find that my shirt and coat were sticking to my shoulders. As she bowed, Anita kept her hand close to her left side.

"My God," said Cora in my ear, "did you see how close that was? The lance actually cut the cloth of her costume."

But the girls turned before I could verify this statement, and ran from the ring. The clapping was deafening, even the people from Bogli's Circus were applauding. But the girls did not reappear to take a bow, and in a few seconds the band changed the music and the curtains parted for the next turn, as Eustace the seal flopped through and into the ring, where the attendants were already arranging the apparatus for the turn.

Somehow, after the previous display, the seal act seemed slow and uninteresting. I realized how much the audience had been shaken in the last five minutes by the way they now felt the urge to talk, to turn to each other with some nervous joke or remark, as if to prove that they each knew there had been no danger in that last act. Actually, there had been very real danger, and they knew it, but people are like that. A slightly hysterical giggle often betrays far higher emotion than the burying of a face in a pair of hands.

Even Cora seemed to feel this, for she turned to me now that Corinne had followed the seal into the ring, with the obvious desire to talk.

"Trying to be a *femme fatale,*" she said, indicating Corinne, who did appear to be performing in a remarkably languid way. "Of course, the seal does rather spoil the act for her, poor dear," went on Cora. "Oh, but how catty you must think me. I simply can't help it. You must admit that she's a very silly little creature, really."

I tried to evade saying anything to this by merely grunting, and pretending to keep my eyes glued on the act. Torrant, I noticed thankfully, had not heard the remark, for he was leaning forward in his seat gazing at Corinne Jackson.

The act followed the usual lines of the seal-act, balancing balls, climbing steps with a ball on its nose, juggling with a loaf of bread and so on. I could see that the people from Bogli's Circus were showing quite open boredom, and this in turn seemed to affect Corinne, whose commands to Eustace grew more and more curt, and her actions even careless. At one point, when the seal was balancing on a narrow strip of board and refused to take up a position she wanted, she walked over to it and lifted it bodily an inch or so farther along. A loud voice from the other side of the ring gave a derisive laugh, which was quickly taken up by the rest of Bogli's artists.

Knowing even the slight amount that we did about Corinne, I could realize the dislike Corinne must have for this act. It could only be her father's influence that made her bring it on. Even the small pieces of fish she had to handle during the tricks must have nauseated her.

My attention was distracted by the figure of Jackson standing at the back of the ring, close to the curtains which concealed the artists' entrance. He seemed to be watching the act with some anxiety, every now and again glancing quickly behind at the curtains, and even once or twice going back to them and peering between them. What could he be expecting from that direction? Whatever it was, it did not interrupt the act, which passed off smoothly, if uneventfully. The applause was polite, except from Bogli's Circus, many of the members of which called into the ring phrases which I could not hear properly. They were probably in circus slang, for I noticed Cora gave a slight chuckle once, as if she had seen a joke. Corinne bowed coldly to the audience and then retired, to be immediately replaced by the three clowns. There seemed to be a slight altercation at the entrance, and one or two of the audience at that side of the ring laughed.

Sid Bolton, who was wearing a long black silky costume, rather like a pantomime dame, flopped down on the ground as he reached the ring, and began to waddle in on his bent elbows and knees in a large imitation of Eustace the seal. In a few seconds he was followed by Eric, who minced coyly to the middle of the ring, and then, taking up a small whip, menaced Sid with it, ordering him in a squeaky voice to mount the stool. Sid shook his head violently, Eric insisted, and then, on a further refusal from the "seal," he threw down the whip in the sawdust and stamped his feet pettishly. I realized suddenly, with the audience, that Corinne's act was being guyed, and a gust of laughter rocked the tent. Finally, Eric walked daintily forward and threw his arms round the prostrate Sid, pretending to attempt to lift him into position.

Young Torrant suddenly stood upright in his place, but Cora grasped him quickly and drew him down. "There was no need for him to do that," he protested.

"Oh, you mustn't mind that sort of thing," said Cora pacifically. "Of course, it's not in the usual act, but I think it's rather clever all the same."

"But it's not right," said Torrant, still trying to free himself from her. "I mean, showing her up in the ring like that. And he's her brother too."

"I should have thought that gave him more of a right than most people," I observed, for quite honestly, I had found the display immensely amusing, even if not in the best of taste. I could only imagine how furious Corinne would be. It might even be a reason for her never appearing in the ring again. Meanwhile, however, it was very funny.

But Eric and Sid had finished their gagging, and had gone on to the routine which I knew: an exchange of slaps, which always seemed to form the bedrock of the circus clown's art. Sid writhed on the ground in mock agony, howling and moaning in an unusually realistic way. Whether it was from previous knowledge of him or not, I felt that this evening he was more than ever annoyed with the part he was playing. Suddenly, in the middle of the act, there was the crack of lightning close over the tent, followed immediately by a roaring burst of thunder. Clem Gail pulled a long face and looked round at the audience.

"Eeee," he said, "what a luvly night for a murder."

Strangely enough, the crowd did not laugh very much at this, and I felt myself being wrenched back to the reality of the situation. The clowning filled in the gap quickly, however, and in a few minutes the crowd were applauding them out of the ring. If I had never seen Clem Gail before, I should have found it impossible to believe that this clown was the same man I knew him to be out of the ring. Not only his manner, and his face, were changed, but his whole bearing were those of another man, of a stranger. It was as if he had become someone else despite himself.

Jackson now came forward to announce, while the apparatus was being erected, Daroga's wire-walking act. The two shining steel trestles were quickly wedged into place, with the wire hanging slackly between them. Jackson was just tightening this when Daroga entered the ring and saluted the audience. Bogli's, who had been giving the most generous applause to the other acts, now remained perfectly silent, and Daroga glanced across at them, almost as if he were commanding them to clap. "Let's see if you're worth it first," shouted a voice. Daroga made as if to threaten the speaker, and then suddenly remembered where he was and walked coolly over to the wire and tested it. He looked almost handsome in his bright cossack costume, with high soft leather boots, embroidered blouse, and astrakhan hat. A small, evil-looking knout dangled from his belt and knocked against his knee as he walked in a way which fascinated me. As he approached the wire, Jackson, who was screwing the supports tighter, said something to him in a low voice. The wire-walker took no notice, but pushed the proprietor out of the way roughly and proceeded to loosen the very wire Jackson had been tightening. The proprietor stood his ground for a moment, and then retreated slowly, almost like a cat, until he was just outside the ring, and then he turned and walked swiftly out of the tent.

I had watched Daroga's act before, and found it amazing that a man of his age was able to perform such feats on the wire. But I soon realized that he was on his mettle this evening, and was doing a number of tricks which were completely new to me. Even Cora Frances seemed impressed when, without effort, he lifted his body clean on to one arm without using his elbow for support.

"You know," she whispered to me, "I had no idea that old Daroga could do a thing like that When I went to Bertram Mills' this season, they told me that Reverbo was the only wire-walker who could do it. Of course," she rattled on, "the somersault on the wire is more difficult—I've seen Colleano do that, and Don Valento, although he's probably not so well known, has some of the best tricks of the lot. But old Daroga, in his time, was as good as any of them. Divine old man. Look at him now."

Daroga was lying on his back on the wire with his hands tucked comfortably behind his head and his feet crossed, and swinging from side to side, almost as if he were half-asleep in a hammock. The band was playing a low lilting tune in time with his swinging, which grew faster and faster, until he suddenly threw himself up on to his feet and continued the swaying from this new position. His body swung with the wire, the center appearing perfectly still, and his legs moving so fast that his body looked like a large letter X. By some arrangement I had not previously noticed, the lights concentrated on him almost like a spot-light, leaving the rest of the tent dim. As his body flicked backward and forward in the strong white light, I suddenly realized what a perfect target the man made. I looked round instinctively, as I thought this, almost as if I might see the sharp-shooter somewhere behind me. But, of course, the ideal position was not inside the tent at all, but outside. How simple it would be for anyone to stand by a hole in the tent wall, fire at Daroga, and then get away long before anyone could get out and trace where the shot came from. The first suspicion would naturally fall on those inside the tent, and during the confusion the assassin could easily either get away or even come into the tent unobserved. At this time of the night, and especially during a violent rain-storm, no one was about outside the tent. My imagination had produced the picture so clearly that I almost anticipated the shot, hearing it ringing in my head. I looked quickly at the wire-walker to see if he had fallen, and then realized that there had been no shot at all—that I had been well on the way towards creating a murder.

A light tap on my shoulder made me start violently and I looked up to see Jackson bending over me. Without saying a word he beckoned me and I followed him into the gangway.

"Mr. Beef," he said quietly, "told me that you have a revolver."

"Beef told you?" I asked incredulously.

"Yes. Would you mind handing it over to me. You must realize that I'm responsible for anything that happens in this tent, and I don't like any of the audience carrying firearms."

"But this is ridiculous," I said. "Beef left me his revolver in case there should be any trouble while he was away. And now you're expecting me to hand it over to you. Well, if it gives you any comfort, I haven't got the thing on me now. And you can believe that or not."

Jackson looked at me for a moment, and then turned abruptly and left the tent. He seemed to believe me. As I was returning to my seat, however, I had the premonition that he might have gone to the wagon to try and find the revolver. Obviously, if I was not carrying the thing, there was only one place where it could be. I quickly followed him out into the open.

It was still raining hard, and the thunder had passed across some miles to the north, where it could still be heard like a dull undertone of guns. I walked towards our wagon, but before I got half-way I saw a figure coming from it. I intercepted him before he had reached the big top. It was Jackson.

"Didn't I see you just come out of our wagon?" I asked.

"That's quite right, Mr. Townsend," answered Jackson coolly. "I went to see if I could find that gun."

"But what right had you . . ." I began indignantly, but the proprietor interrupted.

"Look here, Mr. Townsend," he said reasonably, "there's no reason for you to make all this fuss. I told you before that I didn't like people in the circus carrying firearms, so I've taken charge of this particular gun. You must try to understand my position in this case. Suppose anything happens there in the ring, won't I be responsible? Of course I will. So I'm taking care to avoid all possible accidents, that's all."

"I still don't see," I said coldly, "that that gives you the right to break into my wagon."

"A slight exaggeration," said Jackson with a smile. "Actually, the door was unlocked. But, of course, you are right. I had no legal right to take this gun. But I think I have the justification, under the circumstances. Now I must get back to the ring."

"With my gun in your pocket," I commented.

"Quite. And to put it quite bluntly, there it's going to stay." And with this Jackson gave a brief nod and passed me into the big tent. There was nothing I could do but to return to my seat.

Daroga's wire-walking act had finished, and as I sat down again the comedy ride began. The comedy ride, I discovered from Cora Frances, was one of the traditional acts of the saw-dust ring. There is very little variation in it and Eric's performance followed the usual lines.

The horse ran into the ring, followed by Eric, made up with wig and bulbous nose, so as to be almost unrecognizable. Puffing a fat cigar, he watched the horse running round the ring for a while, and then, handing the cigar to an attendant, he strolled forward and raised his hand confidently to the audience in a gesture which implied that he would now show everybody how a horse should be ridden. The rest of the act was the sheerest slap-stick. Eric leaped over the horse's back, under its hoofs, was thrown off backwards, sideways, and even over its head. He remained completely unruffled, and continued his attempt to mount the running horse, as if one or two failures were the least one could expect in such a task. The crowd rocked with laughter.

By now Jackson was at his place in the center of the ring, cracking his long ring-master's whip. But I noticed from time to time that he kept his left hand buried in his coat-pocket all through the act. His face was cold and unmoving as he flicked the lash of the whip a few feet behind the horse every time it passed; his mind was clearly a long way away, and his actions almost automatic.

At last Eric mounted the horse, and struggled to his feet on its crupper. There was much arm waving and shouting to the crowd, and then he began to undress. At least he began to divest himself of coat after coat, and then waistcoat after waistcoat, tossing them into the center of the ring, until the whole place seemed littered with shed clothing. At the four-teenth waistcoat he revealed a pair of stays fastened tightly round his waist, and the crowd's laughter grew into a roar. These he unbuttoned with difficulty. Immediately, his trousers began to slip gently to his knees, and with a scream of mock embarrassment, he somersaulted out of them, and ran from the ring with his long white shirt trailing behind him.

It seemed quite possible now, with the show nearly half-finished, that Beef had been right when he said nothing would happen that evening. As I looked around the audience, I realized that the early gloom had altogether disappeared, and had been replaced by a real excitement and interest in the performance. It was, without doubt, the best I had ever seen, and I turned to Cora Frances to express the belief that the artists were excelling themselves.

"Aren't they," she replied. "At times, you know, one has the feeling that they are performing from sheer desperation. I've never seen them quite so careless. Even Daroga, usually so steady and quiet, was positively taking his life in his hands this evening. I think it's most awfully thrilling."

Perhaps that was the explanation which I had missed. Were they really throwing themselves at risks in desperation? There was no doubt about the show being an outstanding one, and Cora's reason might be the correct one. She, however, was happily unconscious of the implications of what she had said. Or was she?

The last turn before the interval was the elephants, and as they walked slowly into the ring, Cora nudged me, drawing my attention, no doubt, to her handiwork on their toenails. Daroga followed them on, looking dour and reserved in his Indian costume. But I could tell from the abrupt way he ran through the act, that he was boiling with rage. Once or twice he looked over in our direction, and Cora giggled like a school girl.

"My dear," she whispered. "He's livid with fury. He must know who did them. But it would be just like him to blame it on to the new hand. Just look at the poor lamb. Positively cringing."

The new hand, who remained in the ring during the elephant act, did appear to be behaving very strangely. He kept as far away from Daroga as possible, and also from the elephants, only leading one or another of them when it was absolutely essential. The act started off with the usual climbing on to tubs, dancing, and lifting the wire-walker into the air. Then the Concinis entered for their part of the act, in which they were lifted to the animals' backs in a sort of pyramid.

Very slowly and resentfully the animals took their places and the two girls climbed into position. Then came the turn of the new hand, who should have been lifted to the head of the bigger elephant. The animal curled his trunk around the man's waist, but made no effort to raise him from the ground. Suddenly, the man screamed, a high-pitched fearful scream, and began to pull at the trunk with his hands.

"He's crushing me," he shouted. "I can't breathe."

Jackson leaped forward and began to shout at the elephant, striking at it with the iron hook he was holding, but the animal refused to release the man, lifting him instead high into the air above the wire-walker's head and trumpeting shrilly. The man's screams ceased suddenly and he seemed to go limp. Half of the audience were already on their feet and utterly silent. As if in slow motion, the elephant rolled slowly from side to side. It seemed about to toss the man, like a bit of rubbish, into the audience. A woman screamed. Daroga stood underneath the massive bulk of the animal. Uncannily, the thunder had rolled back almost immediately over the tent, and drowned the sound of elephant and people. Then, slowly, as if ashamed, the elephant gently lowered the new hand to the ground. The girls scrambled down from their positions as quickly as they could, and helped to pull the unconscious man away. Without waiting for an order from Daroga, the two beasts immediately turned and walked quietly, but steadily, from the ring.

As the tension was relieved the audience began to talk rapidly among themselves, although most of them still remained standing, staring at the prostrate man. Jackson came forward and bent over him for a few seconds, and then, when he straightened up, he was holding the man's arm and helping him to rise. Something of a cheer broke from the crowd as the man lifted his pale face, and then, with the almost instinctive action of show-people, he shook his arm loose from the proprietor's and waved it at the audience. When he had walked shakily, but unaided, from the ring, Jackson turned once more to the waiting people.

"It's quite all right, ladies and gentlemen," he said, "no harm has been done. The man only fainted. You have just witnessed an example of the amazing gentleness of these massive brutes in captivity. At the last moment, the elephant would not repay with violence, the kindness of his trainers, but placed the man unharmed, back on the ground. Would you, please, resume your seats. There will now be an interval of ten minutes before the second half of the show."

There was the sound of an incipient jeer from the members of Bogli's Circus, but the rest of the audience seemed satisfied, and their spontaneous clapping soon drowned the one hostile sound. A loud excited buzz of conversation arose, pricked here and there by the cries of attendants selling ice-creams and chocolates.

CHAPTER XXXII

May 3rd (continued).

AFTER a bare ten minutes the band returned to their places and began playing immediately. During the interval it had been more obvious that the storm had by no means passed over, but was describing a sort of circular movement round the district, all the time more or less close to the tober. At some moments the lighting was visible through the tent top and the thunder seemed to burst at the same instant, while at others the vaguest of rumblings was only to be heard in some lull in the music or between the acts. But it no longer seemed to depress the audience, and even the circus staff looked less nervy than they had at the beginning of the evening. After a short introduction from the band, the music changed, and the first act of the second half commenced.

Through the parted curtain at the back of the ring ran eight pure white horses, their necks bent in a proud arc, and their tails almost touching their heels as they ran. Corinne followed them, dressed in a strict black costume and looking more handsome than I had ever seen her. She seemed a different person from the Corinne we had watched in the almost dismal seal act. Perhaps, I thought, she had a feeling for horses. I had been amazed at the one riding act I had seen her do, and here again it seemed as though there were a special sort of sympathy between her and the animals.

The horses were a little disturbed by the storm, and at first they showed some hesitation in the act, snorting, and occasionally jumping nervously when the whip seemed to approach too closely to them. I had once seen such an act completely ruined because one of the horses had been flicked with the lash, but I soon realized that Corinne was far too good a circus artist to lose her temper in the ring. She might have shown boredom, indifference, during an act which was anathema to her, but now I could see the infinite patience, the coaxing, as she tried to give the horses confidence. And she was succeeding. After a few moments she was completely holding the animals' attention, and the act was running smoothly and briskly, as if there was no thunder, no rain, anywhere for a thousand miles. The audience was enthusiastic.

Meanwhile, I had noticed a strange thing happening beside me. Torrant was talking. I had never heard him speak at so great a length or with such intensity, and for once Cora Frances was the listener.

"But she's so lovely," he was saying. "Look at the way she's handling those horses. Of course, to some people, she's snappy and bad-tempered—I mean people who don't see things quite the same way as she does, although I don't mean by that that she's not broad-minded. For instance, once . . . what was I saying? Oh yes, I mean, she's not really bad-tempered by nature. Perhaps to those kinds of people I just mentioned, but that's because she's unhappy here. There are so many things she could do—she could do anything—so why should she stay in this circus when she doesn't want to? She doesn't owe her father anything. What's he ever done for her, I wonder. Anyway, she's repaid him by now."

"My dear," burst in Cora, unable to keep silent any longer, "if you're trying to tell me that Corinne is a sweet-natured girl, then I do so entirely agree with you. But when you reckon with her, you know, you have to reckon with the circus in general."

"Oh, the circus, the circus," interrupted Torrant. "That's what everybody says. But I can't see why circus people should always be considered as something different from others. 'Hath not a Jew eyes?'. . ."

"But really," cried Cora, "I think that's most unfair. There's not the slightest resemblance. Of course I know all about the wandering Jew and all that—but he turned out to be a man called Feuchtwanger didn't he, so there was no real mystery at all to that story. And of course circus people do wander about, I suppose . . ."

"I was quoting," said Torrant, "in a purely figurative way. What I meant was, why should circus people always be looked on as different from other people?"

"Well, I'm sure you say things in the queerest ways," said Cora, a little nettled.

"Then perhaps I express myself badly," answered Torrant. "What I really mean is," and now he seemed to be trying desperately to express himself, "that this sort of life is all wrong for a beautiful girl like Corinne. She ought to have a comfortable home and things like that. You can't imagine how I hate it when I see her out there with that beastly seal, handling fish and being made a fool of by that stupid brother of hers. It's so humiliating."

"That all sounds most exciting and original," said Cora, and I found it hard to believe that she had not her tongue in her cheek, "but you can't imagine what you're up against when you talk like that. I'm afraid it's something far bigger than you are."

"And what's that?" asked Torrant.

"The circus," said Cora. "Oh, I know you think that's so much tommy-rot, but I assure you there *is* something in it. I don't mean that the other people in the circus would try and stop you taking her away. Of course, they'd try, but if she wanted to go they wouldn't have a chance."

"And she does want to go," burst in Torrant. "She's told me so herself, over and over again."

"She may think so now," went on Cora Frances, "but actually, do you think she'd be happy herself away from all this? Of course, she wouldn't. She was born in the circus, and has lived among its people all her life. She'd never be really happy away from it. You take my word for it . . ."

"I know I could make her forget the circus," said Torrant confidently, and turned back to the ring as though there were no more to be said.

Corinne's act was just finishing, and it was clear from the applause that she had redeemed herself in their eyes from the stigma of the seal act. The three clowns rushed on almost before she was out of the ring.

Sid was riding a diminutive donkey, swaying drunkenly from side by side and being propped up by Clem and Eric every time he seemed in danger of falling right off. Only the head and tail of the animal seemed to emerge from under his large figure, and his feet trailed within a couple of inches of the ground on either side.

When it reached the center of the ring the donkey refused to move any farther, despite the ludicrous coaxing of Clem and Eric. Finally, they got behind and tried to push it forward, but the donkey immediately began to move backwards, pushing the two clowns out of the ring, to the huge laughter of the crowd. They abandoned the scheme, and after a short conference approached its head and began to push the animal backwards. As the crowd had anticipated, the donkey walked forward again into the center of the ring. But there once more it stopped.

Somehow, I felt a great sense of relief as I watched the act. Although the three clowns were behaving as drunks, it was quite easy to see how good humored and friendly they were among themselves. The tension seemed definitely to be lifted. With the show nearly over, it was possible to think that perhaps the whole thing had been a mistake on my part. Nothing would happen now. Beef had most probably been right after all. So far I had gone through the performance with taut nerves, expecting all the time some small detail here or there which I must not miss, in case it gave a lead to the tragedy I had been expecting. Now I felt released from that, the whole atmosphere seemed friendlier and less oppressive.

Meanwhile, the act was continuing. Eric seemed to have decided that the donkey would be more likely to move if it were harnessed in a cart, and he had fetched one. It was a small paper and cardboard and plywood affair. But even in the shafts of this the animal refused to move, and the clowns, Sid by this time having dismounted, held another conference. This time they resolved that the only way left was to light a fire under the donkey, and Sid brought along a spirit-stove which, with much drunken gamboling, he managed to light and get into place. In a few seconds the donkey began to stir restlessly, and the clowns capered with glee. Then the donkey moved forward three or four steps, and stopped again, but this time with the flame burning up under the cart, which immediately caught fire. The climax of the act came when the three clowns arrived with huge tubs of water, which they contrived to throw over each other, while the cart burned uninterruptedly to the ground. When all the water was gone, and the cart a charred cinder in the ring, the donkey suddenly pricked up its ears and proceeded to walk sedately from the ring, to the immense mortification of the three clowns.

While the audience was still clapping this act, Cora turned to me and suggested that we should walk round to the artists' entrance and speak to the Dariennes.

"It's their turn next," she said. "I really must go round and wish them luck. You know how the dears love that sort of thing. Won't you come too?"

I could not see any real point in this, but there might conceivably be something I ought not to miss. In any case we might run into Anita. So I agreed, and we dodged down under the long banks of seats and worked our way round to the end of the ring. The Dariennes and Suzanne were standing just inside the curtain talking together when we reached them, and for the moment before they saw us I imagined that something of an argument was going on between them. Cora, however, walked straight over to them and placed one hand on each of the boys' shoulders.

"What, quarreling again?" she asked brightly. "My dear, what a frightful amount of energy you must waste. And just before you're going into the ring, too. That will never do, will it, Mr. Townsend?"

I made an indeterminate noise in my throat, which might be taken as a cough and smiled at Suzanne.

"Oh, it's nothing serious," said Christophe quickly. "One of these little family affairs, you know."

"That's just the point," said Paul. "It is serious. I don't care if everybody does hear it. I don't feel like becoming polite and good mannered just because . . ."

"Paul!" said Suzanne reproachfully.

The elder Darienne seemed about to burst out again, when he suddenly closed his mouth and looked away. There was a short pause, in which we all stood rather uncomfortably avoiding each other's eyes.

"Well, really," said Cora Frances. "You're just like a lot of children with your bickering. Yes, you are. Just like children. I suggest you kiss and make up before you go into the ring."

Luckily, at that moment, the band changed into their music, which was their cue for entering the ring, and without another word either to us or to each other, they went through the curtain.

"How very peculiar," commented Cora. "And I tried to be as cheerful as I could. These people are so unselfconscious that they simply give themselves away in front of everybody. That's what's so charming about them, I suppose. Oh well, let's get back to our seats."

This time we walked slowly round outside the tent, in the

open air. It still rained slightly, and the sky was heavy and black. But there was a fresher feeling in the air, and a slight wind, which would eventually drive the storm away completely. By the front entrance of the big tent we found Ansell directing three or four of the hands who were bringing up the materials for building the lion-cage.

"But what's happened?" I asked. "Is there going to be a lion act after all?"

Ansell grinned. "That's right," he said. "Last minute changes in the program."

"But who's going to show them? You?"

"No. Kurt's crawled out of bed," answered the feeder. "He says he's going into the ring after all."

"That's madness," I insisted. "Why, when I last saw the man he had a fever on him."

"When Kurt makes up his mind," said Ansell, moving away to help the hands, "he takes a bit of persuading."

Bewildered, I followed Cora Frances back to our seats. The Dariennes and Suzanne were up on their trapeze and all the heads of the audience were turned upward, watching the swinging figures. Thank God the next act was the last one. I felt that I could not stand the strain for very much longer of watching and waiting. I turned to Cora Frances and tried to explain what I felt.

"But my dear," she said in a surprised tone, "I thought you were dying for a murder. Really, I'm disappointed in you. Surely, if there's no murder, there's no book to write? And you can't let sentiment interfere with business, can you?"

"I'm afraid," I said stiffly, "that my estimation of the value of human life is a little higher than you seem to suppose. Compared with a tragedy, I cannot see what importance such a minor matter as a book has."

"Well, you *do* surprise me," said Cora.

The Dariennes dipped from side to side of the ring, holding

the attention of the audience in the tent. But somehow I felt that I dared not watch that graceful display. Every face was turned upward, and for that very reason I only snatched occasional glances at them, watching for the rest of the time, the slight movement on the ground below. A motion of the tent-flap at the entrance quickly attracted my attention, and I glanced round to discover that Len Waterman had entered and was standing perfectly still with his eyes fixed on Suzanne. I had never seen the electrician in the tent during the performance before; it was something he never did. Why then should he choose to come in on this night? Could it simply be the Jubilee Performance, or was there something behind it more sinister? My mind flashed back to the day on which the lights had fused and Beef had seemed satisfied that Len had not been to blame. I had already foreseen the recurrence of that, but how did Len's present behavior fit in? Suddenly, I realized with a flash that there was a very clever explanation of Len's presence in the tent just now. Suppose the lights did fuse again, during this act. If Len were in the tent all the time, no suspicion could possibly be attached to him. In other words, could he be here now as a sort of alibi?

Jackson, too, was watching the trapeze artists with complete concentration from his position at the end of the ring. I noticed that he still had his hand in his left-hand coat-pocket, where I suspected my revolver lay. But it was absurd to suppose that he would attempt to use it here in the ring. Anything he did had five hundred witnesses. He would not be such a fool to run that risk, even if he wanted any harm to come to the Dariennes or to Suzanne. But then, again, I realized a curious thing. The attention of the audience was only on the artists in the air. There were, in fact, not five hundred witnesses. There was only one witness of whatever Jackson might do, and that witness was myself. This thought seemed to burden me with an almost unbearable responsibility. How could I be sure of watching everything in the ring, of letting nothing escape me?

"How I would like to know what Bogli's Circus are thinking of this act," Cora's voice suddenly whispered.

"Why especially Bogli's?" I asked without daring to look round.

"Oh, but my dear," went on Cora, "didn't you know? Suzanne used to be with them before she joined up with Jackson. Nobody ever found out quite what happened when she left, but I'm sure there was something behind it. Of course, she hardly ever mentions them—but I think that's suspicious to begin with. I mean, why shouldn't she talk about them? I'm sure if I knew them—just look at them now—I should never be able to keep quiet."

That, I felt, went without saying, but I did not comment on it. I was too relieved, watching the last part of the act and the successful, unharmed descent of the artists to the ground. The applause from the audience seemed, in my distorted state, to be more an appreciation of the safety of the performers than of their performance.

Just near us, as the trapeze act ended, the lion tunnel was being pushed in through the entrance and maneuvered against the cage. The last bolt and nut had been fixed in the cage and Peter Ansell was standing by wiping his hands slowly on a piece of rag, his eyes wandering over the apparatus, as if to make sure nothing had been forgotten. He caught my eye and gave a quick grin, and then turned and began to clamber on top of the tunnel, ready to raise the trap for the lions to run into the cage. But Kurt had not yet appeared in the ring, so Ansell squatted there, his hands on his knees, waiting. I could hear the soft thumping of the three lions walking up and down in the restricted space, and every now and again caught sight of a gleam, as one of them paused to glare out of the barred end of the tunnel. Then, quite unexpectedly, there was the sound of snarling and heavy banging inside the tunnel. The people nearest looked round nervously, and seemed to edge over in their seats, as if to be as far away as possible from the animals. The snarling was quickly developing into a fight, when Ansell leaped off the top of the tunnel and began rattling an iron rod back and forth across the bars. In a few minutes the noise ceased, and he stood looking into the tunnel, holding the bar ready, as if he expected it to commence again.

At that moment the lights changed and Kurt entered the ring. He walked slowly, although perfectly upright, into the center, and then stopped to bow to the audience. His face was white and shadowed, but he seemed to have himself completely under control, holding the coiled whip closely to his side, while he raised the other hand in a sort of salute. Ansell held the gate-top of the tunnel, waiting for him to enter the cage. There was the clang of iron as Kurt entered the cage and slammed the door behind him. He bowed once again to the silent audience, and then turned to Ansell and gave a brief nod. The feeder stood upright on the top of the tunnel, opening the trap-door, and at the same time stamping with his feet on the wood, as I had seen him so often do, to persuade the lions out into the cage.

The two lionesses came out first, and stood for a moment swinging their heads round as if to take in the crowd. Kurt cracked his whip and one of them slunk slowly towards the pedestal at the far side of the cage. The other animal moved slightly, and then turned its head back to the tunnel, as though contemplating a return. Kurt cracked his whip again sharply and advanced towards the lioness, which immediately walked over towards the corner. At that moment the third lion came to the mouth of the tunnel and without pausing leaped straight at the lion-trainer. His head was turned slightly to one side, watching the second beast, and he did not seem to see the danger coming. There was a sudden shout from Ansell, and the two figures fell to the ground together. I was on my feet without realizing the action, and only vaguely conscious of the cries around me from the rest of the audience.

Ansell leaped quickly from the top of the tunnel and snatching up a long two-pronged fork began to jab savagely at the beast. "Fetch the gun!" he shouted to one of the hands standing near, and then, as if realizing that this would be too late, he flung open the door of the cage and himself went in. It seemed a crazy thing to do, but it was undoubtedly the only thing which could save the trainer, who was still lying motionless under the body of the lion. The animal stared for a moment at the new arrival, snarling with its head a little on one side, as if in doubt, and then Ansell took a step forward and prodded it with the prongs of the fork he was still holding. The lion moved back slowly, away from Kurt, and then suddenly turned and leaped into the tunnel, followed by the other two lionesses, which had not moved from their pedestals throughout the incident. One of the hands had the sense to leap on top of the tunnel and quickly drop the trap into place.

Ansell bent over the figure of the trainer for a moment, and then quickly beckoned to Jackson, who was hurrying across the ring. The crowd was perfectly silent, watching the illuminated cage. There seemed to be no word spoken in the whole tent. Then the proprietor rose to his feet and motioned emphatically to the band, and they began to play "God Save the King."

Even then the audience would not leave the tent, but clustered down into the ring watching in horrified silence. At last Ansell and Jackson picked up the limp form and walked slowly through, the crowd falling quickly back on either side, and carried Kurt out of the big top towards his own wagon.

CHAPTER XXXIII

May 3rd–4th.

I WAITED, with the gathered crowd of circus people and members of the audience, outside Kurt's wagon. When the doctor had arrived no one had been allowed in but Jackson. The crowd was fairly silent, murmuring a little among themselves, but for the most part lighting cigarettes and waiting. The circus artists in particular did not seem to wish to discuss the accident.

After quite a short time the proprietor emerged, followed immediately by the doctor. Jackson stood for a moment on the top step of the wagon, as if he contemplated making a short speech, and then seemed to change his mind and walked down toward the crowd.

"Well, how is he?" demanded a voice which I thought I identified as Ginger's.

"He's dead," said Jackson, as if he resented being forced to utter the words, and then walked quickly over towards his wagon.

As the crowd began slowly to separate out, still silent, on the way to their various destinations, I pushed through to the doctor. He was just climbing into his car, which had been drawn up close to the lion-trainer's wagon, and looked up at me with a faint expression of annoyance. He was a middle-aged, carelessly-dressed man, and I could imagine him being called away from a bridge-party only with urgent persuasion. Perhaps I did him an injustice, but, nevertheless, he was not pleased by my intrusion.

"My name is Townsend," I said.

"Never heard of you," the man snapped.

"That is hardly the point," I continued. "But I happen to

be here with this circus in the company of William Beef, the private investigator. I wonder if you would mind telling me something before you leave?"

"And what is that?"

"Can you tell me exactly what killed Kurt?" I asked.

"Good heavens, man," said the doctor in some surprise. "Weren't you in there when it happened? Did you see the condition his head was in? My dear fellow, don't ask silly questions."

"We have reason," I persisted, with justifiable exaggeration, "to suspect foul play."

"Well," the doctor hesitated for a moment, "that's hardly in my line. I did not, of course, make a post-mortem. But I'll stake my reputation that the man died purely and solely from head wounds inflicted by the teeth and claws of a lion."

"Thank you," I said dismally.

"Quite all right, quite all right," snapped the doctor abruptly, and with a scraping of gears he was gone. I walked slowly back to the wagon.

So it was all over, and Kurt had died in the lion-cage. What the doctor had said ruled out the last faint hope I had had; there was no need for a silent shot from the outside of the cage, a poisoned splinter from a blow-pipe. The head wounds had killed him, and had apparently been sufficiently bad to kill any normal man. It was impossible to entertain any other ideas but that the whole thing had been an accident. There was so much that had made it less than that though. For instance, who persuaded Kurt to get out of his bed? That had led in some measure to his death, even if it was not murder. It was as if so many things had combined together. There was the storm, which had undoubtedly upset the lions. There had been the slight scuffle in the tunnel before the show. The animal must have been nervous and angry when the trap had opened, and attacked the first thing he saw—which was Kurt standing in the cage.

What was the use now of Beef's evidence? He had pottered off in his stupid way, just at the moment when he was most needed. It is true there had been no murder, but that made matters even worse for him. Another case in which he had made the wrong conclusions. Luckily, it was away from the normal publicity of the newspapers, and might receive no attention from the public. But the whole affair was so stupid that I felt a sort of fury with the Sergeant for starting the thing, for bringing me up, for even interesting me further in the "case," when my better judgment had told me to pack up and go home many days ago.

It was in this mood that I received Beef some three-quarters of an hour later. He walked into the wagon and sat down with a broad grin.

"Well?" he said, and placed his large red hands on his knees and looked at me with his eyes twinkling.

"So you've come back," I said. "You've actually got back here. The one moment when you might conceivably have been of some use, you were just not here. Well, where have you been?"

"Oh, I dropped into the 'Goat and Compasses' on my way back," said Beef. "Nice little house. Got talking and that, otherwise I might have got back an hour or so ago. Show finished a bit early, didn't it? Anything happened?"

I felt that I must somehow shock him out of this horrible good humor, surprise him, startle him, anything to change his broad grin to a more serious expression.

"There's been an accident," I said coldly. "There's been a death in the circus during the performance. We've seen a head that was nothing but a mess of bloody pulp and white splinters of bone . . ."

The effect on Beef was instantaneous and amazing. His

face seemed to freeze with his mouth slightly open, staring at me for almost a minute before he spoke.

"You don't mean," he said at last, "you don't mean to say that he *went* in after all? You don't mean to tell me that he got up and actually went into that lion-cage after all?"

"How did you know it was Kurt?" I asked. It was my turn to be amazed.

"How did I know!" said Beef scornfully. "Of course I knew. But why didn't you stop him? He told me before I left, in fact he promised me, that he wouldn't get up for the lion act. Do you think I should have *thought* of going away otherwise?"

"But how was I to know anything about that?" I demanded. "You've told me nothing all through the case, and yet you expect me to know everything."

"You shouldn't have needed telling," said Beef unreasonably. "You ought to have stopped him, that's what you ought to have done."

"Beef . . ." I began. But the Sergeant appeared to be thinking of something else.

"Police been?" he asked.

"Oh, I don't know. I expect so. I don't care. You'd better go out and see." I was utterly and completely weary of the whole affair.

"Yes," said Beef. "I can see that I'd better. Well, you get to bed. It'll do you good. I'll look after this from now on." And I took his advice immediately.

But I seemed scarcely to have fallen asleep when I was awakened again by his hand roughly shaking my shoulder.

"Come on," he said. "We've got a lot to do this morning. Come on, get up."

It was quite late in the morning, but the circus had not moved on, so that I had not been disturbed by the starting up of lorries.

"That's right," said Beef to my query. "They've canceled Monday's performance, so that they can stay on here until Tuesday morning and get this thing over and done with."

As I dressed hurriedly, he explained again that he had a lot to do during the day. "And first of all," he concluded, as I followed him down the wagon steps, "I want to go and have a look round the zoo."

The Wild Animal Zoo was deserted when we reached it, although the wooden fronts of the cages had all been taken down. Beef started at the far end and walked carefully along all the cages, peering through into each one without speaking. The solitary lion looked up at him a little resentfully, with the remains of the meat that had been given him that morning still grasped between its forepaws, and then, blinking in the bright sun, put its head down again and continued the meal. One by one, Beef stopped before each cage and seemed to be taking stock of the animals.

"Why on earth are you doing all this?" I asked. "What are you looking for?"

"Well," said Beef with a twinkle in his eye, "I might be looking for someone to take me on at darts." And then, after a pause he added, "But I'm not."

It was obviously useless to attempt to question the Sergeant when he was in this frame of mind. I walked on with him without speaking.

"You see," he went on in a little while, "I like you to have the same chances that I have, if you see what I mean. I mean, it's not fair to keep you in the dark, is it?" And again he chuckled.

When at last we emerged from the zoo, it was to find a middle-aged constable looking for Beef.

"Which of you two gentlemen is Mr. William Beef?" he asked.

"I am," said Beef promptly. "And what might you want?"

"Well, it's like this," said the constable. "I'm the coroner's officer, and I was told to come up and see if you'd got anything what might be useful. . . ."

"Yes, I know all about that," said Beef.

"Of course you do," said the constable. "I've heard a bit about you, you know. In the Force once yourself, weren't you? Until you took up with this here fancy game of private investigation." There was tremendous scorn in those last two words, but Beef did not seem disturbed.

"So you heard of me?" he asked.

"That's right," said the policeman. "You've been held up to me as a sort of a warning, as you might say. 'Course, you won't come to no good on that game. Just look what a pickle you got yourself into in that last business of yours."

"So that's what they say about me in the Force now, is it?" demanded Beef with indignation. "Slandering my name behind my back, that's what it is. Worse than a lot of gossips. Let me tell you, young man, that it takes more than a blue uniform to make an investigator."

The "young man," who could not have been more than three years younger than the Sergeant, seemed to regard this as a rare joke.

"Still," said Beef, "be that as it may, there's something I want to talk to you about, if you don't mind."

"Am I in on this?" I asked, as the two began to walk away.

The Sergeant hesitated, as if in doubt. Then: "No," he said. "You can have your turn after. I won't be long." And talking emphatically he led the policeman off towards, I suspected, the "Goat and Compasses." There was nothing for me to do except waste a bit of time around the ground until he returned.

But before Beef came back, a car drew up at the gate of the tober half an hour later, and two policemen climbed out and walked into the zoo. When they emerged again they were leading Peter Ansell forcibly between them.

CHAPTER XXXIV

May 4th.

BEEF came into the wagon in a state which I can only describe as triumphant. I suspected him of having celebrated something or other with the coroner's officer down at the "Goat and Compasses," though I tactfully refrained from reminding him of it. I might have pointed out to him that, only twelve hours before there had been a tragedy, and that a dead man was lying not fifteen yards from us now. When he spoke, however, it was quietly and soberly.

"You know," he said, "Shakespeare was right."

I had never heard the Sergeant quote from any of his country's literature, and waited with interest to see what hackneyed phrase he would choose.

" 'There is a destiny what shapes our ends, rough hew them how we will,' " he announced. "I'd give a great deal not to have gone away yesterday."

"It's too late to think of that now," I pointed out.

"I know, I know," said Beef. "Still, I could have saved the poor fellow's life if I'd ever had the slightest suspicion that he'd do anything as crazy as show the lions."

"You mean, I suppose, that he wasn't fit enough? That a lion could sense illness, and take advantage of it?"

"Now look here," said Beef impressively, "if I'm going to tell you this story, I'm going to tell it. I don't want you putting in silly suggestions all the time. It may make good reading, but I like to express things clear. We'll go right back to the beginning and you shall hear how it is I've been able to give information to the police about a horrible murder that's been done in Jacobi's Circus."

"But," I began inevitably.

Beef held up his formidable ·traffic-controlling hand. "You heard what I said," he reminded me. "Now sit tight and listen. This is the biggest success I've ever had, and I don't want it spoiled with a lot of sneering remarks from you."

I was determined to interrupt. "All right, Beef," I said. "I'll listen. But, first of all, I'm going to ask you a question. How can you have had your biggest success *when you didn't prevent the man's death?*"

"That was out of my hands," said Beef, "as you shall hear in due course. No one in the world could have guessed that Kurt would get up yesterday and show those lions. Not Lord Simon Plimsol couldn't have," he added bitterly. "Nor Mr. Philo Vance, nor Dr. Thorndyke, nor any other of the detectives whose novels sell ten times what ours do. And if anyone blames me for not having prevented the murder, you can tell them that. No one," his voice ran on towards a rhetorical climax. "Not the Lord Mayor of London, nor the Shah of Persia could have done different. I'm an investigator, and I investigated. After all, do any of them do more than that? Did Sherlock Holmes prevent the murders he had to find out about? Which of them ever stopped their man before he done it? Why, some of them start investigating a murder and have half a dozen more before they make an arrest. I've read cases where a cold-blooded assassin, with the 'keenest brain in the world of investigation' smelling out his doings, has gone so far as to poison, blow up, stab and strangle three or four innocent people before the reader knows who he is. And just to make a better story of it, mark you. Unscrupulous, that is. Human life should come before royalties and cheap editions. Or film rights, for that matter. I don't believe in a lot of blood to give satisfaction to people what pays tuppence in a lending library. And if I could have stopped that poor fellow being killed, I would have, whether you lost your chance of writing a masterpiece or not. And that's more than you can say for many of them. Why, if they was to stop the murderer first, there wouldn't be many murders to write about. And what's more," he added savagely, "there wouldn't be any writers making handsome fortunes telling the tale. Now, I'll tell you the story.

"When I first got that letter from Albert I thought to myself, 'well, that's funny.' Not because I thought there was going to be a murder, but because anyone should have said there was. And anyway, I thought, it would make a nice holiday. I mean, since I've retired from regular duties, I've often wanted to see a bit of the world, and here was my chance . . ."

"So you allowed me," I broke in furiously, "to give up all other work, and the chance of finding a detective who would be taken seriously, to come up and indulge your taste for a holiday."

"Taken seriously?" said Beef. "What do you mean?"

"Well, you know what the *Church Times* said," I argued hotly. " 'To take the egregious Beef seriously has already become impossible. He is a figure of fun. *We cannot swallow your Beef.*' "

Beef leaned back in his chair and looked at me fixedly for a moment. "Do you suppose," he said with a blundering attempt at sarcasm, "that I have any wish to be swallowed by the *Church Times?* You know very well how I feel about parsons."

I waved this nonsense aside impatiently. "The fact remains," I said, "that you are a laughing stock in the world of detection, and that before we started on this business I had my eye on a young lady school-teacher in Murston who, I have been told, solves every interesting crime by an algebraic process which she works out during her scripture classes. She would, I believe, have made an excellent investigator for me to chronicle, instead of wasting my time running in and out of public-houses after you. Yet you calmly inveigled me into following you to Yorkshire because you wanted a holiday."

"Well," explained Beef, "you had a motor-car. I never liked trains, they make me dizzy. But do let's get back to the point, if you want to hear how I solved this extraordinary riddle."

"Yes," I said, "do let's. I have no doubt that, in your own estimation, you have done a remarkable piece of work. Though all I can see is three wasted weeks, culminating in a most unfortunate accident."

Beef paused. "If," he said, "I was to prove conclusively to you that there had been a murder; that I knew there was going to be a murder; that I knew who was going to do it and who was going to be the victim; that I knew why he was going to do it, and how; could you give me a little of the credit which you so readily hand out to all these other brilliant gentlemen?"

I laughed. "If you do all that," I said, "I'll admit that you're a master."

Beef shook his head sadly. "No," he said, "you won't. Not when I tell you. It was perfectly simple, and you had all the evidence I had. It depended on quite plain and obvious things. There was nothing superhuman, nothing compli- cated, nothing that called for Scotland Yard, theories, finger- prints, or microscopes. I solved it because I've got one thing you'll never have, Townsend; not you nor any of your clever crime-solvers—common sense, my boy. Common sense, a bit of experience, observation, and a habit of putting two and two together have got me where I am today. And they've solved this crime, what's more. Yet when I come to tell you how, you'll be turning your nose up again. All right. A prophet's never recognized in his own country. And I don't suppose if I was to tell you what happened to the *Marie Celeste,* who killed Cock Robin, the whole truth about Colonel Dreyfus, and where the flies go to in the winter-time, you'd ever realize that I'm more than what you think I am. Still, perhaps some of your readers are more intelligent than what you are, and'll see that it needed Beef to get at the truth of this. So you may as well write it up.

"Now the first thing I realized when we came up on this circus was that we were dealing with unusual people. All the way through you've been laughing at me for learning circus words, and for treating the circus as something apart. Well, it is something apart. I don't mean as the people in it are monsters, or freaks, or anything like that, but just that they're a bit different from the sort of people you usually mix with. They couldn't help it, living the way they do. You could make as many New Year resolutions as you liked and it wouldn't change you much. But if you changed your way of living . . . that's what makes people different. So I knew, directly I decided to come along to the circus, that the people would be something a little different from what I'd been used to. And that's the first thing I set about finding out. I wanted to know just how much, and what it meant in a case like this. And what I found out was this. Take this language of theirs first. It's a sort of umbrella, as you might say. Something to shelter under, that's what it is. It wasn't so very long ago that people used to look down on circus people, and think they were no better than gypsies or thieves. So, like other people when they're sneered at by society, they got into a corner out of the way. Or in other words, they worked up this special language of theirs so that no one could understand what they were talking about unless they wanted them to. A sort of retreat, that's what it is. People in towns didn't think very much of the circus people, so what's more natural than that the people in the circus shouldn't think very much of the rest of us. Tit for tat, you see. They live in a world all their own, and they don't have too much to do with anybody else if they can help it.

"But when I'd got to understand that, I didn't think, as you did, that every little bit of jealously and nasty feeling among these people was going to lead to one killing another. But I did see that they were worth watching. Why, I've learned more about human nature, watching the people on this show, than I learned in five years traffic-directing in the Force. I'm getting on to fifty, you know, but I'm only just feeling my way when it comes to the human heart. For instance, those clowns.

"Now you noticed Sid Bolton in that fight we had with Bogli's Circus; vicious he was, as if he owed someone a grudge. Well, in a way, so he did. How would you like to be sat up in a tent for silly folk to laugh at because you was fat? You'd hate them, like Sid Bolton does. But if you came out of the job and went on with your ordinary life after you might forget it, or it might only show every now and again. But Sid Bolton joined the circus, so he goes on not liking people. Like these here agitators you hear so much about, he's got a grudge against the world. It hasn't treated him fair, see, so he likes to spit in its face now and again. But that doesn't mean he'd go about wanting to kill some special man or woman. That's not what he feels. When he gets people alone he likes them, and when he gets them in a crowd, he doesn't, and that's all there is to it.

"With young Clem Gail, it's much the same. Only he's got a different reason. Now you went and listened to him when he was with that girl. Did you notice anything peculiar about that?"

"They were very romantic," I said.

"He didn't tell her what he really did in the circus," said Beef with emphasis. "That's what gave me the key to him. And why didn't he? Because of his face, that's why. Because the only time anybody clapped him or said he was good, was when he had that hideous make-up on, and because when he came out of the ring nobody ever recognized him. He's a well-set-up young chap, is Clem Gail, and it galls him that he lives what you might call two lives. Now I know what you're thinking. You're thinking about that little game they had in the ring when they all set to slapping each other. But you got that all wrong. In the first place, Clem was a bit drunk, and he was wild with everybody and showed it. And in the second place, he was wild with Cora Frances, and who wouldn't be? Hanging round him like she hangs round everybody. But you don't think that because he took a smack at her he wanted to do her in, do you? 'Course he didn't. Why, if that was true, half the husbands in the world would be under arrest at this minute, *and* their wives would be coming round to try to get them out. You can't go suspecting people of wanting to commit a murder just because they show a healthy dislike for somebody what well deserves it."

"But," I interrupted, "what about Eric's enmity for his sister?"

Beef gave a huge guffaw and slapped his thigh. "There you go again," he said. "Enmity for his sister! I don't know where you get all these ideas from. Couldn't you see that he was just like a schoolboy? He was enjoying himself—pulling her leg a bit, like I pull yours sometimes. He has the time of his life, young Eric does. Larking about like a regular kid."

"All right," I said irritably, "don't rub it in. But what about some of the others. Jackson and Daroga for instance? You can't say there wasn't something going on between them."

"Of course there was something going on between them," retorted Beef quickly, "but it wasn't what you thought. You got the right idea, but you exaggerated it, like you always do."

"Do you mean to say that Daroga wasn't blackmailing Jackson?" I asked in surprise.

"Well, in a way he was, and in another way he wasn't. I'll explain it to you," said Beef. "We'd better start off with that button what I picked up in Jackson's wagon and what you thought must belong to Daroga. Now you saw for yourself that it wasn't likely to have been Daroga's because it had writing on it in Russian, and he'd left Russia when he was quite a tot. But Jackson said it was his—so why shouldn't it be?"

"And why should Jackson own a Russian button?" I asked.

"Well, there might be any sort of ordinary explanation to that," answered Beef. "But as it happens, the answer is very interesting—and also very simple. You see, Jackson happens to be a Russian himself. You noticed how he dodged my question when I asked him what he'd been doing before he started the circus business? The reason was that he was in Russia, and he didn't want us to know."

"But why not?" I asked. "That's not a crime, is it?"

"No, it's not a crime," said Beef. "But it is a crime to stay in this country without registering yourself or taking out naturalization papers for more than a certain amount of time. And that's what he'd done. And that's what Daroga knew he'd done. You see, it was that little button what gave it away. You remember it had the Russian word for artist or actor on it? Well, that meant he belonged to one of these here organizations or unions or whatnot, like there's so many of."

"So he was blackmailing him after all?" I exclaimed.

"There you go," said Beef, "running away with an idea again. I wouldn't call it blackmailing him. He had a sort of a hold over him, that's all. As a matter of fact, Jackson took a lot of care of Daroga—more than what he did of any of the other artists, anyway. Look at the way he kept an eye on his wire-walking apparatus. What you thought was suspicious and sinister. But you know the sort of man Jackson is; a bit of a Tartar to get on with, nasty way with him, bad-tempered, likes to order people around. Well, Daroga couldn't stand that, so when he finds out that Jackson's keeping something quiet, then he uses it to have a bit of peace from his nagging. That's all there was to it."

"And what about that little incident when Daroga built up on the wrong tober?" I asked.

"Exactly," agreed Beef. "Didn't that just go to show what it was Daroga wanted? He liked to feel free, that he had a bit of a say in the doings of the circus and wasn't always to be ordered around like the others were. Some people are like that. They just can't stand being told what to do.

"But you ought to have seen what a useful man Daroga was to the circus. Jackson's got a good business head on his shoulders, and he wouldn't do anything that might make Daroga clear off, as you might say. So he has to put up with Daroga, knowing about him being an unregistered alien, so as to keep him in the show. He's a handy wire-walker, as you've seen for yourself, and what's more, he knows how to manage those elephants. Of course, I admit that Daroga had a pretty strong hold over old Jackson. Didn't need more than a word from him in the right quarters, and Jackson would have been bundled straight out of the country. But where you went wrong was in the way you thought that hold was being used. There wasn't no money in it, nor nothing that might have caused a murder. Daroga was quite happy so long as he didn't get badgered about by Jackson to do this and to do that. And so long as he knew Jackson's secret he was safe from that. Jackson didn't want Daroga to leave the circus, and he knew that if he treated him right he wouldn't go and split to the police. So really they were both perfectly satisfied with things as they were, and there wasn't no cause for one of them to try and do in the other like what you seemed to think they would."

"It seems to me," I observed, "that all you're doing is to show me why no one in the circus could have even wanted to commit a murder."

"I wouldn't need to," retorted the Sergeant, "if it wasn't for the funny ideas you've got hold of. But there was a murder, just the same. Which we'll come to all in good time."

"But," I objected, "you can't deny that there were attempts at a murder before this. What about the affair when Helen stabbed Anita, and later when the lights failed? How do you account for those?"

"We'll take those one at a time," said Beef calmly. "Now what you ought to have seen was that that little dust-up between Helen and Anita was all there was to it. I mean, that was the beginning and the end of it. You know as well as I do that those two sisters were really fond of each other, and that neither of them wanted such a thing to happen again. But you wouldn't believe that. You thought something else might happen between them. But you must have missed one very curious little thing which told me that everything had settled down, and that there wouldn't be any more trouble. Because, you see, when Helen stabbed her sister she did just what was wanted—she made everything all right."

"I don't see what you're getting at," I said.

"Didn't you notice that after the wound had healed up it left a scar?" asked Beef. "And what's more, Anita did a funny thing what most women wouldn't have done. When she got better she didn't wear clothes that would cover the scar; in fact, she might almost have been proud of it the way she let everybody see it. Why do you think that was? A way of getting her own back on her sister? Not a bit of it. She knew that the reason for Helen going for her like she did was because they were both exactly alike, because they were twins and Helen felt she didn't have a soul of her own. That's what it was. And the scar, you see, made all the difference. Every time Helen saw that scar she knew that she and Anita had something a little different about them. So you see, there wasn't any chance of any more trouble between them."

"And what about hypnotism?" I demanded. "Anita told me that old Margot was a hypnotist."

"Hypnotism," said Beef scornfully. "That's just the sort of thing you take a pleasure in. French idea, that is. What if the old girl did do a bit of mind-reading on the stage at one time or another? That didn't mean she was likely to crawl around making people do all sorts of things they weren't responsible for. You want to get some of these romantic ideas out of your head and get to the bottom of things some time. Why, Anita told you herself it was only a simple sort of hypnotism what couldn't do no harm to anyone. But of course, you never believe what you're told."

"In other words," I said bitterly, "I've been making a fool of myself all this time. But I still think that there was something suspicious in the way those lights fused right in the middle of the trapeze act."

"That," said Beef, "is because you never took the trouble to think about it. Now as a matter of fact, the reason why that little job couldn't have been done on purpose was because it *did* come at such a peculiar time. Suppose you was outside the tent by the lighting lorry and you wanted to turn them out just when someone was flying through the air. How would you go about it? You see, it's impossible. Suzanne was only in the air about two seconds at the most, and Len Waterman couldn't have run around to have a look in the tent and then run back and pulled the fuse out in that time. And if it had happened at any other time, even just when she was preparing to let go a split second before, they would have stopped the act until the lights came on again. And another thing. Did you ever take the trouble to find out how often those lights fused? Or if they had ever fused before?"

"No," I admitted, "I didn't."

"Exactly," said Beef. "But I did. And I found out that they'd gone wrong three times this season, twice in the afternoon and once in the evening. The wires were so patched up and mucked about with that you couldn't expect anything else. Didn't you notice that none of the people in the actual circus were at all suspicious about them fusing? They weren't. They took it all a day's work, like they would a drop of rain or a bit of bad luck. And a third reason why you were wrong about that was that Len Waterman wasn't the sort of man who would do a thing like that. I admit that he was jealous of young Darienne, and that he was still a bit in love with Suzanne. But that's not the way he would have tried to get even with them. Even if he'd wanted to get even."

"But there's one other thing about Len and Christophe that you seem to have forgotten," I told him, "and that is the little affair when we were having that fight with Bogli's Circus. If you remember, they had a quarrel then."

"And why not?" demanded Beef. "Trouble with you is that you want everything explained for you. When Christophe and Len started that little bit of a scrap that day it was because they were circus people, that's why it was. Nothing else. Circus folk love a bundle now and again. They don't worry about who it is they're fighting, so long as it's a fight. But it doesn't mean anything—not the way you think it means."

"And how about Bogli's Circus itself?" I asked. "Perhaps there was nothing much in the scrap they had, but why did they turn up to the performance, and why were they so critical all the time? They couldn't have come just to enjoy the show. Cora Frances told me that Suzanne used to be with them before she joined Jacobi's. Was there anything in that?"

"Now look here," said Beef, shaking his large forefinger at me. "I've told you before that you just don't understand circus people. Now if you like, there's a sort of rivalry between the two circuses, but the point is, it's friendly. They're people with the same sort of ideas, the same way of living, and the same job. When one circus comes over to see the show of the other, it's friendly, see? It was a bit unusual cutting their own performance, but then the Jubilee show was a special affair, and it was a very nice action to come over and watch it. And as for being critical, they weren't half so critical as what you are of me all the time."

"But that's different," I protested. "I'm your friend and I believe you like to know what I think. I mean, if you can't be frank with your friends, who can you be frank with?"

"And that explains the business of Bogli's Circus very nicely," commented Beef. "Only why you have to have it pointed out to you first, I can't see. Still, let's get on with this business. We'll take the Dariennes next, and that affair between Christophe and Suzanne.

"Now you know brothers are funny. Sometimes they're as close as you like, and at other times they simply hate the sight of each other. I've noticed it many a time. It all depends, I suppose, on the way they're brought up. Well, with those Dariennes, they never had no parents and they had to get along together. Got sort of to rely on each other, I expect. Then, as you heard, Paul was ill, and there was no one to look after him, only his brother. Well, that made a bit of a difference to them. I don't say it wasn't unusual, mind you. But it was something you could understand. They were the sort of brothers you just couldn't imagine not being together all the time. And then this Suzanne comes along and falls for young Christophe. What could be more natural than that he should be worried about it? In the first place, Christophe knew it wouldn't go down too well with his brother, so he kept it from him as long as he could. Suzanne was a bit jealous of the way Paul and Christophe were always together, case of love me, love my dog, as you might say. And, of course, Paul didn't like the idea because he'd become so dependent on his brother. And there they were at sixes and sevens when along we come to the circus on the look-out for a murder. But there was nothing like that about them. They had their little tiffs now and again, but it was nothing that couldn't be straightened out with a bit of care. As a matter of fact," continued Beef, grinning at me, "I did a bit of straightening there myself, and I can tell you that everything's all right. I just got that Paul alone for a while and gave him a good talking to. What with having a bit more experience than him in the ways of life and in the ways of women in particular, I soon got him round to see my point of view. I only had to show him that this wouldn't break up the act, or take Christophe away altogether, and he began to see daylight. Now he doesn't mind how soon they get married. So you can see I've done some good somewhere, anyway."

"Since you seem to have found everybody on the circus had a heart of gold and wouldn't have committed a murder whatever the situation," I said coldly, "I'm surprised that you stayed so long. I suppose you couldn't even find something sinister in Cora Frances?"

"Oh yes, I could," answered the Sergeant quickly. "I saw right away that she was a dangerous baggage."

"In what way?" I asked.

Beef paused. "Well," he said slowly, "I may be a bit old-fashioned in my ideas, but directly she came poking her nose into the circus I knew we were going to have trouble with her. Look at the way she behaves! All that paint and powder all over her face, and throwing her money about! And the way she runs around after some of the men. Doesn't seem to care whether it's Clem Gail or young Darienne. Women like that ought never to be allowed out. Sending telegrams!" Beef's scorn was burning. "Repeating things between people what she ought to have kept to herself! And the way she turned her nose up when she found we were here, and she couldn't have the circus all to herself, that should have showed you what she was. Then there were those elephants all done up silly. Fancy anyone messing about with the acts like that!"

"Now there's one person," I said, "I'm very anxious to hear your opinion of. And that's Tug Wilson."

"Ah," said Beef. "Now there you had something to be said for you. I had my eye on him as soon as we set foot in this circus. When I saw the way he handled them elephants when they ducked poor Albert, it did make me think. But there was no real harm in him, as it happened. Throwed a nice dart, too."

"But that phrase he used," I said. "That surely had some significance?"

"What phrase?" asked Beef.

"When he said 'The ghost walks tomorrow' to Ginger."

Beef leaned back in his chair and his enormous laughter seemed to fill the wagon. "The ghost walks," he chuckled to himself.

"I with you'd let me into this joke," I snapped. "I don't happen to see anything funny."

"You will," promised Beef. "Would you like me to tell you what he meant?"

"I most certainly should," I answered.

"Well, if you'd learned a bit more circus language, like what I have," lectured the Sergeant, "you'd know that 'the ghost walks' is circus slang for 'pay-day.' See?"

There was nothing I could say to this, so I sat patiently waiting for the Sergeant to tire of his merriment and continue with his explanation of the case.

CHAPTER XXXV

BEEF stopped laughing at last and pulled out his handkerchief, but whether to wipe away tears or perspiration I was not sufficiently interested to observe.

"I promised myself a good laugh," he said, "over you being took in by that 'ghost walks' business, and I've had it. So now I'll tell you about the murder. You still think, though, that if I prove to you I knew the who, how and why of that murder, I'm a genius, don't you?"

I nodded impatiently.

"However simple they are?"

"Unless you knew something I didn't," I asserted.

"Well, here goes then. Do you remember that day when we went across to see Ansell?"

"Yes," I said.

Beef leaned forward as though he were going to accuse me of the murder. "And do you remember what he was doing?"

"Of course I do," I said huffily, for neither my observation nor my memory is as bad as Beef thinks. "He was digging."

Beef leaned back. "Ah," he said, as though with tremendous relief. "He was digging."

"Well, what about it?" I asked.

"You may well ask about it. That was the key to the whole thing. *Digging.* Did it never occur to you to ask yourself why a man with a traveling circus should be digging the ground with a spade?"

I sat up. "Of course," I gasped. "A corpse."

Beef did not even laugh. "Don't be silly," he said, "there wasn't no corpse. At least," he added, as though something had occurred to him, "not the corpse of a human being."

"What, had one of the monkeys died?" I asked.

"No," said Beef, "a horse."

"A horse? But, good heavens, we should have heard about that."

"Not about this one, you wouldn't," said Beef, and settled down to talk. "Now let's consider Mr. Ansell for a moment. He'd been educated at what he called a 'public school,' meaning, I suppose, one of the most private and exclusive colleges in England. He'd been brought up to consider himself a gentleman, and there he was sweeping kangaroo droppings out of a cage. Didn't that seem funny to you? He hadn't seen his parents for fifteen years. Now, I'm not one who's always talking about parents and children, but I never believe much in a young fellow what's got parents and doesn't take the trouble to go and see them. Then he said he's been in prison, and half a minute later he was talking about one of your highbrow writers, whose name, I have no doubt, you can remember, if only because it had no importance whatever in the case."

"Ernest Hemingway," I murmured.

"That's it. But there was funnier things than that. What did he do when that tiger got out and there was a young lady present? Shut himself up in a cage, didn't he, and wouldn't be shifted? That told me something when I considered him as a possible murderer. I knew that if he did go for somebody else, it wouldn't be straight out with a butcher's knife, as you might say, but round the corner, subtle, secret. He said he'd been on this job for over a year. Why? He'd never stuck another job as long as that. He wasn't a circus man, and the circus people didn't like him. What was he after? It didn't take me long to find that out. He was after Corinne Jackson as sure as eggs is eggs.

"Well, there you have the chap, and what made me suspicious of him, and the first real clue I had. As soon as I saw him digging I puzzled my old brain. He wasn't burying one of the animals because none of them hadn't died—I found that out. He certainly wasn't burying rubbish because of all the crowd that left their refuse lying about the fields we stood in, Ansell was the worst. He never troubled to put anything away. Then what was he burying? That's what I had to find out, and that's what I have found out.

"There are three people in this story," said Beef. "Ansell, Kurt, and Corinne Jackson. And I'm not sure Corinne wasn't the worst. I never liked a woman without a heart, as you might say. She didn't care two straws for any of them. She didn't care which it was, Kurt or Ansell or that young fool Torrant, so long as they got her away from the show. She had no one else to turn to, no money of her own, and very little chance of getting a job without her father getting it for her. So all she wanted was a man who'd marry her and take her away. There was three of them willing. But only one had the money."

"Torrant," I suggested.

"Torrant! He couldn't have bought her an engagament ring. No, Kurt had the money."

"How do you know?" I asked.

"You shall see," said Beef. "But how I came to suspect it was like this. Didn't you notice anything queer about the way he guarded his wagon? Never left it unlocked for a moment. It was the only one we couldn't get into. Don't you remember that morning when he as good as turned us away? Besides, he was the sort who would have money. Never spent any to speak of. Do you know he was the only man in the whole show who never asked me to have a drink?"

Beef might have been accusing Kurt himself of the murder, so solemnly did he bring out this preposterous accusation. "So there you have it. A man with money, tight and careful, going in with the lions every night; a young fellow who visits the show, decent and respectable; and another who's been brought up as a gentleman, who's been rag-tagging around the world, in and out of prison, and who's stuck this job. And all three of them in love with one girl. And each of them been promised that as soon as he takes her away from the circus, she's his.

"What's the result? Well, I should have thought even you might have guessed it. The 'gentleman' says to himself, 'If I could find a way of getting rid of Kurt without arousing suspicion *and* getting my fingers on his money, I'm as good as home.' So he sets about thinking of a way, and being the clever underhand young brute he was, he gets hold of a way which would have fooled anyone in the world except the man what ought to be recognized as the greatest investigator of all time, and who sits before you now, thirsty, but unashamed."

Beef gave a long, satisfied gasp. "I'll tell you how he decided to do it. He decided to kill Kurt with his own lions. Who could say anything then? He wasn't in the cage. He had hundreds of witnesses to prove that he hadn't egged them on. He didn't frighten the lions, and he didn't do anything to their apparatus which could have been found out afterwards even if there hadn't been an immediate investigation."

"Then what did he do?" I asked.

"He dug," said Beef.

"What do you mean, he dug?"

"I told you. He was burying the corpse of a horse. Only, of course, you jumped to conclusions and thought it was one of the circus horses. It was an old, old horse he was burying what had come from the knackers' yards days before. When we walked across that morning he was burying the horse meat what he should have been giving to the lions."

"Good God!" I exclaimed, beginning at last to see light through the tortuous ways of Beef's explanation.

Once again Beef held up his hand. "That's nothing," he said. "That was only part of the way I found out what he was up to. It's very doubtful whether you could get a lion to turn on its trainer simply by making it hungry. But it would help. Ansell never meant to take any chances. That was part of his plan, and the part I got on to quickest.

"Did you notice something interesting Kurt told us one morning about wounds on a lion? He said that if you was to wound a lion it wouldn't bleed or even show the wound, because of the skin being loose, as it were. Well, that's another thing Ansell knew, and another part of his plan, as you will see in a minute. But the real trick lay in something you wasn't even interested in, though I pointed it out at the time. There was a fourth lion, just the same size and color as the third. I thought to myself when I saw it that I shouldn't have been able to tell them apart. Like as two peas, they was, or like as Helen and Anita. What Mr. Ansell decided to do was to send the fourth lion out into the cage when Kurt was in there ready to start the performance. And that's exactly what he did."

I was leaning forward genuinely impressed.

"You see the beauty of the plan? There was no one in the circus who'd know it was the strange lion. And Ansell had shifted them round that very morning so that when the men moved the tunnel up it was just as usual. Then Ansell knew that whatever scrapping went on between the lions, there wouldn't be any scar showing until long after the thing had been dismissed as an accident and a verdict of accidental death given at the inquest. Then, after that, what was a scar on a spare lion? Even if anyone did notice it? The lions would all be short-tempered and hungry, and with the strange one among them the chances were that all three would go for Kurt. It's a wonder, really, that they didn't, and it speaks well for Kurt as a lion-trainer. But after all, one's enough, and it wouldn't take no Sir Bernard Spilsbury to see that Kurt's death was quick and sudden as soon as ever that lion, which had never been trained, which had never had a man in with him, which was known to be a ferocious and uncontrollable brute, popped out of the tunnel and on to him in a flash.

"Mind you," added Beef, "he nearly had a slip up. Kurt's illness was as genuine as the day is long. But who was to think he'd go and get up for the performance with a temperature like that? I thought I was as safe as houses to leave him there, even knowing all I did. I went back to half a dozen of the last tobers to check up on the buried horse meat and I managed that very nice. But I never dreamed that Kurt would go and put his head in the lion's mouth, as you might appropriately say.

"Of course," Beef continued, "we've a bit more evidence to collect yet. We've examined the fourth lion and found just a suspicion of a scratch on his head. But the three lions had quite a good scrap in the tunnel, so I've no doubt the weals will come up nicely before the adjourned inquest, and it'll be those weals that'll hang Mr. Ansell. And besides that, what do you think he done? *Just* as I foresaw. After you'd gone off to bed last night, you couldn't understand my creeping about, could you? Old Beef wasting his time again, you thought. Ah, but was I? I got hold of young Ginger, who I thought would be as reliable a witness as any, and we watched Kurt's wagon. Would you believe it? As sure as fate across comes Ansell and in he goes, even with the body lying there mangled and horrible. He must be a cold-blooded brute, that Ansell. And he must have known where the money was too, because he was out in five minutes with the packet in his hand. We found it under his mattress today. Oh yes, we've got enough on him. Or shall have before the trial comes up."

"And Corinne?" I asked. "Was Corinne in it?"

"Not, as you might say, *in* it," returned Beef. "She never thought there'd be a murder. But any girl who runs about with three men at the same time is playing with fire, in my opinion."

"What about Gypsy Margot?" I asked as cynically as I could. "How do you account for her extraordinary prescience?"

"I don't know what that means," said Beef, "but what I think about her is this. There's no doubt that she was brainy and clever and that. You could tell that from the way she talked. 'Course, she picked up a lot of that from books, but I should call her the smartest old baggage in the show. All right. But it's pretty clear she doesn't like the circus, and especially she doesn't like the proprietor. We know why— because he took the circus off her brother's hands years ago and she'd never forgiven him. Even though it was all legal and above board, as I don't doubt it was, still she doesn't like the idea of her brother's circus being run by a man like Jackson. And then, she gets it put in the contract of sale that she's to be allowed to put up her booth on the field whenever she likes. At first you can take it that it was a kind of keeping her eye on things. She didn't like to feel that the circus was going to rack and ruin. But then later, when she got too old to do much work on the musical-hall stage, she made it permanent with the circus and her two daughters put on their act. But all this time it must have been rankling that the old circus wasn't what it used to be, and she must have begun to think that perhaps it would be a good idea if the whole thing busted up. So she predicted a murder. And she told it to Albert. Now for some reason or other Albert seems to be the fool of the show. So why should she tell it to him? Because, you see, he was the only one who would believe her and spread it around. If she'd told anybody else they would have laughed at her and forgotten all about it. But the way she did it, the news spread round very slowly, and did just what she wanted —to make people nervous."

"And why did she choose the Jubilee performance as the last date?" I asked.

"Well, it was as good a date as any, wasn't it? And her idea was, no doubt, to make the people so nervous about murders and so on that the Jubilee show was a flop. You know there are always one or two little accidents in a circus during the season, and normally no one thinks twice about them after they've happened. But when everybody's looking for a murder they begin to think each of those accidents is an attempt at one. Just like you did. But, of course, old Margot was a clever old girl, and I wouldn't put it past her to have noticed something of what was going on between Kurt and Ansell. But she didn't know anything else about it than that."

"Well," I said, "I suppose once more I've got to congratulate you."

Beef beamed. "I thought you would. Well, you couldn't help it really, could you? I mean, it sounds so simple when I tell it, but the simplest things are the hardest, very often. You had all the evidence that I had when I made up my mind that Ansell was going to murder Kurt and how he was going to do it. And I don't believe you even suspected it."

"I can only hope," I returned, "that the reader will not have suspected it either."

"Oh, him," said Beef. "He'll have been jumping about from one to another suspecting each in turn. But that's what you mean him to do, isn't it?"

"I suppose so," I said, and added thoughtfully: "I shall call it *Case With Four Clowns*. That should help to mislead him."

"Four clowns?" said Beef. "How do you make that out? There were only three clowns in the ring."

"Yes, in the ring," I said, and left him gaping.

THE END